MONEY
&
GREED

MONEY & GREED

UNAVOIDABLE CONSEQUENCES

JORGE RIVERA

Hamilton Rand Publishers

London—New York—Los Angeles

Hamilton Rand Publishers
London—New York—Los Angeles

MONEY & GREED

Available in bookstores. Independent booksellers. Barnes and Noble. Online retailers. Accessible formats: ePub, Mobi, iPad, iBook, and Kindle. Amazon.com Apple.com BarnesandNoble.com Distributed worldwide to academia and libraries by Baker and Taylor, and Ingram.

Available to purchase online from www.HamiltonRandPublishers.org

Library of Congress Cataloging-in-Publication Data applied for and is on file with Library of Congress.

ISBN 978-0-9975223-3-4 (Hardback) Export Edition.

ISBN 978-0-9975223-4-1 (Softcover)

ISBN 978-0-9975223-5-8 (eBook)

Printed in the United States of America

January 2017
First Edition

10 9 8 7 6 5 4 3 2 1

Dedication

LOVE, my family, and friends.

Acknowledgments

One of the most pleasant parts of finishing a book is to thank those who contributed, in different ways to its making.

My humble thanks to my COUNSELOR. Also to the following: Abraham Jenkins. Lucia Castañeda. Alice Peterson. Ana Patricia Graham. Bobby Hines. Candice Bertman. Charles Rogers. Chayton Miller. David Bernal. David Rutledge. Elvira Figueroa. Galina Polevaya. Gilbert Claure. Greg Norris, Gregory McCully. Josephine Wareta. Johana Saenz. Karen Tamblyn. Kelly Larson. Lucille Drew. Maria Maya, Maria Van Auken. Marisol Hermosillo. Mary Beth Welch.Michele Moore. Michelle Rogaway. Monique Besson. Monique Gale. Roger Todd. Rona Getty. Sike Azu-Irondi. Tamara Matheson. Sheila Golden. William Perry. Wendy Muralles. Editors: Arthur O'Malley, Lucille Molina, and Vince O'Hara. Photography: Bud Smith. Book Designer: Susan Hashimoto.

Chapter 1

At nine o'clock in the morning on the first Monday of March, an unexpectedly high storm was pouring rain in La Grange, a charming Kentucky train town of 8,000 people. A couple in their mid-50s, Marjorie and Robert Cabot were still asleep in bed when the bell rang and rang on their front door woke them. Marjorie got out of bed and with some difficulty walked to the front bedroom window. She moved the blinds and looked down to see who was outside. "Oh God!" she exclaimed to her husband. "It's the police!"

She secured her robe and turned on the nightstand light. Nervous and still half asleep she headed toward the door. The police officer outside rang the bell once more. She wondered what could be so important. Slowly and carefully she took the six steps downward leading to the front of the house and opened the door.

The police officer was adjusting the collar of his raincoat. Lowering his head to avoid the rain on his face he said, "Sorry to disturb this early Madam. We are collaborating in a multi-agency investigation of the Louisville Midtown Bank. According to the investigators, Robert Cabot and Marjorie Cabot have a special medical needs trust and long-term medical care account in this bank. The investigators would appreciate it if you could be available to speak to them today. Due to the severe weather they would come and interview you here. However, if you prefer to go to the police station, I can make arrangements for an officer to take you there and bring you back home when the interview is over. It shouldn't take too long." The police handed Marjorie a business card. When Marjorie did not immediately respond, he said, "When you're ready, please give us a call with your decision."

Marjorie had begun to perspire. She brought her left hand with a closed fist to her chest, squinted at the card and fearfully asked, "What is happening with the bank?" We have our retirement account and all our money there!"

"I can't comment on that Madam," the officer replied over his shoulder as he departed into the intense downpour.

Marjorie looked at the card and realized her reading glasses were upstairs on the nightstand. Then she glanced up to catch a glimpse of the departing police officer. She trembled fearfully as she turned and with a fainting voice called, "Honey! Come here read this card. Our bank is being investigated."

Her husband, Bob, a former city attorney, had been severely injured in a car accident several years before. His hearing and speech were impaired, and the movement of his legs was limited. He could tell his wife was upset but had difficulty moving fast enough from the bedroom with his walker. Slurring some of his words he yelled, "What'd you say? We're what?"

Responding in frustration, Marjorie shouted, "Our bank is going belly-up." By this time Marjorie was crying and at the same time making an extraordinary effort to rush back upstairs for her glasses. She shouted to Bob "Stay put! I don't want you to fall." Bob stopped and with an angry expression watched Marjorie. When she reached the top of the stairs, he was in her way.

"Please. I need my glasses. Don't just stare, move, and go!" Then, feeling a little remorse at her abruptness, she continued, "thank you, honey." As she passed, she lightly touched Bob on his left arm. Bob came out of his paralysis and in an inappropriately loud voice he said, "What the hell...! I am going to turn on the coffee while you calm down."

Marjorie sat on the edge of her bed and read the card. She broke in a cold sweat, had a sharp pain in her chest and trembled, she wondered what was going on and how she would pay their medical bills if indeed something had happened to their money.

After a few minutes, the aroma of hazelnut coffee permeated the house. Bob shouted, "Honey the coffee is ready! Bring the card and let me see it." There was no response. After another few minutes, Bob turned around and with his walker hurried as best he could towards the bedroom. As he entered the room, he saw Marjorie laying on the floor. Bob dropped the walker and tried to run, but his leg gave out and instead he fell on top of her, "Honey! Honey, honey!" Then, he realized she was unconscious. With an extraordinary effort, he reached to the right side of Marjorie, grabbed the cell phone on the floor and punched 911.

"La Grange Police"—answered a female dispatcher.

Bob was beginning to panic as his wife lay there limp and apparently lifeless. "You bastards killed my wife!"

In a soothing voice, the dispatcher said, "Sir, please tell me what is going on. Is someone injured?"

"You bastards killed my wife! Get the ambulance here now!"

"Sir, what is your address? Is the telephone you are calling from in your house?"

"The phone is in my hand; I'm in my house. You bastards killed my wife!" Bob shouted.

"An ambulance is on its way, Sir. Now tell me, is your wife bleeding?

"No! I didn't hurt her."

"Is she breathing?"

"I can't hear well. Said Bob. How can I tell if she is breathing? She's just laying on the floor; she's uncovered."

"Sir, please do as I ask." The dispatcher's calming voice was finally starting to connect with Bob. "Place your hand under her nose and tell me if you feel any air sensation."

"Okay!" Then, after a pause, Bob's voice, now softer, "She's alive!"

3

"Is she hurt?"

"She's laying on the floor; she's not moving. I'm on top of her; I can't get up, I can't move my legs, my walker is by the door, please help, hurry, hurry! Please!"

The fire department; the police, and an ambulance arrived. A team of two paramedics and two firefighters ran to the door and found it unlocked. One firefighter went down to check the basement and the others run upstairs. The team searching the upper floor checked the kitchen, the dining room, living room, and bathroom and then reached the second bedroom door. One firefighter called on his radio, "Aid mutual truck, a couple in their mid-50s on the northeast of the second floor, dual equipment, and one plastic board now."

The paramedics carefully moved Bob away from Marjorie and then placed them each on a gurney for transportation to the ambulance. Paramedics took Marjorie's vital signs and gave her CPR. They then put an oxygen mask over her nose and mouth. Marjorie did not respond. Her arms and legs remained motionless. A second attendant pulled out the defibrillator, but within seconds, Marjorie began breathing. Rapidly, the paramedics applied a "Miami J Collar," to protect her neck from any additional trauma.

The ambulance took the couple to Good Samaritan Hospital, located less than a mile away, where the emergency room team of physicians and nurses were already waiting. Suddenly, the receiving team saw three ambulances following one another approach the unloading ramp!

With a calm voice, and a surprised look on his face Dr. Hunt, the team trauma physician, asked: "What's going on?" A male voice in the background yelled, "Two more calls. School kids, thirteen and fourteen. They collided head-on in the hallway of the middle school. Both are conscious and alert, vitals normal. The attending crew is applying hand pressure to control bleeding of head injuries.

In the hallway of the ER, the medical crew transporting Marjorie stopped and yielded priority position to the teams bringing the head injuries. Dr. Hunt examined the younger boy, and Dr. Garret, the physician in residence, took care of the fourteen-year-old. On initial examination they considered both injuries to be superficial; nonetheless, they ordered computerize tomography studies to rule out head trauma. Dr. Hunt signaled Dr. Garret to go ahead with the physician assistant and stop the bleeding and complete the suturing while he turned his attention to Marjorie.

Upon arrival to the ER, the trauma team had inserted a small, flexible tube into Marjorie's mouth and down her windpipe; then they attached it to a ventilator to protect the airway and assist breathing. During the initial exam, Dr. Hunt concluded that Marjorie had fainted, and when she fell she hit her head and had become paralyzed from her neck down. Deeply concerned he sent Marjorie for a CT-scan. The results confirmed his suspicions: C3 fracture with spinal cord compression. Hunt instructed the trauma team coordinator to call the spine surgeon, a Dr. Rasmussen.

After a brief consultation with Dr. Hunt Dr. Rasmussen ordered the patient airlifted to the Orthopedic Hospital in Louisville. The ER coordinator immediately called the air medical emergency response unit at the Louisville Airport and directed the dispatcher to send a helicopter to pick up a surgical patient at Good Samaritan in La Grange. He notified the dispatcher that time was of the essence.

Within an hour, the helicopter landed at Good Samaritan. The air ambulance crew consisted of a pilot and copilot, a physician, and a certified critical care transport nurse. The weather was cold, 31 degrees Fahrenheit. Marjorie rode on a gurney, covered with rain protector canopy, and a warm blanket. She was rolled to the northeast parking lot to the heliport and secured onboard. Dr. Hunt and the trauma team returned to the ER. While inside the building, in a voice reflecting uneasiness, Dr. Hunt told Eden, the physician assistant, "That patient's chances of recovering from quadriplegic paralysis are minimal at best, and there's a high risk of infection. Most likely she will remain quadriplegic and dependent on a breathing machine."

Eden nodded, "Her poor husband. Oops…! Let me check on Mr. Cabot." She tapped the door, and entered the room where Bob remained asleep from the intravenous sedative given to him upon arrival, Eden checked his pulse and heart condition. All showed normal.

While Marjorie was airborne, the physician onboard was transmitting vital information to the trauma team waiting at the Orthopedic Hospital. The helicopter landed and Marjorie was rushed to the trauma unit. The team evaluated Marjorie's airway; it was open and transparent; abdominal muscles were active in her breathing process. Her blood pressure was low. The nurse administered a rapid intravenous infusion of fluid with a normal saline solution. Marjorie was rushed to the radiology department for a second CT-scan to rule out internal bleeding. When the radiologist, Dr. Van Hausen evaluated the study he saw that the spleen was ruptured. He transmitted his findings to Dr. Gates, the general surgeon and Dr. Haynes, the anesthesiologist as they formulated the plan of action. They decided that Dr. Gates should remove the little spleen first, then Dr. Rasmussen would proceed with cervical fusion stabilization.

Immediately, Dr. Gates ordered his surgical team to the operating room. Dr. Haynes administered general anesthesia while sounding caution about the high risk of performing two such significant procedures on the same day. He was concerned because each required a different position of Marjorie's body on the operating table. The spine decompression and cervical stabilization procedure took longer, and it was hard to estimate the amount of blood loss that would result. Therefore, Dr. Gates elected a minimally invasive technique for the splenectomy.

Gates successfully removed Marjorie's spleen. As the physician assistant closed the incisions, the doctor noted his concerns about the risk of blood loss and the formation of blood clots. At the same time, he was having doubts as to whether Dr. Rasmussen should proceed immediately with the cervical stabilization. He finally decided it was best to continue as planned, so he ordered the surgical coordinator to notify Dr. Rasmussen to be ready for Marjorie in twenty minutes. Meanwhile, the anesthesiologist reviewed Marjorie's unconscious condition and assessed the possible alterations that occurred during the first surgical intervention. All seemed well. Marjorie was ready for Dr. Rasmussen to proceed to stabilize the cervical spine.

Dr. Rasmussen's surgical team moved in and took over the operating room. The assistant surgeon accessed the updated electronic medical record and with a sense of caution read Dr. Gates surgical notes. He was especially worried by the sentence: "This patient is on blood thinner medication due to a recently diagnosed irregular heartbeat. Her blood condition prolongs the bleeding time." The assistant surgeon concluded that Marjorie was at high risk of bleeding on the table and that the odds of saving her life were reduced. He called the physician assistant to alert Dr. Rasmussen to the potential complications. However, Dr. Rasmussen did not respond to the assistant's page. He was not in the building. It turned out that he had left during the first procedure to take delivery of a new Bentley, he had been anxiously awaiting for weeks, and the transaction had taken longer than anticipated.

To the team, the next ten minutes felt like an eternity. As anxiety mounted, no one spoke. There was no background music playing as was usual and customary for Dr. Rasmussen. The surgeon's position was empty. All systems were on. Marjorie was carefully repositioned on the operating table. Surgical prepping and draping was in motion! The team was in the state of profound uncertainty. However, showing no exterior clues of distress— where was Dr. Rasmussen?

Finally, the surgeon assistant said in a loud voice that carried, "Are we ready?" He glanced towards the surgeon's location and saw Dr. Rasmussen furiously drying his hands as he arrived. The doctor seemed calm as he initiated the cervical fusion stabilization but the ambiance in the surgical theater was glacial and tense, Dr. Rasmussen was emotionless, although uncharacteristic beads of perspiration dotted his forehead. During the surgery, Marjorie's blood pressure fell. Circulation was replaced with a saline, standard solution to correct the decreasing blood pressure. Nobody could predict how it would affect her brain, or why she was registering such low blood pressure. The procedure was finally finished. Marjorie remained with the tube inserted into her windpipe, and she was sent post-operatively to the intensive care unit for close observation. In a few hours, Marjorie was becoming feverish while remaining peaceful under sedation.

Chapter 2
TUESDAY, MARCH 4, 2014

By seven-thirty in the morning, despite standard laboratory results, Marjorie's temperature was rising, and she was becoming agitated. The source of her fever was unknown. The ICU team was becoming concerned and could not extract the tube from her windpipe. They decided to keep her under sedation until her temperature returned to normal. The suspense was tangible as the nurses exchanged probable causes, and the physicians discussed possible outcomes.

Later in the evening, the physician in charge, Dr. Beck, examined Marjorie and ordered an ultrasound of her legs. He determined a blood clot was moving to her lungs, affecting her regular breathing. Her case had no prospects of improving. Soon afterward, he instructed the supervising nurse to contact the admitting department to determine if there was a Kentucky Living Will Directive and who was the appointed executor.

Now the ethical question was how long to keep Marjorie on a ventilator. Also, there was a matter of seeking authority to disconnect her from the machine.

Dr. Beck decided to maintain Marjorie on the ventilator for another seven days, hoping for a sign of improvement. He asked Joyce, the discharge nurse, to find out if Marjorie's husband was still at Good

Samaritan Hospital, and who besides her husband should be notified regarding the case and pending decision of when to disconnect her from the machine. The fact that Marjorie was at the Orthopedic Hospital in Louisville, and her husband at a different hospital in La Grange complicated the interaction between Dr. Beck and Marjorie's husband, Bob. Joyce contacted Good Samaritan Hospital and found that Bob was still a patient there. She also found the name of the next of kin, their son Ronald Cabot, and reported these findings to Dr. Beck. He instructed her to call Mr. Cabot to come to the Orthopedic Hospital to meet with him as soon as possible. Joyce range the number and someone picked up almost immediately.

"Hello…, may I speak to Mr. Ronald Cabot?"

"I'm the."

"Hi, my name is Joyce, and I'm the discharge nurse supervisor here at the Orthopedic Hospital in Louisville. I regret to inform you that your mother is in intensive care, and the attending physician, Dr. Beck asks if you can come to the hospital to meet with him to discuss Mrs. Cabot's condition." There was a moment of silence on the other line.

"This morning, I was informed that both of my parents were at the Good Samaritan Hospital, in La Grange," Ronald said. "I've already arranged a replacement on my court case so I could be at Good Samaritan at noon. Why was she moved to the Orthopedic Hospital?" He sounded a little frustrated.

"Unfortunately due to patient privacy laws, I am not permitted to discuss details," Joyce responded patiently. "However, Dr. Beck will be able to fill you in on the situation today at three in the afternoon. Please come to the ICU Department and ask for Dr. Beck."

"Thanks, I'm on my way." The dial tone sounded abruptly as Ronald hung up.

Later that day Ronald arrived at the information desk at the Orthopedic Hospital.

Ronald Cabot was 34, handsome, and single, five foot nine, brown eyes, short black hair, white skin, athletic body, and with a husky tone of voice and the skills to use it well. He was a graduate of the University of Kentucky with a master's degree in government and law. With this level of knowledge and no small amount of natural ability, Ronald had become assistant to the State of Kentucky Attorney General. He was a baseball fan, liked country music and square dancing, played guitar and was an avid reader of historical law cases and poetry.

The receptionist stared at the computer screen, then turned towards Ronald, "Let me locate Dr. Beck," she told him. A few minutes later she instructed; "Please sign this visitor record, and affix this label to your coat. Then take the elevator to the second floor and go left. When in front of the ICU sign on the double doors, look to your right. You'll see a blue square button, push it to open the doors and go into the ICU department. Dr. Beck knows you're coming." He took the form and followed her directions. When he reached the ICU, he approached the receptionist.

"Hi, I'm Ronald Cabot, I'm here to see Dr. Beck."

"One moment please, he will be with you in a few minutes," he responded without looking up,

The few minutes that Ronald sat waiting for Dr. Beck seemed to go on forever. Finally, a tall, robust looking man asked in a baritone voice; "Are you Mr. Cabot?"

"Yes, I am," Ronald replied. "How's my mother? May I see her?"

"Come with me." Ronald followed Dr. Beck into a room where Marjorie was laying peacefully in a soft looking bed. She had a tube in her windpipe, and intravenous solutions connected to both her arms. Wires were plugged into monitors and extended to her forehead and chest. This equipment gave Ronald the sickening premonition that his mother was dying. He speechlessly caressed the side of her head as tears began to freely flow down his face.

The scene made Dr. Beck vaguely uncomfortable, and he felt compelled to break the silence. "Yesterday afternoon, Mrs. Cabot was transported here by helicopter from Good Samaritan Hospital in La Grange," he explained. "Upon arrival, her condition was diagnosed as

C3 fracture with spinal cord compression, resulting from a fall at home. A second CT-scan revealed a ruptured spleen. The general surgeon removed the spleen and the spine surgeon stabilized the cervical spine." Ronald continued to look down at his mother, barely hearing Dr. Beck's words. "Let's go to my office and talk about the reason I asked you here," he murmured.

While walking down the hall to Dr. Beck's office, Ronald asked, "Is she going to make it?" They arrived at a big polished door.

"Here we are, would you like some water, or to use the restroom?" Asked Dr. Beck.

"Thanks, doctor, I'm okay."

After they had been seated in his office, Dr. Beck continued. "Your mother's medical history of a previous deep vein thrombosis became our primary concern. About three-thirty this morning her temperature began rising, and she became agitated. The source of fever was unknown. We decided to keep her sedated until the temperature became normal. Unfortunately, the temperature continued to increase with no real explanation despite three comparable laboratory test results."

Ronald listened silently. He looked visibly overwhelmed and in distress, and his left hand began to tremble. He took a deep breath and finally said, "Dr. Beck, I understand your position and respect your medical counsel. However, God is the giver of life. My mother was used by God to give me my life, and she raised me and put me through law school. Even though I have the lawful authority to disconnect her from the ventilator, I don't have the moral power to end my mother's life. I do, however, have the authority to ask for second and third opinions, and then I'll find out why this happened to her.

Dr. Beck nodded. "Please feel free to seek independent medical advice before taking any action. We'll continue to monitor your mother and look for signs of improvement. You already spoke to Joyce; she'll contact you if there are any new developments." Dr. Beck stood up, and after a moment Ronald did too. They shook hands over the desk. "Thanks for coming, Ronald. I wish you the very best."

Ronald promptly departed for Good Samaritan Hospital to visit his father and get the details of what had happened. He worried as he headed up the forested I-71 corridor all the way to La Grange, and wondered how he was going to handle the situation, especially with his father's medical conditions and the need for 24/7 in-home care. After forty-five minutes Ronald arrived at Good Samaritan. He asked for his father at an information desk much like the one at the Orthopedic Hospital, and received his room number, 304. Before entering his father's room Ronald freshened up so as to not to alarm his father with his puffy eyes and pallid face. Ronald dreaded having to tell him the reason for his visit.

He knocked three times on the door.

"Come in!" a weak voice finally called from the other side.

"Hey, Dad!" Ronald greeted his father as he entered the ward. How ya feelin'?"

As Bob looked up at his son his sad expression was transformed. "I've been sleeping so much I woke up and didn't know who or where I was! He said in a slurred voice. "I tried to get up but they've got all these darned tubes in me," he sighed. "Anyways, how's your Mom?" Ronald decided he had to tell him immediately.

"She's in the ICU, Dad, and they don't know if she'll even make it. What the hell happened?"

Bob's eyes cleared up somewhat. "I don't know," he cooed, his voice becoming more coherent. "All I remember is that it was raining, the police came to the house, and some cop gave Marge a card, and she couldn't read it. That woman always forgets her glasses. She was mad as hell! Came upstairs and fell in the bedroom. She couldn't move. I . . . I wasn't there. I didn't see it. I tried to help but just fell right on top of her," he snorted. "Next thing I know I'm right here in this bed. How long? I don't know that either. Today, here I am watching the ceiling wondering am I next?" His face looked ill and drawn. Ronald sat down next to him.

"No Dad, you're not next. I'm going to talk with the nurse to find out what the hell happened, and why you're here..," he paused. "How're you feeling?"

With difficulty, Bob replied, "I'm starving. There's nothing to eat around here."

In a soft tone of voice, Ronald said; "I'm going to go find some food for you, Dad. I'll be right back." Ronald patted his father on the hand and walked out of the room.

Bob waited in the dark ward for what seemed like a long time. Suddenly he heard a knock on the door. A friendly looking woman, in her mid- forties, burst into the room. "I was on my way here when I met your son," she said cheerfully, a broad smile on her face. "He told me you were a little hungry Mr. Cabot."

"Heck, yes! I'm more than a little hungry," Bob told her, becoming animated at the prospect of food. "I haven't eaten for days! Leave a nice big plate will ya, and if some other guy doesn't want his, I'll have that too."

The dietitian chuckled as she arranged the bed for Bob to eat. "I'll keep your request in mind, Mr. Cabot," she said smiling.

"Thanks, honey, can't wait to see you again!"

Meanwhile, the supervising nurse was giving Ronald the details of Bob's medical condition, along with Marjorie's initial arrival and admission time to the Good Samaritan Hospital. She also informed him that Bob would be ready to go home once they found someone to take care of him, as she understood Marjorie would be remaining at the Orthopedic Hospital.

After digesting this news, Ronald returned to Bob's room. "Hey, Dad! I see you're enjoying lunch."

In a cheerier, yet still slurred voice Bob responded; "Heck yes! It's real good, and the nurse told me that if anyone else didn't want their grub she'd let me have it!"

"She said all that? Or are you just so hungry you imagine things?" Ronald laughed. "Look, Dad, I'm going to go to your house and find the card the police gave to Mom. I'll come back after that's done and

I've checked on Mom."

"Thanks, son. Tell her that I love her, no matter what."

Ronald approached Bob's bed, touching him on his forehead goodbye. As he opened the door to leave, he looked back.

"I'll tell Mom," he said. "Take care Dad."

Ronald drove to his parent's house. The first thing he noticed after he arrived was the mess left by the first responders. Next to a first story window, he found the business card the police officer had left. This had triggered the whole series of events and landed both his parents in the hospital. Feeling the need to know more, he immediately drove to the police department. There he asked for the station chief. A uniformed man walked out to receive him.

"Hello, I am Major Willis," he said extending his hand. "The station chief isn't in today. What can I do for you?"

"Thank you, I'm Ronald Cabot, the son of Robert and Marjorie Cabot," Ronald introduced himself. "I am here as their emergency contact. They reside at 4908 Talbott Road. I understand that yesterday there was an incident that occurred shortly after Officer Adams visited my parent's house and gave my mother his card." Ronald showed Major Willis the business card left by Officer Adams.

"Oh . . . yeah . . . I know this case. Besides being the emergency contact, do you have a power of attorney?"

"As a matter of fact, I do. Here's a certified copy," said Ronald as he pulled the paperwork from his coat. Major Willis took it from him and gave a cursory look-over. "May I make a copy, so I can discuss more details with you?" he asked Ronald.

In a tone of voice that bordered on the smooth side of impatience, Ronald replied, "Yes, please. I need to find out what landed both of my parents in the hospital."

After a brief read of a power of attorney, Willis called his secretary and asked her to make a copy and bring both copies to his office. "Mr. Cabot, please come with me," he told Ronald after hanging up. "I'll fill you in with all the details we know as of now. We're collaborating in a multi-agency investigation of the Louisville Midtown Bank. According to the investigators, Mr. and Mrs. Cabot have a special needs trust, retirement savings, and long-term medical care accounts there." He motioned for Ronald to sit down in a chair in front of his desk,

"The case investigators from The Special Inspector General wanted to interview them. Officer Adams were sent to their house, to find out if they would be willing to come to the station or whether we should conduct the interview at their place. Right afterward we received an emergency call from your father. He said that he and your mother had fallen. First respondents were sent, and your parents were taken to Good Samaritan Hospital."

Ronald nodded and then he said. "Is there an incident report available?"

"You can pick one up at nine tomorrow morning." "Thank you," Ronald stood and shook Major's hand. "I'll be back tomorrow."

Ronald, as a staff attorney for the Attorney General's Office, was familiar with the Special Inspector General's functions. He was not, however, aware of the particular investigation Willis had mentioned and many of his questions remained unanswered. A quick glance at the highway indicated that the traffic back to Louisville would stop and go.

Too distressed to deal with traffic he decided to return to his parent's home to tidy up. He wanted some time alone to think about the unavoidable consequences of Bob's need for in-home care. What would he do if his mother never recovered...? He also mulled Dr. Beck's earlier comments at the ICU. An hour later, with the house is in proper order, Ronald finally felt able to relax. He determined that the best course of action was to visit his father and discuss Marjorie's critical condition.

He returned to his father's ward and knocked on the door. "Hey, Dad, have you had dinner yet?" he asked as he walked into the room.

Bob looked worried, and his speech had become less coherent than earlier in the day. "Heck, yes! But still so hungry..... When're we going to go home?"

"That's why I'm here." Ronald pulled up a chair and sat down by his father's bed. "I talked to your supervising nurse, and she said you can be relocated as soon as I find some in-home care."

In an angry slur, Bob burst out, "What do you mean by relocation and in-home care…? That sounds like Roosevelt's Executive Order 9066. Prison camp!"

Ronald affectionately touched his father's arm. "Dad, Mom, is in intensive care," he crooned. "We don't know how long she's going to be there, and I can't take care of you. I'm going to find you a nice place to stay until she recovers."

"Is she that bad?"

"Yeah, Dad. I talked to the doctor in charge and well . . . He's not that hopeful." There Ronald's eyes started to tear.

Bob looked shocked. "So, what's going to happen to me?" he asked in a flat voice.

"Well, Dad, for now, you're going to stay here a few days. I'll make sure they take good care of you while you get some rest and recover your strength. This'll be the best place for you while I sort everything out." Bob looked away, upset. "Dad you know I live alone!" Ronald slowly said. "If things were different, I'd discharge you right now and take you with me, but I can't take care of you!"

Bob had begun to cry. "You're a good son," he choked out with some difficulty. "Go check on your Mom, and just make sure they take care of me." Hearing this, Ronald broke down and began to weep too. He hugged his father, and for a moment the two men expressed their grief without words. Bob ended the hug and looked at his son sorrowfully. "Son, you are the strength of this family," he said, shaking. "It's up to you to find out what's going on. Find out about the bank situation, find why it went belly up. I promise I'll stay here and not cause any trouble. Just please . . . Fix this."

Ronald smiled. "Thanks for your vote of confidence, Dad. I'll see you tomorrow."

When he was finally back in his apartment, Ronald began to

connect the information he had learned in the past day.

The information from Major Willis, the preliminary oral reports from Dr. Beck, the supervising nurse at Good Samaritan Hospital and Bob's description of the event, he played everything over and over in his head. What he thought of most was Bob's comment, "Find out about the bank situation, find, why it went belly up?" Near exhaustion, Ronald made a list of priorities for his investigation the next day. First, he would visit his mother, and request a copy of her medical records, including the surgical notes. Second, obtain a copy of the incident report from the police station. Finally, he would, visit his father and get a copy of his medical records, including a transcript of the transfer of care from his mother to the Orthopedic Hospital. After all that, he would determine the best of course of action if his mother never got better. He knew it was a distinct possibility.

Chapter 3
WEDNESDAY, MARCH 5, 2014

At eight thirty the following morning Ronald met with his boss, Mr. Curtis, to inform him of the situation and ask for his approval to appoint Rona Hogan, an associate familiar with his cases, to cover while he investigated his parent's situation. He not only faced the arduous task of fixing his parent's problems, but also their hospitalization and incapacitation. Mr. Curtis expressed his condolences and immediately approved Ronald's request. Feeling especially sympathetic, he also offered the services of the Special Inspector General for the Trouble Asset Relief Program to help Ronald with his investigation. Ronald left the Attorney General's Office with a conviction that would soon make everything the way it had been.

From there he drove to the Orthopedic Hospital to visit his mother. He greeted her, hoping for a hand signal or any other acknowledgment of his existence, but Marjorie was still unresponsive. She was still on life support devices and had a tube inserted into her windpipe. He sat by his mother's bed, caressed her arm, and began to talk as if she could hear. "Mom I don't know what happened. I'll investigate and do everything that I can to make sure you get out of here. And Dad—or my dear Bob as you call him—is going to be okay too."

Ronald began crying and soon his pale blue shirt was visibly wet.

Almost unable to speak, but choking out the words as best he could he continued, "Mom, I don't know if you can even hear me. But, if somehow you can, I want you to know how much I love you. You've done so much for me, and I'll always be grateful for it." He wiped some of his tears away and took her hand.

"When I was a baby, you held me, and fed me, while I cried. When I was a boy, you taught me to love God, and made me better when I got hurt." He squeezed her hand. "You helped with my homework when I was in school. I remember when you took me to baseball practice and cheered no matter how bad I was. When I went to college, you stayed up all night making coffee for me while I studied for my finals. You'd cover for me when I would get home at one in the morning. You were so happy when I gave the keynote speech at my graduation." Marjorie was still motionless. The only sign of life was the beeping heart monitor behind her.

"Three years ago after the car accident," Ronald continued tearfully, "when prominent city attorney Bob Cabot became physically and mentally limited, you dropped everything and took care of him. Your love and devotion were evident, and for all these acts of courage and sacrifice, I love you and admire." Ronald broke down sobbing, unable to continue. His crying was so loud that the ICU nurse rushed into the IC2 to make sure everyone was okay. She checked the monitors and took Marjorie's pulse and left after giving Ronald a sympathetic smile. Ronald stood, breathing slowly to regain his composure before leaving the room. He found the ICU supervising nurse and asked her, "Has my mother show any signs of improvement?"

"Dr. Beck checked on her at seven thirty AM. No change, I'm afraid," the nurse replied.

Ronald was torn between staying with his mother and going out to find the information he needed. "Thanks, I'll be back tonight," he finally said.

Ronald departed for the police station to pick up the incident report. He arrived forty-five minutes later to find Major Willis standing by the window. "Hello," Willis greeted him. "I just signed off on the incident report." He offered the report to Ronald. "Feel free to call me if you need anything else, you have my card."

"Thank you." Ronald began to flip through the report on the walk back to his car. It quickly became apparent that he needed to talk with Mr. Curtis to arrange a meeting with the investigators from The Special Inspector General for the Trouble Asset Relief Program. First, however, he needed to talk with the discharge nurse at Good Samaritan Hospital to transfer Bob's in-home care to the nursing department. Ronald had already researched the nursing homes ratings in the area and had found that Good Samaritan had five-star ratings in the categories of health inspections, nurse staffing, and measures of medical care. He arrived at the hospital and asked for the discharge nurse on duty.

"That'd be Ms. Maya," said the attendant. She peered past him and then added, "There she is, just a moment, please." Ronald turned and saw the nurse walking towards him.

"Hello, Ms. Maya, I'm Ronald Cabot, the son of Robert Cabot in 304," Ronald introduced himself.

"Nice to meet you," she replied, shaking his hand. "I'm familiar with your father's case. We're ready to discharge him once we're advised who will be taking care of him."

"My mother's in intensive care at the Orthopedic Hospital, and I can't do it. I've decided that it'd be best for him to stay here, and I want to know if there's any way he can be transferred to your nursing department," Ronald asked imploringly.

Maya nodded. "Let me find out. I'll let you know as soon as possible, but it you might not hear from me until tomorrow. I think that his condition qualifies him to be in our "rehabilitation department.""

"I'd appreciate all you can do to minimize my father's trauma. Do whatever you need to do, and call me with the decision," Ronald told her.

"I'll be in touch with you as soon as I have the signed authorization from the director of this department. Upon approval, do I have your consent to proceed with the move?"

"Yes, you have my authorization."

Ronald left for his office. Once there, he sought out Mr. Curtis and asked him for an introduction to his contact at The Special Inspector General for the Trouble Asset Relief Program. He explained that he needed to find out why the investigators had such an interest in talking to his parents.

Mr. Curtis could see that Ronald was very affected by the condition of his parents. "I'll have my secretary call The Special Inspector General's office and arrange for your visit." He said. Then, with a sympathetic nod, "Ronald... I hope you get to the bottom of this."

Mr. Curtis then instructed his secretary place the call, and she was able to arrange an appointment with special agent Smith who was in charge of that case. Because Agent Smith was booked all morning the meeting had to be scheduled for 3:00 pm the next day.

After this had been done Mr. Curtis asked Ronald, "Is there anything else I can do to help you?"

Ronald looked at his boss appreciating the support he was receiving. "There is. I'd like to have a bit of your time to summarize my conversations with Rona about the cases she's taking over." Curtis scratched his head.

"I have to go to Frankfort this afternoon. I have an hour and twenty minutes before I need to leave. Let's get lunch at Jack Fry's up in the Highlands, and we can talk about whether Rona needs any help."

Mr. Curtis used an official vehicle for transportation, and it was waiting in front of the building when the two men emerged. The driver held the door open for Mr. Curtis as Ronald got on the other side.

Once they were underway, Ronald began to summarize his most famous case, "This is case number 21278. It's been on the calendar since 2012, and we have a hearing in New York upcoming. Rona is the second person in charge of the investigation. She's fully prepared and able to assume my responsibilities," Ronald explained. "However, due to the nature of the case, you may want to consider bringing in another person to fast track it and be on standby just in case there's an emergency like today. So far we've arrested here in Kentucky—three—three terrorists. They're in jail where they belong. Hopefully, they'll give us the information we can share with other agencies."

Curtis rubbed his temples. "The policy now is to make it clear we'll hunt any terrorists we know of, and hold countries that harbor them accountable for their actions." Ronald nodded as Curtis continued, "We need to prevent any terrorist activity here on the home front, and we can only do this through aggressive investigations and swift and appropriate punishment. Although we've committed significant resources to homeland security, there's still a lot of work to be done." The two men sat in silence for a moment as the car stopped at a signal. Then Curtis continued, "I'm happy with the changing culture of the FBI. These days, one in three FBI employees is directly involved with efforts to track down every lead we have relating to terrorist activity. Our investigations are moving forward, and as we do so, state and local agencies continue enforcement fairly and in full."

"Well," Ronald said, "In the context of your statement, during the scheduled hearing in New York we will call the material witness. We'll give them a chance to participate in the war against terror by telling us what they know. When appropriate, we will recommend applying immigration laws. We are interviewing people on a voluntary basis. We are saying, "Welcome to America. You have come to our country why don't you help make it safe? Why don't you share information with us? Why don't you help us to protect innocent people, women, children, and men? Why don't you help us value life? As you enjoy, the freedoms of our country help us to protect those freedoms."

Curtis listened very attentively, his eyes never leaving Ronald's face. "There should be no doubt as to our intentions. Anyone who plots to harm the people of Kentucky and of the United States will be stopped and punished. Protecting the innocent against violence is a solemn duty of my office, and it's our most important responsibility."

The driver stopped the car in front of a restaurant. "Gentlemen, here we are," he announced. "I'll wait here till you're ready to go."

"Thanks, Joe," Curtis said. "We'll be at least an hour. Why don't you grab some lunch too." Ronald and Curtis walked into the restaurant, where the host greeted Curtis by name. He showed them to a table in a quiet corner of the restaurant. "Your secretary called and notified me that you have limited time today. Therefore, your order is our priority," he told Curtis. "May I bring you something to drink?

After both men had ordered iced teas, Curtis got down to business.

"After listening to your summary, I've decided to appoint Lucas Norton to help Rona. Norton is an expert and he'll take care of business so you can focus on fixing your family's problems. Take whatever long you need Ronald and don't hesitate to ask me for anything. Your father was a colleague of mine, and I'll do everything I can to help."

Ronald nodded. "I'm very grateful. This takes a load off my mind."

"Let's order now," Curtis said, seeing the waiter approaching with their teas.

"May I take your order sir?" he said politely to Curtis, and he sat the drinks on their table.

"I'll have your best sirloin steak, medium rare with a loaded baked potato and a house salad," Curtis ordered. Ronald ordered the New York Steak, and their food came more quickly than Ronald had ever seen at a high-end restaurant. They dug in immediately, concentrating on their meal and finishing in time for their various engagements. After they had finished Curtis signed the bill, and they returned to the car. Joe was waiting just where he had left them.

Once seated inside Curtis pulled out his phone and placed a call. "Lucas, are you in the office?"

"Hello, sir. I'm still here, what can I do for you?" Norton responded.

"Clear your calendar for today, please. I'm assigning you to work on Ronald Cabot's case number 21278. You'll work with someone called

Rona Hogan. I'm dropping Ronald off at the office in shortly. He'll fill you in on everything else."

"We'll be ready when Ronald gets here, sir," Lucas responded.

"Thank you," Ronald told Curtis after Lucas had hung up. "I really appreciate you putting Lucas on the case. His subject area expertise will add a new dimension to the case. We'll definitely put those terrorists away."

When the car pulled in front of Curtis' building Ronald gathered his things and shook Curtis' hand. "Thank you again, sir, I can't begin to tell you how much I appreciate your help."

"Don't worry about," responded Curtis with a smile, and then his car drove off.

Ronald took the elevator to the 7th floor. He saw Rona's back as she entered the conference room and he followed her in. There he found Rona and Lucas already sitting down. "Hey guys, thanks for taking thirty minutes of your time to meet with me. It's important I bring you both up to speed with the case."

"What's going on? Am I being replaced?" Rona asked stiffly.

"No, no, no!" exclaimed Ronald, shaking his head. "The fact is my folks had an accident and ended up in two separate hospitals. My mother is in the ICU at the Orthopedic Hospital here in town, and my father is at Good Samaritan Hospital in La Grange. You guys can imagine what a pain that is logistical, not to mention emotionally, but that's not all. All my parent's assets are under investigation by The Special Inspector General for the Trouble Asset Relief Program, and I need to find out what's going on."

"Oh s***!" Lucas swore. "That's a problem. Those guys are deadly." Rona gave him a questioning look.

"I worked with them for eight months in D.C," he explained. Then he added, "Yeah they're tough, they're meticulous and systematic, and those guys would only move forward with a case when they're one hundred percent sure they're right and get a conviction. They won't stop or negotiate till they get what they want. And that's bad for whoever gets the sharp end of the stick."

Rona whistled. "And that's why we're here?" asked Rona.

"No, Rona, you're here to take my place in the 21278 case. Lucas will take yours. Please go ahead and brief Lucas. Tomorrow afternoon I meet here with the lead investigator. My parents as one of the multiple plaintiffs against the Louisville Midtown Bank. Meanwhile, can I ask you, if I need some specific guidance, could I call on either of you for clarification? Is that okay with you?"

In unison, Lucas and Rona responded. "Count on us!" "Thanks," Ronald said gratefully. "I'll keep you guys posted."

"Okay, I'll take it from here. Go get ready for your meeting," Rona told Ronald.

"Okay, see you guys" Ronald left the room with a wave.

Chapter 4
THURSDAY, MARCH 6, 2014

At 3:00 p.m. the next day Ronald headed to the field office of The Special Inspector General for the Trouble Asset Relief Program to meet with Smith, the lead investigator on the case. After a brief introduction and an inspection of Ronald's power of attorney, Ronald got straight to the point. "Please tell me what particular issue made my parents targets of investigation in this case?"

Smith paused before answering, then in a friendly tone, "In the last eighteen months we've received several complaints against the Louisville Midtown Bank. These complaints have come from three sources." He began to count them off on his fingers. "First, students with their future education accounts; second, elderly people who entrusted the bank with their life savings and retirement funds; and third, we've had complaints from individuals with special medical needs who deposited their comprehensive medical accounts in the bank. My superior, the Special Inspector General, ordered a full audit and put me in charge. My missions are to determine whether the bank has violated the terms and conditions of the federal bailout agreements of 2007-2008 and investigate the complaints lodged against the bank." He paused and studied Ronald for a second and then continued.

"During the discovery process, we have identified some bank

customers who reside in small towns within this state. These clients match the account profiles of the populations that have filed formal complaints. That's why we asked to interview the Cabot's regarding their accounts. As you know, we never had the opportunity. While waiting for them at the La Grange police station, we were notified that they were in the hospital. Thus, I'm most pleased you are here and have the authority to speak for them in this case."

Ronald stood and extended his hand to Smith. "Thank you, Mr. Smith for telling all this," he said measuredly. "I'm still investigating what happened to my parents, but once I certify particular facts, I'll be available for the interview my parents were never able to get to."

"Sounds good," Mr. Smith said with a smile. "How long do you think it'll take you to complete your investigation?"

Ronald scratched his chin. "It'll just be a matter of account verification, shouldn't take too long. But right now my parents are the priority. They're in different hospitals and some of the problems are severe." Mr. Smith nodded and murmured his condolences. Ronald continued; "My father has special medical needs and my mother is unconscious in the ICU, so I have my hands pretty full. Once I get everything sorted out with them, I'll be able to focus on the banking situation. Is it okay if I get back to you to set up a meeting?"

"Of course!" Smith said. He jumped up and began to rummage around his desk. Smith held a business card and quickly wrote a telephone number on it. Then he gave it to Ronald "I understand completely. I included my cell number. Get back to me whenever you can." The two men shook hands again.

"I really appreciate your understanding," Ronald thanked him. "I'll be seeing you soon."

Ronald then headed to the Orthopedic Hospital. Upon arrival, he checked with the nurse in charge of Marjorie and learned that his mother's condition remained static, walked to IC2 to see her and found her in the same position as the day before… Then Ronald noticed two additional monitors with connecting wires extending from her legs. He sat by her, and like the night before, he tenderly touched her arm and spoke to her knowing that she could not hear a word he said. "Hear me, please show me a sign you can hear me, and I'll be happy," As he spoke he could feel his eyes involuntarily tearing.

He remembered the nurse's words "No change." He sighed sadly and left his Mom's room, feeling unhappy with everything. He headed back to La Grange to meet with Maya at Good Samaritan Hospital. She had called and left a message during his meeting with Smith.

"Hi Ms. Maya, I understand you have good news for me," Ronald greeted her.

"Yes," she replied. "Your father has been accepted by our Rehabilitation Department- he's being moved to room 223 by the way," she added. "More good news for you—all his costs are covered by his medical insurance." Ronald sighed inwardly with relief. "If you have any questions at all, feel free to contact me," said Maya.

Ronald thanked her vigorously, equal parts relieved that his father's situation was being sorted and appreciative that the hospital had acted so quickly.

He knocked on the door to room 223 and entered his father's new room. "Hey, Dad! How'ya doing?" He looked around the room. "Ms. Maya and I got you this new room! How do you like it so far?"

"I think I'll like it here!" Mr. Cabot chirped although Ronald noted he was still slurring his words badly. "The first thing Ms. Maya did was bring me a menu for my food tomorrow! Can you believe that son? A menu!" He looked positively beatific. "How's your Mom?" he asked, more seriously.

"I visited Mom before coming to see you today. She's the same," Ronald replied sadly. "By the way, Dad, can you tell me anything about your banking relationship with the Louisville Midtown Bank?" Bob's good mood seemed to evaporate.

"I just remember that the day after we signed the settlement agreement with the insurance company, we received a check for a lot of money; it may have been over one and a half million dollars," Bob said flatly. "You suggested we deposit these funds in an interest-earning comprehensive medical account with that bank, I don't remember the name of the bank or the fellow that helped us. All I remember was that he had animal heads hanging on the wall of his big ol' office. Creepy." At that moment someone knocked on the door.

"May I come in?" Maya's voice sounds from across the door. Bob grunted his approval, and she entered the room. "How're you doing Bob?" she asked him.

"I'm okay," he responded. "Is it dinner time yet?"

Maya shook her head and smiled at him. "Not yet, but soon." She turned to Ronald. "Mr. Cabot, I remembered that we have some consent forms that need signing. Would you mind? It's for your father's medical records." Ms. Maya handed him a clipboard with the forms attached and a pen. Ronald quickly reviewed the forms and then signed at the spaces the administrator pointed out.

"Thanks, Ms. Maya," he said returning the clipboard. She nodded and left the room, leaving them able to continue their conversation.

"So, Dad, do you remember any other business with the bank?"

In the same sad monotone, Bob responded, "You can find any other financial information you need in the safe at the house. You have the combination."

Thanks, Dad, I'll come visit you tomorrow after I see Mom."

"Good luck, Son, and watch out for the bad guys."

Ronald departed knowing that he had copies of the documents his father mentioned at his apartment. He decided to stop by the Louisville Midtown Bank tomorrow to get the facts on Bob and Marjorie's accounts. It was something that needed to be done before Ronald could do anything else. That night he found he had trouble sleeping. Finally, he got up and made himself some herbal tea with honey. He picked up the newspaper from the day before and began reading...

Chapter 5
FRIDAY, MARCH 7, 2014

Ronald finally managed to fall asleep around three in the morning, but almost immediately afterward his phone began to ring. He groaned and answered sleepily;

"Hello...?"

"Mr. Cabot?" A female voice said on the other line. "This is Daniella, the ICU supervising nurse at the Orthopedic Hospital. Dr. Beck would like to meet with you right away."

"I'm on my way!" Any trace of fatigue vanished, and Ronald leaped up to get ready. His mind was anticipating the worse and on the way to the hospital he prayed for God's wisdom and courage to face and accept the inevitable.

In the hallway leading to the ICU, Dr. Beck was standing with two other doctors, in serious conversation. Upon seeing Ronald walk out of the elevator, Dr. Beck signaled him to follow him to his office. The two other doctors left in the opposite direction. Dr. Beck motioned Ronald to sit down and took a seat across from him. He looked tired and distressed.

"Mr. Cabot," he began, "last night, around eleven-thirty, I checked up on your mother and found there was no change to her condition. At two-thirty this morning, however, the nurse noted her vitals beginning to slowly decline. She immediately called me, and I rushed over to examine her. I found your mother with her eyes open, looking back, and right then she stopped breathing. I ordered defibrillation, but we were unable to revive her. Mr. Cabot… your mother passed away at two-forty-seven today." Dr. Beck's voice was tight, almost brittle as if he was about to break down.

Ronald lowered his head and placed his hands over his ears. "Can I see her now?"

"Yes, upon her death she was moved to 201," said Dr. Beck.

Ronald found himself walking to room 201. He saw the sign right in front of him, but it seemed to be miles away.

"Authorized Personnel Only," it read, but he opened the door anyways and walked in.

He was immediately hit by the freezing temperature in the room. Inside it was dim, and he could barely see a curtain, halfway drawn. Ronald stopped for a moment, unsure what to do next. From behind the curtain, he could pick out half of Marjorie's body, neatly covered by a white sheet. He wandered to the curtain, forcing his body to move. His arms and legs were shaking. In a single, violent movement he whipped the curtain away, revealing his mother's body. She was pale but looked peaceful, and her arms were crossed gently over her chest.

Next to her lifeless body, Ronald slowly dropped to his knees and quietly began to pray; "Lord, she is absent from this world but in your presence. Grant me the strength to tell my father and guide me to the truth of what caused my mother's death. Amen!" He stood up and remained a short time by his mother's gurney. He could no longer cry. Slowly he realized that while his mother was no longer with him, she was now with the Lord, basking in His glory. A feeling of peace replaced his sorrow.

It was six-thirty a.m. when Ronald returned to his apartment. He tried to get some rest but found that he still could not sleep, so he got up to get started his day. Ronald sat down to eat breakfast but had no appetite. He tried to think of what he was going to do that day, but he couldn't focus on anything. He got dressed and decided to dress in black to mourn his mother. He noted the time and impulsively decided to call Josephine. She was a television producer and a close friend of Ronald's, and he knew she would be arriving home from work about that time. Her phone rang five times, then went to voicemail. "You've reached Josephine. Unfortunately, I'm unable to pick up the phone right now, please leave a message. Beep…"

"This is Ronald," he spoke to the recording. "My mom… died this morning. Please call me."

At seven-twenty Ronald was in the shower when he heard a loud knocking on his door. "This is Josephine, open the door!" A voice yelled from outside. The knocking intensified. "Are you okay Ronald? Open the door!" Ronald hurried the shower pulling on a navy blue bathrobe. She continued knocking as he rushed up the hallway. "This is Josephine! Open up, or I see. . ." Ronald yanked the door open, cutting her off midsentence. He stood there, still dripping from his shower.

Josephine hugged Ronald hard and held him close for a minute. They finally broke apart, and she looked up at him and said solemnly; "What can I say to make you feel better at a time like this?"

Ronald began to sob, unable to control himself. "I'm so glad you're here—I lost track of time after leaving you the message—and I didn't know if you'd come," he said tearfully. "I don't know how to do this alone I . . . Need a friend. I need you. How is a Son supposed to take the death of his Mom?"

By now the tears were freely flowing freely on Josephine's face as well. "I'm here," she whispered. "I've known you nine years, and I've never seen you like this… I can't imagine what you're going through, but I'm here, and I'll help any way I can." She patted him on the cheek. "Go dry off, get ready, I'll make some coffee, and we can talk."

Fifteen minutes later, they were sitting down together around two steaming mugs of coffee. Ronald felt better. "There's nothing like the smell of fresh coffee," he said. Thanks, Josephine". "How am I going to tell Dad about Mom?" He continued despondently

"Is Doctor Wyatt still treating your dad?" Josephine asked calmly.

"Yeah, he is."

"Let's finish our cups. Then I'll help you organize yourself."

"I'd really appreciate that, it's been hard to focus lately," Ronald thanked her.

"Well, first I'd call Dr. Wyatt and ask for his advice," Josephine said, sipping at her coffee. "He's the best qualified to know Bob's physical and mental condition and how the news about your mom will affect him."

"That's true, he has been treating dad for almost three years now," Ronald said thoughtfully.

"Do you want me to go with you to talk to him?"

"Thanks, Josephine, but this is something I think I need to deal with alone. It's going to take a lot of adjusting."

"I agree with you," she said sympathetically. "I'm here for you anytime you need me. That is, anytime except between midnight and six-thirty in the morning." She drained her cup, and they both stood up. As she was walking out the door, she looked back and said, "May the Counselor of peace guide your steps. Call me!" Later that morning, Ronald called White Rock Funeral Home, where funeral arrangements for his parents had been made three years before. He notified the director of Marjorie's death and arranged for her body to be moved from the hospital to the funeral home and to be prepared for burial.

This made Ronald realize that his feelings of loss were more intense than could ever have imagined and that he would need professional help on how to deliver the news to his father. He called Dr. Wyatt, the psychiatrist who had been treating his father the last three years. He wanted to know how he could minimize the trauma to his father when he told him of his wife's death.

Dr. Wyatt expressed his sympathy and agreed to see Ronald immediately.

"Hello, Dr. Wyatt," Ronald greeted him as he walked into his office.

"I appreciate you meeting me on such short notice. As I explained, my mother passed away this morning in the Orthopedic Hospital, as a result of a sudden fall at home, and my father is at Good Samaritan Hospital as a consequence of the same incident. You've known my Dad for many years now, and I wanted to ask your advice on how to break it to him."

"Of course, you have my full support!" Dr. Wyatt said as he motioned for Ronald to sit down. "Let me go over it real quick. I've known Bob for many years—I'm not sure if you know, but we've known each other since he was city attorney. He's a good man, your father. He was always so quick-witted—and people liked him." Dr. Wyatt sighed heavily. "He was my friend- but then he became my patient. That car accident—it changed him. His mind is still lucid sometimes, but his ability to speak and understand is limited. The only way to tell him about Marjorie's death is the truth. How you deliver that truth is the issue." He looked at Ronald, his eyes full of sadness and compassion. "Would you like me to go with you to deliver the news?"

Ronald is speechless for a moment, profoundly moved by Dr. Wyatt's offer. "How should we do it?" he finally asked.

"First, you need to know what Bob opens up some and feels better when I talk to him about the good ol' days. That way he'll be more receptive and initiate more conversations. It's also a good gauge to see what sort of mental state he happens to be in that day. My advice is to go to the hospital one hour after lunch time. Bob will be calm, and the shock can be minimized. Start a conversation with a short story about an experience you all shared and where, in the end, Bob was the hero. Then, bring up another good experience, but this time with Marjorie the principal character. Then tell him how happy you are with his care at that hospital, especially the food he likes. Bring up how bad your Mom's situation was, say how she was connected to multiple monitors, how a tube was jammed into her windpipe, how she couldn't move or speak. She could only be fed intravenously. Tell him how she was suffering but couldn't express how much. Stop there and wait for his response." Ronald nodded as a lump began to form in his throat.

"I'll tell Bob the actual news," Dr. Wyatt continued solemnly. "I'll say to him that you're going to take care of him. After we deliver the news, we should both stay there as long as we can and talk about good times, especially with Marjorie and the family. These memories will trigger the right parts of his brain."

"Thanks, Dr. Wyatt, I really appreciate your advice and I and accept you offer," Ronald said, and then stood up and offered the doctor his hand.

Dr. Wyatt shook it firmly and told Ronald; "I'll meet you in the lobby of Good Samaritan Hospital at two-fifteen this afternoon."

Ronald was there waiting for him at the appointed time and place.

"Hello Dr. Wyatt, thank you for coming," he said as Dr. Wyatt walked up to him.

"I'm glad to be here," Dr. Wyatt responded politely. "What's Bob's room number?

"He's in 223."

"Alright Ronald, you go ahead, I'll catch up in a minute or two."

"Okay, I'll be in inside."

Ronald knocked on the door, dreading what he would have to do inside. "Hey, Dad!" he said as cheerfully as possible. "How was lunch?"

"Oh Boy did Ms. Maya do a good job," Bob replied in his usual happy, slurred way. "Everything was good, and nice big portions too! Can you take me to visit your Mom today?" Bob asked suddenly.

This surprise question hit Ronald like a fist to the stomach, and he went straight to Dr. Wyatt's plan, slightly revised. "Well, Dad, I don't know if that's possible," he whispered, trying hard to keep his voice steady. "Last night, after seeing you, I stopped by to see if Mom had gotten any better. She was still hooked up to a bunch of machines, and had a breathing tube coming out of her throat." Ronald paused, and then in a very calm and controlled voice. "Mom couldn't move, or even talk. She was suffering, but she couldn't even say so. Her eyes were closed, but I could tell that she had a peaceful expression despite everything." He looked down at his father sadly. "The nurse had been in the ICU specialty for twenty years, and she told me it wasn't a good sign Mom was still out."

Ronald could see tears beginning to form in his father's eyes. "Look, son," Robert Cabot murmured, his voice clearer than ever. "Since the car accident I have suffered more that I am able to express. I love my wife so, so much, and I don't want her to be a vegetable like I was. I'd rather the Lord take her home than see her suffer another day." He began to tremble, and some of the tears welling in his eyes moved down his cheek.

Bob was speaking with the authority and conviction of a former city attorney, and Ronald was shocked that his father could still speak so sanely.

At that moment, there was a short rap on the door and Dr. Wyatt burst in. "Hey, Bob!"

"Hey! What's up doc...?" Bob said, sounding a little confused again.

"How're you feeling?" Dr. Wyatt inquired.

"I'm okay, but I wanna know how Marge is." Bob's moment of sanity had clearly passed.

"This morning I met with Ronald in my office, and we agreed that I should come to see you and talk to you about what's going on," Dr. Wyatt answered

As Dr. Wyatt was speaking, someone else began knocking on the door.

It was Maya. "Good afternoon Bob!" she greeted Bob in her usual happy way. She turned and looked surprised to see Dr. Wyatt there. "I'm sorry sir, but I don't think we're acquainted yet. What's your name?

"Hello, I am Dr. Wyatt," the doctor responded, shaking her hand. "I'm Bob's treating psychiatrist." Maya laughed. "Well, that makes more sense! Happy to meet you, Doctor Wyatt."

She turned to Ronald. "I'm here to see if I have your permission to bring our chaplain, Pastor Melick, and introduce him to Bob," she said, more seriously. "He's the spiritual strength of this department and everyone likes him." Bob apparently overhead, and raised himself on his elbows to respond. "You're hev'n sent Maya," he announced, now barely coherent. "We were just talkin' 'bout Marge- that's ma wife- and we both wan' meet this Pasteuuur."

"I'll call him now," Maya said quickly, looking a little worried.

"Thanks, Ms. Maya," Ronald said. "May I speak to you for a second?"

She nodded. "Let's go to my office and then we can bring the chaplain up to meet Bob." On the way she asked Ronald why he was visiting his father so early, and he gave her the news. Maya looked distressed as they entered her office. "Well it was all in the hands of the Lord," she told Ronald and picked up the phone to call pastor Melick.

Shortly he was there at the door. "Good afternoon," Melick greeted them. "How may I be of service?"

Maya introduced Ronald and the reason for her request for Melick to meet with Bob.

Ronald briefly discussed his family background and Bob's situation. He also told the pastor about Dr. Wyatt and quickly went over why his father was in this hospital, and why his mother had died in a different one.

"Let we pray in silence for wisdom, guidance, discernment, and strength before meeting your father," Melick said after a long pause.

A few minutes later Ronald and Melick showed up in Bob's room, where they found Dr. Wyatt deep in conversation with Bob.

"Dad, Doctor Wyatt, this is Pastor Melick," he introduced the chaplain.

Bob sat up in his bed. He looked sorrowful, but once again his words had regained some clarity. "After you had left, Dr. Wyatt and I prayed for wisdom, and I came to the conclusion that I do not have the moral authority to approve the medical termination of my wife's life." It was difficult for him to form the words properly, but he forged on; "We have enough money in the bank to keep her in the hospital until the Lord decides to take her home. We have enough money saved in the individual medical needs account to pay for my care, so my son doesn't have to take care of me or worry about my care."

Ronald went up to the bed and squeezed his father's right shoulder. At the same time Dr. Wyatt moved forward to the opposite side of the bed and placed his hand on Bob's left shoulder, and Melick stood at the foot of Bob's bed. "Mr. Cabot, the Lord hears your prayer. He is showing compassion for you and your son, and took your wife to be by his early side this . . ."

Bob's arms shot up, and he exclaimed; "Praise the Lord for His love and compassion!" He then he fell back on his pillow and fainted. Ronald immediately rushed to the door. "Nurse! Nurse!" he shouted. In a matter of seconds, the attending nurse was at Bob's side. She took his vital signs and, ignoring everyone else in the room, yelled out "Doctor Kent! Doctor Kent!" A physician quickly entered the room, and after examining Bob ordered the oxygen to be activated and placed a mask over his nose and mouth. Within a couple of minutes, Bob was conscious again. He was, however, totally disoriented and unsure of where he was or what was going on. The physician gave Bob a mild sedative and told Ronald that his father would be okay. "He needs sleep to recover." He murmured, then exited the room.

Dr. Wyatt, Ronald, and Melick remained in the room for another fifteen minutes until Bob finally dozed off to sleep. "Please let me know if there is anything else I can do to help," he said, breaking the heavy silence in the room. "I'll check back on Bob, pray with him when he awakens." He shook Dr. Wyatt's hand, preparing to leave. Before walking out the door, however, he turned back to Ronald. "Mr. Cabot, you go in peace and take care of all the matters you need to attend to. There are no patients in any major distress in the hospital today. Therefore, I will keep company with your father as long as necessary to make sure he will be spiritually sound and secure in the ultimate reality that he will eventually accompany his wife to her final resting place."

"Thank you, Pastor. We were blessed to have you here today. I'll be back in the afternoon."

"Amen, may the Lord guide you," Melick responded formally.

Dr. Wyatt signaled Ronald to follow Melick out. As they were walking, Ronald thanked Dr. Wyatt for coming with him. "I feel a new sense of strength. I'm really glad you came along."

Dr. Wyatt patted Ronald's shoulder. "Please call me and let me know how you are doing," he said warmly. "I'll come back tomorrow to see Bob when I finish at the clinic. Have a good afternoon Ron."

They parted ways, and Ronald headed to the funeral home to determine the available days and times for the services and burial. From there he went back to his apartment and drafted a list of people to be notified of his mother's passing and the funeral arrangements. After finishing the list, he called Josephine and asked her to make the calls for him.

At seven that evening, Ronald returned to the hospital to visit his father. As he approached the door, he could hear Bob talking to pastor Melick about what he was going to do if the bank situation actually had gone wrong. Ronald remained outside for a few more minutes unwilling to interrupt, and using the time to assess his father's state of mind.

Finally, he knocked and entered the room. "Hey, Dad, good evening Pastor Melick," he greeted them. "I'm glad you're both here. How are you two doing?"

"I am grateful to get to know your father and blessed that I was called to serve at this critical time," said Melick. Bob sat up and gestured for Ronald to come closer.

"Come here son," he said affectionately, "let me hold you for a moment and tell you how much I love you and appreciate you for what you did for your mother and all you are doing for me," His words were slurred, but still bright enough.

Ronald was again taken completely by surprise. He couldn't help himself and began to cry in his father's arms. "Thank you, Dad. I love you, and I promise I'll make everything turn out alright," he managed to choke out.

Speaking slowly, but completely lucidly, Bob said, "Pastor, Melick was with me right after I woke, and we spent most of the afternoon in prayer, and talking about how I remembered your mother saying, "The bank is going belly up." We know you have the legal training to investigate what is happening to the bank and where our money is." He looked at his son seriously, and once again the attorney Robert Cabot was speaking. "Then, you need to take whatever legal action you deem necessary to protect me and our interests." "Yes, Dad I will do all I can to get to the bottom of this, by the way, tomorrow will be in Frankfort meeting with a classmate an expert on this matters, I won't be here, Then he departed with padding his father's shoulder. I'll see you on Sunday."

In the same tone of voice, slurring some of his words, "That's Okay son, I'll need more rest."

JORGE RIVERA

Chapter 6
SUNDAY, MARCH 9, 2014

At seven in the morning, Josephine arrived at Ronald's apartment. The strong aroma of coffee hit her nostrils immediately. "Ron!" she called out. "You making coffee? I'm exhausted and would love a cup." Ronald appeared from the kitchen, holding a steaming mug.

"Would you like some toast?" he asked, handing her a cup. Josephine accepted the cup with a smile and shook her head. "Let's drink this then and talk for a second. Then I'll drive you home, you look way too tired to drive." Ronald returned to the kitchen to get another cup, and returned to find Josephine sound asleep on his couch. He covered her with a blanket and wrote a short note that he placed on the table by her. It read; "I'm going to La Grange to have breakfast with dad. Call when you wake up. Love, Ronald."

He arrived at the hospital, and upon opening the door to Bob's room he was met with a sight he never expected to see. Bob was walking around the room with a walker, completely mobile and healthy-looking. "Hey guy!" he said to cheerily. "Let me tell ya it's been a circus here lately!" He was still slurring some, but he sounded better than he had in a long time. "First at seven I find Josephine on the morning news! Our Josephine imagine that! Then at eight, the doc walked in to visit me and surprised me with the good news that tomorrow is the funeral and Marjorie will have military honors! At nine, five nurses arrived with my new walker, these flowers and that coffee cake. They walked singing Happy Birthday! Now at ten-thirty, you are here! I feel blessed."

Ronald stood speechless. He did not know how to react or what to say with Bob using his new walker. He saw the flowers and the cut coffee cake on the table.

"Oh... my goodness...," today is your Birthday! Congratulations! Ronald took a step forward and gripped his father's shoulders. 'I love you, Dad, Happy Birthday.'

Back at Ronald's apartment, Josephine woke up disoriented; her shoes were off, and to the side, her overcoat was on the chair facing the couch, her purse, and phone on the center table. She felt very strange and immediately picked up her phone and called Ronald. He did not get, so Josephine left a message asking him where he was. She called again, and another time after that, and still there was no response. Finally on the fourth time, right before it went to voicemail, she heard his voice say, "Hello?"

"This is Josephine where are you?!" she said sharply, expressing her frustration.

"Did you sleep well?" Ronald asked, ignoring her question.

"What do you mean? I asked where you are!" she said raising her voice.

"Didn't you see my note?" he said, sounding surprised.

"What note?"

"I left you a note right between your purse and telephone letting you know where I am."

"There's no note, Ron!"

"It's there, believes me. You don't have to get angry."

Josephine was about answered when she saw a small scrap of paper under the table.

"Oh... dear..., I am so sorry," she mumbled, "it's right here in the table one sec." She picked up the note and read it. Are you with your dad."

"I am here at the hospital with Dad celebrating his birthday," Ronald said, relieved. "The best news is that Dr. Wyatt came to visit him early this morning and while here he kindly took care of our forthcoming issue."

"Okay I'm going to stop by the flower shop, I'll be there in about forty-five minutes," Josephine said and hung up the phone. Around forty-five minutes later, she there wished Bob a happy birthday.

"Thanks, Jo," Bob wheezed, sounding a little more tired now after visiting with the family for so long. "How do you like my new transport?" He pointed at his walker.

"It has a handbrake and a seat, that's all you need!" she observed.

"If you guys don't mind I think I'm going to get a little shut-eye," Bob said groggily.

"Yeah Dad, you need to rest," Ronald told him. "I'll bring your clothes for the funeral in a bit," Josephine said goodbye and left the hospital.

At seven-thirty that evening Ronald returned with the promised change of clothes. He opened the door and entered. "Hey, Da-" his usual greeting was cut off by a loud shushing noise, from Dr. Wyatt, who was sitting at the foot of Bob's bed.

Ronald nodded, taking a seat next to him. "I prescribed a light antianxiety agent for your dad so to be alert and calm tomorrow," Dr. Wyatt whispered.

"I appreciate it, doctor," Ronald thanked him. "I'll leave these here then."

The two men left Bob asleep. On the way to the elevator, they agreed to meet at nine in the morning in the lobby to determine the plan of action, as the funeral would be a crucial test for Bob's state of mind and emotional readiness to handle the ultimate test of his love for Marjorie.

JORGE RIVERA

Chapter 7
MONDAY, MARCH 10, 2014

At 9:00 a.m. Dr. Wyatt met with Ronald and Josephine in the hospital lobby. After a brief conversation, Dr. Wyatt suggested that Ronald goes up to Bob's room first, and see if Bob is up and dressed and ready for everyone to show up.

Ronald entered Bob's room and found him up and dressed. "Hey, Dad!" He said, "You look like you're all ready to go."

"I got a good night's sleep that's why," Bob told his son, his words nearly distinct. "The nurse helped me get ready and got me an excellent big breakfast so I'd be willing for say goodbye to my Marjorie."

"Sounds good Dad," Ronald said, sitting down. "Is there anything else you need before I call everyone else up?"

"Yeah, after the ceremony and everything I want us to come back here and have some time together, just the family."

"No problem dad," Ronald murmured. "We'll do that."

Soon afterward everyone else came up to join Ronald in Bob's room.

"Bob!" Dr. Wyatt greeted him pleasantly, "we were talking downstairs with Josephine, and we thought we'd come up here and speak to you about the good ol' times."

"Yes, sharing memories of Marjorie with all of you would help me get through the day," and I don't even remember most of the people there anyways."

"Most will be exchanging the usual pleasantries anyways," Josephine observed. "It will be hard for them to really understand how you guys will be feeling. Better to talk about the personal things now. This is our time to be with Bob; this is our time for closeness, and this is our time for mutual support."

"Dad I'm going talk with the staff about refreshments for when we come back here, maybe make it like a little wake," Ronald said to Bob. He left the room and came back shortly, looking happy. "Yeah the nurse who's been taking care of Dad is great, she arranged everything. They'll have everything ready for when we return."

Oops! It's time to go!" Josephine announced suddenly.

The day of Marjorie's funeral was a bright but cold day, about thirty degrees, cold for mid-morning in the middle of March. Including family, fifty-seven people were in attendance including elected officials, civic leaders, and close friends.

A U.S. Army honor guard detail of eight fired three rifle volleys to honor Marjorie, who, as a dentist had served at one time as the Fort Knox Medical Officer. Colonel McGuire, the base commander, presented Bob with a folded U.S. flag to drape over her coffin.

After the funeral and a brief reception, Ronald, Dr. Wyatt, Josephine and five other close friends gathered around Bob in Good Samaritan Hospital. As the mourners exchanged condolences and talked about Marjorie's life, Bob suddenly sat straight up, his eyes bright and knowing. "So who's going to be charged for Marjorie's death?" he asked. The room went dead silent.

Chapter 8
WHO WAS RESPONSIBLE?

Who was responsible for Marjorie's death? Was it the bank, or the spine surgeon?

The real-life stories in this novel reveal the need for love and financial security. The treasonable conspiracy involved top executives and innocent people. Who was responsible for the unavoidable consequences?

Larry Jordan, Chief Executive Officer of the Louisville Midtown Bank. His crimes included conspiracy to commit securities fraud, wire fraud, making false entries in the bank's records, and making false statements to U.S government authorities. He defrauded the bank, its stockholders, savings, and deposit investments clients. Larry also defrauded the special medical needs trust funds, the elderly's retirement accounts, student college education funds, and the U.S. government of more than $300 million.

Larry was 56 years old, six-foot-three, with sandy hair, blue eyes, a tenor voice and a trim, athletic body. He was a bit reserved with new people yet had exceptional interpersonal skills. Larry was a graduate of the University of Toronto with a Master's degree in accounting and finance. He was also a hunter of large animals, and close friends called him the 'Big Game' sharp shooter. They knew little, however, of his wild secret double life. He was married to Barbara, a former Miss Kentucky. Although they had been married twenty-six years, Barbara retained the young body of her youth, with blonde hair and big hazel eyes. She was intelligent and socially active, taking part in many charitable activities raising money for the new Children's Hospital in La Grange. They had a daughter Megan, 21 and son Ralph, 19, both University of Kentucky students. Neither suspected that Larry's troubled past included gambling addiction.

Nancy McArthur turned 50 on December 23, 2014, the day of Larry Jordan's arrest by the Special Inspector General for the Troubled Asset Relief Program and the FBI. She was five foot ten inches tall, with beautiful olive skin, shoulder-length straight black hair, pronounced cheekbones and large cat-like green eyes. Nancy had the aura of a high-fashion model, dressed like one, and acted with good business manners. Her warm personality and interpersonal skills had won many high-profile private bank clients. Some would even bring her flowers and expensive presents. This attention suited her taste for fine art, which was the focus of her lavish four-bedroom home in the gated Creek Nest neighborhood, just seventeen minutes' drive from the bank. She would often be away from the bank, negotiating new investments and had asked Larry for an assistant to cover her duties while she was away.

Margaret Gianelli, 23, was five foot nine inches tall, with a gorgeous, round face, brown eyes, shoulder-length wavy sandy hair, soft white flawless skin, long legs and well-shaped arms. Margaret was spontaneous, had a unique sense of humor, and good listening and communicating skills. She was a graduate of the University of Kentucky with a Master's degree in political science. Margaret had served as an intern with the U.S. Treasury in Washington D.C. She returned to Kentucky and had been working in the Louisville Midtown Bank for a year. She was living in Woodland Hills, near Louisville, with her parents and brother. Margaret had a boyfriend, Jonathan, a lawyer. She was an accomplished golfer, liked music, going out with friends, and reading historical novels and following current events.

Earlier on that life-changing day, Larry called Nancy to his office and asked, "Please call Margaret Gianelli, and she's that girl executive assistant to Gil in our investor relations. John Muller, the real estate developer, our largest single investor in the last three years, especially recommended her for the job to assist you. Gianelli worked part-time for Muller while attending university, he said she was an excellent communicator, with multitasking abilities, and would be an asset to you, Nancy."

Nancy did not ask any questions, but just nodded and complied. "Margaret Gianelli? This is Nancy Mc Arthur, the executive secretary to Mr. Jordan. He would like to see you in his office in fifteen minutes."

"Am I fired?" Margaret's voice said from the other line, sounding flat and emotionless.

"Oh no, I don't think so," Nancy reassured her. "That's HR's job. He didn't say why he wanted to see you, so just freshen up and look your best. Be on time. He is a stickler about timeliness."

After Margaret, hung up the phone she began to panic, and rushed to the bathroom to check her makeup and apply more where needed.

Ten minutes later she looked at her wristwatch and exclaimed; "Oh God I'll be late!" She ran to the elevator, pushed the up button, and watched the elevator as it descended, 17, 16, and 15. It felt like an eternity, and she could not get her heart to stop pounding in her chest as she imagined what would happen if she were late. The elevator finally stopped, and she was relieved to see no one was in it. Margaret touched the button to the 20 floor, adjusted her blue, above-the-knee skirt, and tightened her light pink long sleeve, open collar blouse. In no time at all, the elevator doors opened, and she found herself in front of Nancy's desk.

"Good morning, I am Margaret, are you Nancy?" she asked the handsome woman sitting behind it.

Nancy nodded and smiled. She regarded Margaret and said, "you look more mature than I expected, how old are you?"

"I just turned 23 yesterday, and this is my first full-time job." She looked down at herself, suddenly doubtful. "Do I look okay?"

"You look beautiful, don't worry dear," Nancy said with a smile. "Please go through that double door and introduce yourself to Mr. Jordan." Nancy moved ahead, opened the door for Margaret and announced, "Here is Margaret, Mr. Jordan. Larry looked up from his desk. "How do you do Margaret?"

"I'm fine Mr. Jordan, thank you."

"This morning I briefly talked with Gil in the investor relations department. She has given me an excellent report of how well you are coming along during your first year with our bank," Larry told her, to be friendly. Margaret nodded and smiled, as her right foot tapped crazily on the floor. She was very nervous. Larry wanted to test her interpersonal skills and ability to handle confidential matters. So, he decided to give her an out of the ordinary assignment that either would make her the ideal candidate to help Nancy or would be a good sign to seek another person.

"Are you familiar with the shopping center where Saks Fifth Avenue is located? " Larry asked suddenly. Margaret sat up straighter. She had not expected such a question. "Oh yes sir!" she exclaimed. "I go there often to window shop."

"Right, then would you consider running an errand for me, going to a store and picking up a gift I ordered for my wife?"

"Oh course sir, it's no problem at all," she said, relieved.

Larry picked up the telephone and called Carlos, his personal driver. "Carlos, please come to my office, I would like you to drive Ms. Gianelli, our new assistant, to the store. She'll tell you where to pick up a package. I want you to park the car in the valet parking and wait for her until she brings the box to the car, and then bring her back and walk with her to the sixth floor."

"Mr. Jordan, how do I recognize Ms. Gianelli?" Carlos asked.

"Just come up, she's in my office."

"Yes Sir, I will be there in five minutes, I need to come up from downstairs."

Larry hung up the phone and looked at Margaret with a broad smile on his face. "Okay Margaret this is important but really easy," he said jovially. "All you need to do is go to Victoria's Secret store, ask for Ms. Goodrich, introduce yourself and hand her this envelope. Wait until she gives you a bag with a package inside. It's a surprise gift for my wife! Bring the bag to the car. If Carlos asks you where you were or what you were doing only, say "A shopping favor for Mr. Jordan." When he brings you back to the office, take the gift to your desk and keep it there until I call you this afternoon and tell you where to deliver it for me."

Margaret could not help but raise an eyebrow. "I understand," she said hesitantly. At that moment Carlos came into the office.

"This is Carlos Torres, my driver," Larry introduced him. "He's been driving professionally for fifteen years, you'll be safe with him." Larry chuckled.

"Thank you, Mr. Jordan," Margaret said as she stood up. "I'll be back to deliver it when you call." Carlos and Margaret rode the elevator in silence. They walked to the front of the building where a black Lincoln town car was waiting. Carlos opened the right rear door for Margaret, closed it, walked around to the driver side, and asked, "Where are we going, Ms. Margaret?"

Margaret felt important and empowered, running what was obviously a special errand for her boss. At this point, she doubted it was actually a gift for his wife. "To Saks Fifth Avenue store. In the new shopping center, located at the outlet shops of the Blue Grass, please," she responded, immediately realizing she sounded pompous.

"Of course, Ms. Margaret.... Do you mean Sacks OFF 5th?"

"Yes.., that one," she said quickly, a little red. Before she could really think about what she was saying she suddenly asked; "Carlos, you haven't said a word since the elevator, why?"

Carlos regarded her for a moment.

"I was hired for this job, fifteen years ago," he finally responded. "On my first day of work I was told: "You have eyes, but you can't see.

Ears, but you can't hear. Mouth but you can't speak." As you can see Ms. Margaret, I am still the driver, and my job is secure with the bank."

"Thank you"—Margaret said politely, but her mind began to conjure wild fantasies of what she was picking up, and the sort of things that Mr. Jordan was involved in. Wow, Lingerie! I am now an insider to the top man, what is he all about? He looks so stoic and formal that to most people command respect. Am I special? Why am I feeling this way? She felt like a secret agent, picking up . . .

Suddenly, she heard Carlos' voice. "Ms. Margaret we're here." She looked around, a little confused. "Wow! I must've lost track of time. Okay wait here, I won't take long at all."

Carlos stopped the car at the valet reserved parking, opened the right rear door, and watched Margaret disappear into the crowd.

Forty-five minutes later, Margaret reappeared walking slowly towards the parked car, shouldering a Walt Disney tote bag while licking at an ice cream cone.

"Ms. Margaret, how is your ice cream?" Carlos inquired, a little ironically. "Did your mission go well?"

"Yeah this is good, it's gelato actually, and yes, all went according to plan," she responded.

"Now where do you need to go?"

"To my house on Mimic Way, off the Flat Rock Road, in the Polo Fields near the Polo Fields Golf and Country Club, I'll tell you which one's my house when we get near."

"Alright, we'll be there in about twenty-five minutes," Carlos said.

"Thanks, Carlos. Can you turn on the music to a classical station or something?"

"I can do better than that," Carlos chuckled. "Open the central console by your left elbow and chose from there, and I'll play it for you."

"Wow, this is great!" Margaret exclaimed as she went through the available music. I love Rachmaninoff, especially Piano Concerto Number Two.

"Ms. Margaret, enjoy and let me know where to stop," Carlos said. Margaret nodded, feeling embarrassed that she had allowed herself to talk so much.

She continued her private fantasies, imagining romantic sex scenarios of Mr. Jordan and his wife while listening to Chopin's Concerto Number Two. Her decision to divert the driver to her house was a calculated one. She knew that if she walked to the sixth floor of the bank with a Disney bag after being absent for over an hour and twenty minutes, it would trigger all kinds of questions from her female co-workers. These would jeopardize her new insider privileges.

"Oh, Carlos, Carlos," she leaned forward. "It's that light blue house second from the right corner. You can park in the driveway. I won't be a minute."

When she returned, carrying the same shoulder Disney tote bag Carlos opened the car door and asked, "Where to now Ms. Margaret?"

"To the office, please."

"What other music would you like me to play for you?" Carlos asked. Margaret mulled over it for a second.

"I spent a year studying Spanish in Salamanca, Spain, and I fell in love with Spanish boleros," she said finally. Do you know anything like that?"

"Not in the car console programming. However, I have a CD in the trunk. May I stop so I can put in a CD of a famous bolero by the Mexican songwriter Consuelo Velasquez? She wrote this song in 1940, and she became celebrated in Mexico, Latin America, and the world," Carlos explained. "Vasquez earned the Latin Grammy in 2001, and she became a member of the Hall of Fame."

"That'd be perfect!" Margaret said excitedly.

The music was playing. Both sat quietly as over the car speakers the memorable lyrics of Velasquez play- Besame... Besame mucho... Como si fuera esta noche la ultima vez.... Besame ... This hypnotizing rendition by Tino Rossi brought Margaret back to her exciting time in Salamanca while Carlos—who knew what she was thinking.

Suddenly Carlos announced they had arrived his voice sounding harsh and abrupt after Rossi's smooth baritone. He parked the car and looked over at Margaret, who was gathering her things. "Maybe I can lend you this CD and perhaps some others one day," he said.

"Oh!" is all Margaret can say, caught off guard by Carlos' sudden change. "Thank you!"

He got out, opened the right rear door, and offered his hand to help Margaret with the bag. She kept held in the bag but took his hand to help her keep her balance as she got out. They walked together to the bank entrance.

Before pressing the elevator up button, Carlos said, "I was directed by Mr. Jordan to walk you to the sixth floor."

"Thank you, Carlos, but that's not necessary; I have to make a special stop on the way."

"Understood. It was a pleasure serving you, Ms. Margaret."

Chapter 9
DISGUISED

Margaret decided that instead of going to her desk, as initially instructed, she would go back to the office of Mr. Jordan to give him the results of her assignment. She stopped by Nancy's office to ask if Mr. Jordan was available.

Ignoring Margaret's question, Nancy asked, "What is in the bag?"

"The book Mr. Jordan told me to find for him," Margaret lied calmly.

The answer seemed to satisfy Nancy, who called Larry to let him know Margaret had arrived. "Please send Margaret in," he said over the intercom.

Margaret walked in to find Larry sitting on the front edge of his massive mahogany desk, with his right leg on the floor and the left slightly a few inches above the ground. His face was completely neutral, but Margaret with her experience in politics could sense a poker face when she saw one.

Margaret confidently entered and stood in the middle of the room, four feet from her boss. "Mr. Jordan, upon completing my assignment I decided that instead of going to the 6th Floor and facing a lot of questions from my co-workers, I would go to my house and switch out the package with a book I've been reading. And that's what I did. Carlos is the only one that might suspect, and he told me about him "Don't see nor tell policy." Larry's strong features suddenly relaxed, as if the weight of the world had been taken off his shoulders.

"Thank you! I really appreciate your competence," he said with surprising candor. "Please tell me everything that happened."

"It all went perfectly," Margaret said confidently. "The package is secure in my house and available whenever you need it. I bought the bag to distract attention from whatever was inside, here's the receipt." She handed it to him. "Everyone in the office, even Carlos, is curious about what's inside, but let me assure you that I didn't take a single peek of the package. My father was in the Foreign Service, and he always taught me how important it is to be prudent and keep my eyes and ears open while using common sense and staying out of things I'm not a part of." Larry's relief was palpable. He felt one hundred percent certain he had picked the right person for the job.

"Margaret you're an exceptional young lady, and you've impressed me," he told her. "I'm going to have Nancy compensate you for the bag and book. Now excuse me, please. I need to make a call."

Margaret thanked him and left the room. He called Nancy and asked her to pay her for the items Margate had bought. "I'll do that sir. Shall I pay her from the discretionary fund?" Nancy asked.

"Yes, please. Also, call Gil, her supervisor and tell her that I'm recommending Margaret to become the girl Friday for your office, the Board of Directors and this office. I want you to know that Margaret achieved in two hours what Barbara, Megan, and Ralph could not do for the last six months."

There was a pause, and Larry could sense Nancy's surprise. "Understood Sir," she said finally. Larry walked to the door to call Margaret back in.

"Margaret thanks again," he told her, visibly pleased. "I've promoted you to be an assistant here on the executive floor. Nancy will familiarize you with your new job and its responsibilities."

"Thank you, Sir!" Margaret blurted out.

Larry nodded then continued; "I am not only impressed but pleasantly surprised by how efficiently you completed your first assignment with the executive office. Let me call Nancy to direct John the facilities supervisor to arrange your new office, it'll be right next to mine which gives you direct access to me and the boardroom. Open that door and take a look!" Margaret went over to the polished wooden door he was pointing at and opened it.

"Wow!" she exclaimed. "I can see the golf course from here!" She noticed Larry had raised his eyebrows quizzically. "Oh I really enjoy golf," she explained. "Although I haven't been able to afford it since I left school, my parents won't pay for my games anymore."

She sighed, feeling sentimental and longing to smell the fresh-cut grass on the practice course early in the morning. She thought of standing on the first tee, sighting the ball, landing to the left of the sand trap 250 yards away, of feeling the light weight of her "Ping" one-iron club on her left hand, the cross wind, the fairway . . .

"Hey! Are you daydreaming?" Larry's voice cut off her thoughts. She turned to Larry, embarrassed, with an apology on her lips, but she found he had a broad smile on his face. By now Nancy had arrived and stood in silence while Larry was looking at Margaret with a particular admiration.

"There's a lot to do if you want to move to this floor by next week, said Nancy. I'll take you through it. We need to give notice to Gil, then we need to stop by HR and ask Karen to authorize your move to the executive floor, and then we'll go to security to issue your new "full access" badge. After that, we'll go to the executive dining room, so I can introduce you to everyone. Make sure to make friends with all of them, you're going to be asking them to do the impossible pretty often, and you'll need them on your right side."

By then, Margaret was getting a little worried about what the opportunity offered to her actually involved. Seeing Nancy work, seeing her tackle seemingly impossible tasks with astounding speed, began to make her very nervous, and she started sweating while her pulse accelerated. Margaret decided that she would play dumb with Nancy so she would explain as much as possible to her. On the elevator ride back down to the lower levels, she asked Nancy; "What's this new badge do for me?"

"The new badge will give you 24/7 access to the entire building," Nancy replied, "but you'll have to go through some screening before you can get it. After the investor's department, and HR, we'll go to security and have you fingerprinted. Once results are back from the FBI, a biometrics measurement will take place, and then they'll give you your new ID with your new access badge. You'll be able to go anywhere in the building, no questions asked, and you'll need to do is face the biometrics camera so that it recognizes your features, and when the light turns green, any door will open for you—that simple, yet totally secure."

Margaret whistled, impressed. "The security in this bank is fantastic... I never thought I'd have my face scanned like that it's like I'm in a spy movie or something!" She laughed in a purposefully empty-headed way. Nancy looked at her, and Margaret could tell that she had interpreted her airhead act as a cover for fear.

"I've been working with this bank for twenty-two years and as executive secretary to Mr. Jordan for the last fifteen," Nancy told her. The day I was promoted to the executive floor, I was as scared as you are today; I was so nervous and almost ready to tell my previous supervisor to forget the move and let me remain in my old department! I was enjoying a good relationship with my co- workers and those individual clients paid really well."

Margaret was intrigued, and more than a little suspicious.—"Who are private clients?" she asked Nancy.

"Individual clients are bank customers with a lot of money, at least a million dollars to officially be considered a private client," Nancy explained. "And to deal with them, you have to be a licensed Register Representative offering securities, or also known as Register Agent. This license allows you to sell stocks and bonds to private clients, who are also qualified investors. I have the largest portfolio of investment customers of anyone in the bank," she added proudly. "I've built these relationships over my twenty-two years with the bank. Long ago before my time in the bank, I was working for an investment-banking firm here in town. This was an upgrade for me and one I'm enjoying every day."

Margaret pretended to be distracted with the elevator buttons, but she listened to every word Nancy said. Without giving any sign of tiring, Nancy gave more information about her career in investment banking and with the Louisville Midtown Bank. Margaret continued her act, prompting Nancy on when she felt she was going to stop talking. Despite her calm demeanor, Margaret was feeling intimidated by the whole thing and wishing the day could be over so could go home and rest, and evaluate and organize her thoughts. She also wanted to ask her father for his own impression of what had happened during the day, and his opinion of her new job.

Margaret suddenly found herself out of the elevator and in front of Gil's office. "Here we are, please go to your desk and make a list of pending issues," Nancy said kindly.

Margaret promptly went to her desk and recorded her unfinished tasks, checked her mailbox and began writing an email to Ms. Gil Taylor—" Ms. Taylor, I've been promoted by Mr. Jordan to be the assistant to Ms. Nancy Mc Arthur's executive office. Thank you for the opportunity to work under your direction, should you ever need anything, please do not hesitate to call me; I am available to you by phone anytime during working hours. Sincerely, Margaret." She printed out the Memorandum and delivered it to Taylor's office, and printed out a copy to give to Nancy. She then walked out to report to Nancy, who had been waiting outside. "I checked my mail and inbox. No tasks pending for today," she said confidently. Ms. Taylor appeared suddenly from her office and to congratulate Margaret and wished her luck with her new job. Margaret gave her a tight hug and left with Nancy.

As Margaret walked by her former co-worker and friend's desk on

the way to the elevator, she whispered, "Call me tonight, big news!"
While waiting for the elevator to come up to their floor, Nancy said,
"Margaret that memo was unexpected and a touch of class. I am
pleased with the way you are handling your surprise departure. I like
that a lot!"

At the Human Resources Department, Nancy spoke for Margaret.
"Hello Karen, I am here with Margaret Gianelli, at the request of Mr.
Jordan. I just need your approval and documentation for Margaret's
promotion to the executive office, and authorization for the Security
Chief to issue Margaret an all-access ID badge."

"Hum…lucky you, Margaret!—Karen said. "Please give me an hour,
and I will have all documents ready for your transfer, and we'll make
the Security Chief aware of your visit."

"Let's go to the executive dining room while Karen completes the
paperwork, and I'll give you a run down about each person there,"
Nancy told Margaret. "The members of the Board of Directors, Mr.
Jordan and the executive officers, along with the bank's private clients,
are often guests there. You'll be in charge of keeping the guest happy
and the staff smiling. Board meetings will often extend to eight in the
evening. The schedule is quite demanding. Don't be concerned with the
pay. Your salary for that pay period will increase anytime you work more
than ten hours. Also, you'll receive a bonus during board meetings."

"What do you mean by more than ten hours?" Margaret asked
suddenly, a little disquieted. "Please, Ms. McArthur, explain this to me
because I do not want to become a 24/7 bank employee at any price. I
love to work here, and I'm excited and happy with the promotion.
However, I will have to reconsider the whole idea if I have to be
available on a 24/7 basis. I have a boyfriend that I love, have my parents,
have a life, and I won't give it up for double or even triple pay." Margaret
realized with dismay she had lost her composure—her face was getting
hot and her hands—were clenched at her sides.

"Margaret, it's okay, I think we've had a misunderstanding of the
situation, and I've accidentally give you the wrong impression," Nancy

reassured her. "We call the spring-Annual meetings a big deal. This is a time when the bank stockholders, not all of them but a substantial number of these come to the bank. They meet with the executive team, hear a summary of operations, and vote on the next year's business plan. This report is discussed and voted on at the spring-Annual meetings, it is published on September 30th of each year. During this time, we are to cater to stockholder's wishes and make them feel good about being the owners of this bank. We hire a professional event coordinator company that specializes in managing all aspects of these banking activities including communications, promotion, hospitality, transportation and logistics. These meetings take place here at the bank, on the 40th- floor penthouse. You will have the opportunity to see it on Monday, for the view of the city from this floor is spectacular!"

She continued- "I handle the outcome of these meetings, and you will be my shadow and assistant to bring the upcoming April meetings to a new level. Typically, on those three days, I arrive at six in the morning and leave at six in the evening. During this time each year, you will have bonus compensation because you are on call to work twelve hours—Oh! Karen is calling." Nancy picked up her phone. "Hello, Karen! Are you ready for us?" Karen's voice was inaudible from the other line. "We'll be down right away," Nancy answered to whatever Karen had said. "See you in a few minutes." She hung up and turned to Margaret with a thumbs up, looking excited. "its official Maggie, you're part of the executive office! The deal with security will only take fifteen minutes; the chief will order a new picture of you, and electronically then send your fingerprints to the FBI. I assume you haven't had had any encounter with the law?

"Ah...yes!" Margaret responded. A sudden chill went up Nancy's spine, but after only a short pause, Margaret continued—"the only time I had a face-to-face with the law was one night I got lost after leaving the Valhalla Golf Club."

"Tell me about it!" Nancy said cautiously.

"It was last summer, after playing my final tournament of golf with the University team," Margaret explained. "We stayed late to celebrate, and I left after dark. Accidentally, after leaving the club, I turned left on Highway 60 instead of turning right towards my home in Woodland Hills. I had driven for 45 minutes before I realized I was lost and could not see how to turn back. I stopped the car on the shoulder of the highway to find my phone and see where I was my location. It was dark and lonely, and I started getting scared, so I locked all my doors. I was attempting to get my GPS to work, but I didn't have any signal. I started panicking. I began to sweat, and my heart began to jump on my chest like a scared rabbit. Then, I remember my father he always said, "When in trouble pray." I started praying and asked the Lord for help," Margaret smiled at the memory that had long lost its terror. "I promised Him I will go to church Sunday, Tuesday, Wednesday and any day he wanted me to, if only he'd get me home safe! And then suddenly, in my rearview mirror, I saw a bunch of blue lights, and I heard a voice say over a loudspeaker; "This is the Kentucky State Police!" I froze right then, and before I knew it there was a bright flashlight in my face, I heard a voice say 'Are you, okay Madam?'

"With relief, I responded. "I am a scared officer." Then, I told him what had happened, and he was sympathetic. He confirmed that this was a poor cell phone reception area, and he comforted me by saying no one lives here other than all kinds of large, animals that sometimes are the cause of accidents. I thanked him and asked him how to get home. I ended up following him back to Woodland Hills." She finished her story and looked at Nancy. "That was my only encounter with the law." Nancy had to hold back an audible sigh of relief "Well I don't think you'll have a problem there," she said. They had arrived with security.

"Ah, here we are. Charles, good morning," she greeted the man at the front desk. "This is Margaret Gianelli, the new member of the executive team."

"Hello Ms. Gianelli, please go to the next door office to your left. The Deputy Chief is waiting to supervise your photo shoot, and he will conduct an electronic Live-scan. Do you have any questions?"

"No Sir, I don't" Margaret answered mildly.

A few minutes later Margaret returned from the Deputy Chief's office wearing a "Temporary" All access ID badge with her new picture.

"Thank you, Charles, have an excellent day," Nancy said. She continued. "It's noontime, and the National City Tower building will be like a beehive, with people going and coming in all directions. We're lucky we're going to the exec dining room, it's usually quiet there. It's operated under the guidance of one of the best Italian Chefs, Mario Corelli; he's been under contract since 1990." They stopped in front of the restaurant door.

"Your job is to win over the dining room staff, and I feel you could do that job even better than I have. Let's go inside." Nancy opened the door for Margaret, and they walked in to meet the host. "Is Mario in today?" Nancy asked him.

"Yes, he is," the host responded politely. I'll let him know you're here. Will you be dining with us today?"

"Yes, a table is for four, please."

"This way," The host showed them to a table for four.

"Table for four!" Margaret murmurs, intrigued. "Who's joining us?

Nancy placed her paperwork and notebook on a chair to her left and signaled Margaret to take the chair facing her. Then she presses a single digit o her iPhone and says—"Mr. Jordan, Margaret and I are in the dining room do you have plans for lunch? If not, I'll order for you right now!"

JORGE RIVERA

Chapter 10
SPECIAL ACCESS

"Is Mr. Jordan coming to have lunch with us now?" Margaret asked curiously.

"He'll call me back and let me know," Nancy responded. "He's kind of busy towards the end of the week—especially Friday that's when we cram to get everything done."

Mario walked up to Nancy's table. He was tall, handsome, and with his black hair and delicate, arched eyebrows, he looked classically Italian. "Good afternoon ladies, how are you?"

"Good Mario, how about yourself? He gave a perfunctory nod and Nancy continued- "This is Margaret Gianelli, my new shadow, and assistant to the executive office. I'm showing her the ropes so she can start taking over a lot of what I do, for example how to deal with those snobs from the government relief program. You know how they are, taking over our offices and asking for this and that document—and so hard to feed! I'm thinking about just letting them eat Big Macs this year."

"That's no good!" Mario exclaimed. "We'll make them feel like they're at home here at the dining room, cook just like their mothers would. Anyways, are you planning to have lunch with Mr. Jordan today? I'm already preparing Vitello al burro e capers for Mr. Jordan. We know his tastes."

"That sounds right for us too." Nancy's phone began ringing, and she excused herself.

While Nancy was on the phone, Mario asked Margaret; "How do you like working with the executive office? There's a lot to do to keep stockholders and their guests happy, but it's a job we all do together, it's not difficult at all."

"Thanks, Mario, I'd really like it if you could give me a tour of the place and introduce me to the staff while Nancy's on the phone."

"Let us go and meet my crew!" Mario responded enthusiastically. Fifteen minutes later; Mario and Margaret returned, but Nancy was still away on the telephone. Mario offered Margaret a glass of white wine while waiting for Nancy, but Margaret politely declined. Mario excused himself and added—"I will finish the preliminary preparation of the Vitello in case Mr. Jordan decides to have lunch with us!" Almost immediately after Mario left the table, Nancy returned.

"Sorry for taking so long," she apologized, sitting down. "Mr. Jordan was explaining to me that the government people called, and they'll be here Monday. It's bad news because Mr. Jordan is scheduled to travel on that day." She took off her glasses and rubbed at the corners of her eyes. "We were expecting their visit in two weeks. Not now!"

"Is Mr. Jordan coming to lunch…?" Margaret asked.

"Mr. Jordan, the Chief Financial Officer Mr. Lubec and the bank's internal Auditor Mr. Jones will be having lunch with us. Mr. Jordan wants all of us to hear the situation briefing, so we are all on the same page."

"Wow, this job is turning out to be something else," Margaret observed. "Only two hours in and I've been given a tour of an executive dining room, and now I'm going to be part of a high-level meeting with a bunch of the higher ups, sure beats sorting mail from investors!" Nancy smiled.

Larry and two other men arrived soon afterward. "Hello Margaret, these are Mr. Roy Lubec and Mr. Keith Jones," Larry introduced the two men. "We'll eat first, then get down to business."

Roy Lubec was Chief Financial Officer of the Louisville Midtown Bank. He was 59 years' old, five-foot-eight, one hundred seventy-five pounds, with black hair, brown eyes, a harsh and grating voice, and a stocky body. He'd been married to Bertha for twenty-seven years. She was a former army sergeant and very active in various community projects and charitable activities. They had a son, Jerry, 23, a computer programmer. Neither suspected Roy's drinking problem and gambling addiction. Roy was a real estate investor and especially enjoyed horse racing.

Keith Jones was the internal auditor of the Louisville Midtown Bank. He was 58 years old, five-foot-eleven, one hundred sixty pounds with shiny white hair and hazel eyes and a soothing voice and a slender build. He'd been married to Elizabeth, a retired high school teacher, for twenty-five years. She was also active in local programs for people with disabilities. She had a cold personality and kept a tight hold on her family. They had a daughter, Jennifer, 24, a social sciences researcher at the University of Louisville. Keith was an avid chess player.

"Hello Nancy, what do we have today?" Larry asked Nancy.

"Veal and whatever Mario brings with it. It's always a surprise."

Mario came at that moment with a dish. "Gentlemen, I have something special for you," he announced. "This is the first time I made this for you and the executive office team,—it's an appetizer of dry-cured smoked ham, we call it in Italian prosciutto affumicato."

"Thanks, Mario sounds delicious," Larry said, although it was obvious his mind was somewhere else.

"No problem, Sir!" Mario and some other waiters served them their meal. No one spoke as they ate, and the atmosphere was tense.

Margaret paid close attention to everything happening around her, observing everyone's habits and demeanor. Finally, they were done, and the waiters took their dirty plates away and served the coffee. Margaret noticed Nancy looking inquisitively at Larry as if to ask "What the hell is going on?"

After they were done with their coffees, Larry immediately began his briefing without preamble. "I was notified two hours ago that the government people from the bailout program had to move their scheduled visit to our bank up by two weeks due to scheduling conflicts. I am not pleased with this change because next Monday I was going to Georgetown in the Cayman Islands to complete the buyout of the Caribbean Bank. This transaction would give our private clients additional options and benefits from the freedom to trade internationally with little or no fees attached to each transaction."

"You don't have to cancel your plans, after all, these people will only deal with my office and Keith's," Roy interjected. "Also, Nancy has most of your reports completed. There are just the last week trades that need to be "Manicured" and put in place. Therefore, I can't see any reason to postpone your travel. I already submitted to the Caribbean Bank the last of the financial statements requested."

At this point, Margaret made a mental note of the term "Manicured" and what it could possibly mean in this context.

Keith agreed with Roy, and added, "As far as I am concerned, these people may be late in preparing their reports. To make things look right, they chose to advance their time to remove our "Packet.""

"Please forgive me but I think Mr. Jordan should stay put and, at least receive them in person," Nancy said. "Then he can go to the Cayman Islands."

Margaret made a mental note of the factions beginning to emerge in the discussion, and what "Packet" could be. She realized that her experience in banking and investing terminology was limited and that she could be reading too much into the statements being made. She was feeling a little anxious but also strangely calm, as if she was an entirely neutral observer with nothing to do with the matters being discussed.

Suddenly, Larry, turned towards Margaret and asked, "If you had the power and ultimate decision in this situation, what would you do?"

Margaret was utterly shocked by the question, and for a moment she was speechless. "Mr. Jordan, I am going to answer your question solely based on my political science education," she finally answered. "My response is a verbatim quote from one of my professors. "First, the experience is the best insurance policy against the adverse effects of a surprise, because it allows people to recognize what's happening during the unexpected event and, therefore, respond earlier and more efficiently. So, Mr. Jordan, your presence would reduce the level of chaos, keeping everyone confident and calm."

"Margaret you continue to amaze me!" Larry exclaimed. "You're becoming a valuable asset to the executive office. I appreciate your candid response." Larry suddenly stood, clearly ending the conversation there. "Thanks for having lunch with me. I'll see you all next week."

The meal ended. Nancy and Margaret continued the tour of the executive dining room without any further discussion about the lunch. Margaret's first day with the executive office ended in Nancy's room at 4:00 p.m. "Margaret your first day on the job was an exceptional success," Nancy congratulated her. "I appreciated the way you handled Ms. Taylor and your response to Mr. Jordan. Go home and enjoy your weekend."

As Margaret was departing, Larry called Nancy and asked her to send Margaret to his office.

Immediately Nancy ran towards the elevator, and touched Margaret on her right shoulder, "Mr. Jordan wants to see you for a minute before you go. He's waiting in his office, go right in."

Margaret returned and went to Larry's office. "You called me Sir?"

"Yes, Margaret" Larry responded. "Would you please call Carlos and arrange him to drive you to your house to pick up the package. When you return, come right into my office and put it in one of my drawers. Nancy and I will be in the dining room where we usually work on Fridays."

"No problem sir," Margaret said without hesitation, and immediately left. As she exited the elevator on the ground floor, she saw Carlos waiting for her.

"I am at your service Ms. Margaret." He told her politely.

"Hello, Carlos. Please take me to my house, I left a document that Mr. Jordan needs right away."

"Let's go then before the traffic gets too bad."

In the car Margaret gave wing to her imagination, wondering about the package and thinking that Larry's wife must be a lucky woman. The round-trip took just under an hour. Margaret entered the bank with a Barnes & Noble bag which contained the package from Victoria's Secret. She deposited the box in Larry's office as instructed.

Chapter 11
DANGER

"Hey you! Who are you?!" A voice yelled suddenly behind Margaret. She spun around to find the cleaning lady behind her. "What are you doing in Mr. Jordan's office?"

Margaret was caught off guard but quickly recalled what a teacher long ago had taught her—the first step in the response loop is to recognize that a surprise is occurring. She said.

"Oh, hi. I'm Margaret Gianelli, Nancy's new assistant. I'm here on orders from Mr. Jordan to deliver a document to his desk."

Margaret's confident air disarmed the cleaning lady's suspicions. "Okay," she responded and started to wipe Nancy's desk.

Margaret was shaking a bit, for having been caught and having to lie. This made her very uncomfortable. Then she went down to the basement parking lot and sat in her car for ten minutes to calm down. She then drove home.

"Hi mom!" she called out as she entered her house. "When's Dad coming?"

Why?" responded Janet, her mother.

"I need to talk to him. I got a promotion today, and I'm exhausted from the day's events."

"That's wonderful. Are you happy with the move? Are you hungry?"

"Yes, I'm excited about the new job, and no, thanks, I'm not hungry yet. I'm going to take a shower and a quick nap before dad gets home. Wake me up when he gets here." Margaret did not want her mother to ask too many questions.

Forty minutes later while dozing, Margaret heard "Honey I'm home!" Without hesitation, she jumped out of bed, rushed downstairs and hugged her father. She whispered in his ear "I need to talk to you in private."

Harry, her father, nodded and in a louder voice, repeated, "Honey I'm home!"

Bobby, Margaret's little brother, was running in from the backyard with his dog Rome and rushed to his father. Rome, the dog, was obviously excited, tail wagging rapidly. "Rome stop! Let us move," Harry remarked, lovingly pushing the dog away and fixing Bobby's falling pants, as he took his overcoat off and grabbed a blue sweater, all at the same time. Then Harry saw a ball by the door. He scooped it up, and Harry, Bobby, and Rome rushed to the outside patio. There were a few throws back and forth between the players with the dog as part of Bobby's team.

Margaret stood by the door and watched, tapping her right foot on the floor as if keeping pace with a Caribbean tune. Fifteen minutes later, when Harry was running with the ball towards the house, she waved her right hand and looked up. Harry acknowledged her call by placing his right hand on his head and tossing the ball back to Bobby for his catch. As Harry was walking away, he called out in a loud tone of voice; "I'm taking Margaret with me to the Club. We'll be back for dinner."

From a distance Janet yelled from the kitchen, "Okay, don't be late, I'll have dinner ready at seven-thirty."

Where are you guys going? Bobby asked. "Can I go too?" At the same time, Margaret was holding Rome at bay while he tried to lick her face. Everybody was doing something in the opposite direction of what Margaret was expecting. Now Bobby was holding onto to Rome by the collar and pushing Margaret away, he yelled, "Mom! Come here, please,

please!" Then Janet showed up on the scene, holding a large spoon with her left hand and a chicken leg coated with flour on the other "What's going on here?"—She asked while kissing Harry and with her left foot pushing Rome away.

Margaret was laughing, but deep down she felt a little frustrated. "Mom, I'm going with dad to the club to talk about my new job—is that okay with you?"

"Go, go you guys and let me finish dinner," she waved them away. "Bobby! Come help me get this flour off the floor!"

Father and daughter walked away in the direction of the club, which was less than a quarter mile away. Harry asked, "What's going on? You look different, are you in trouble?"

"No! I think some other people are in big trouble," said Margaret.

"That sounds interesting. I'm listening."

Margaret eagerly gave her father a summary of the day's events and her interpretation of Carlos statement. "You have eyes, but you can't see; ears, but you can't hear; mouth but you can't speak" Without pausing between statements she continued; "what's the meaning of 'full access' business and the Victoria Secret lingerie? Why the intimacy between Nancy and Mr. Jordan? Why a surprise visit from government auditors? And then there was their weird lingo during the lunch, and Mr. Jordan asking my opinion on the Cayman Islands."

Margaret stopped talking and grabbed Harry's right hand. Harry noticed her tight grip and that her hand was slightly cold. He softly said, "Sweetheart, based on what you are saying and my thirty-three years of diplomatic service experience, most of it chasing the money, it appears to me that the whole bunch is in trouble, and you are right in the middle of it."

He continued, "Let me teach you something that hopefully will last the rest of your life. Two types of professions typically respond to chaos in the environment. The tactical, for example, the Navy SEAL, and SWAT captain. The other is the strategic, the ambassador, and the chief executive officer."

"Wow! Dad, how come you never talked to me about these things?" Margaret asked him. "Well," he said calmly, "Because there never was a need, besides you've never experienced what you experienced today."

"Please, tell me more."

"Response time affects how these people prepare for and respond to surprises. The SEAL and the SWAT for example often have to respond within seconds or minutes much like the heart surgeon, the emergency room doctor, the improv actor or football coach. These people must plan their responses in advance or improvise on the spot. They are skilled in touch labor: they work with their hands."

"In contrast, the ambassador, the public works engineer, or the chief executive officer have more time to plan and organize their response following the surprise. Mostly, the strategist is recognized as a knowledge worker who provides value for their intellectual capital and relationships." The sun was getting low in the sky as they walked and the light was turning a deeper color. "As you can see Margaret, in this context you are a 'knowledge' worker. You see sweetheart, your response to Mr. Jordan was founded on your political science education. Quoting your professor, you gave him a reassuring feeling of comfort to manage the environmental chaos caused by news of the surprise audit. With your observations and keen attention to details and your rapid promotion to the executive office, you may become Mr. Jordan's secret weapon or his executioner. Their talk of 'manicured' business and of the 'packet' worries me because, in my experience, those words sound and smell much like money laundering or bank fraud!"

"I knew it! I knew it!" Margaret exclaimed in a high-pitched voice. "I knew you would understand. I know you'll guide me and protect me, and not just because I'm your "Golfing Queen.""

Harry took Margaret's hand and brought her to his chest almost as if they were waltzing. He held her tight for a minute or two, without telling her of the danger he perceived ahead.

They arrived at the club, then stopped for a moment, Harry noticed tears rolling down Margaret's rosy cheeks, beginning to smear her makeup. She couldn't stop crying and began to weep more and more. Harry held her for a little longer. "Let's go back home the long way so you can unwind and calm down," he said soothingly. Then he took her by the shoulders and looked into her eyes.

"You need to remain calm," he told her, a sharper edge in his voice. "Your mother can't get wind of this situation; otherwise, she may ruin the government investigation by talking to her friends. You know how much your mom worries, that's why from the beginning of our marriage we agreed she would need to trust me and not ask specific questions about my job. Do you remember when you were about sixteen you would ask me always about my travels and why I wouldn't be there for your birthday parties?"

Margaret nodded, pulling her hair away from her eyes. "Sure I do."

"Well, now that you've accidentally stepped into a lion's cage it's time for you to know what I was doing. I was tracking money used by our enemies to fund their attacks against the United States."

"I finally know. From time to time, I would hear you on the phone, in the very early morning or very late at night, saying stuff like chasing the money. I never connected those words to anything I could point my finger too, but today, oh boy!" Margaret gushed. "Not only do I understand some of it but I feel that your life has more meaning that people will ever know. Can I begin to write your memoirs?"

"I am not dead yet!" her father laughed.

"However, there is only one person authorized to bring all this to light, unfortunately, for both of us, it can't happen until I am in the furnace."

"Wow! Dad, like Shadrach, Meshach, and Abednego? Those guys were men of valor, but not in the United States government, or its army."

"Something like that," Harry said evasively. "How are you feeling? We don't want your mother to perceive anything is up or asking questions. Also be careful with Bobby, he's growing up to be real smart. He treats Rome like a trained handler, I swear he can make that dog do anything. So for us to talk privately here's what I suggest: after dinner say you'd like to watch Life is Beautiful. Your mom won't want to and will probably go upstairs saying she is tired, and by that time Bobby will go up too. That'll give us a chance to talk."

"Yes, Dad," Margaret said. They embraced one more time then headed for home.

When they came through the front door, Harry announced their arrival by shouting, "Honey! We're back and hungry, is dinner ready yet?"

Before dinner, Margaret went to her room, and upon returning and sitting down at the table, she looked at her mother and asked; "May I say grace today?"

"Of course, honey, go ahead," Janet said.

"Father God You are the Creator, omnipresent, You are everywhere, You see everything, read every heart and know the truth even if I do not. However, I trust You, believe in Your word, and I have faith You will protect me, my family, friends, the government officials, and my dog Rome."

"Amen!" the family chanted in unison. "Let's eat!" said Harry.

Over dinner, Harry and Margaret stayed away from topics such as Margaret's work, and most of the conversation was small talk. Once they had finished eating, Margaret suggested they watch Life is Beautiful. Bobby ignored her and quickly asked; "May I be excused, please?" He and Rome ran upstairs to wrestle a bit; the nightly prelude to taking a shower and soon after that Bobby was in bed.

Ten minutes into the movie, Janet was half sleep. She stood up. "I'm going to bed," she announced. "Please excuse me, I have seen this movie so many times, good night!"

Chapter 12
STRATEGY

"That actually worked Dad, everyone's out just like you said," Margaret noted.

Harry grinned. "Let's have some green tea. Bring it to my office in the baseman, and turn off all the lights so we know if someone's coming." Margaret complied and brought the tea.

"Dad! Here's the tea. Careful, it's hot!" she warned.

"Thanks, honey, please close the door and hang the "do not disturb" sign on it."

"Dad, please know that I have total, and I do mean complete, confidence in your advice. I'll do what you tell me to do and keep my eyes and ears open and my mouth shut like you've always said. We can meet as many times as we need for you to fully explain what to do about the danger you perceive."

"This is not a matter of perception," Harry stated matter-of-factly, "it's a question of experience. From now on, you need to pay close attention to everything that is said around you, especially when it's about the government inspectors or anything you think sounds suspicious."

"I understand."

"From now on until the inspectors complete their audit, come down here after everyone's asleep and give me a summary of everything you've observed that day on this encrypted fidelity recorder." He produced it from a drawer. "You must speak to it in a whisper because it's designed for recording sensitive matters without being heard within eight feet. However, when decoded, you'll sound like the news anchorwoman from WHAS 1 on the eleven o'clock news." He continued, "Now let's go back a year when you did the internship at the U.S. Treasury. Tell me what you were doing there and how it led you to end up at the Louisville Midtown Bank."

"Well, there is Mr. Ellis at the Office of the Inspector General," Margaret began to say slowly. "He's some big deal; I really don't know too much about him, other that his title is Special Counsel to the Inspector General. At the time of my internship, all I knew was that the work assigned to me came to my desk and was placed in the inbox by the mail clerk. The transmittal document indicated what was I to do when due, and in what format I was to deliver my work to Mr. Ellis." She took a sip of tea and wrinkled her brow trying to remember everything. "When I handed over my finished work, all he would say was 'Thank you, Margaret.' He is an old person like you. Oops!" she exclaimed, covering her mouth. "I didn't mean you are an 'Oldie,' But he is old enough, older than me. He was always thinking and sometimes he looked like he was in another world. One time, I observed him, and I saw him reading and scribbling all over some papers on his desk, all of the sudden he would yell in a loud voice, 'I knew it! I knew it!'

"Check this out," she said. "One the day, I was passing by his desk and heard him say, "I knew it!" Then I turned to him and asked him what he knew exactly. Without hesitation, he told me, "You know Margaret you are observant and quick to think." I was surprised and turned my head a little to show I was confused. Mr. Ellis signaled with his right arm extended pointing to the chair to the right side of his desk, inviting me to sit down. Then, without any preamble, Mr. Ellis began, 'Margaret, I'm in the thinking business. Thinking is how I spend my time; it's my bread and butter.' So I said to him, "I can also think Mr. Ellis.' 'Good,' he said, 'that gives me hope for the young. Their brains are fresh and little used, ready to be developed. It takes one to recognize a real potential.' I said, 'Wow! Mr. Ellis,'' 'Are you trying to tell me that we young can't think?' He said no. He said everyone that is breathing thinks, the problem is not whether or not you can think, and it is how you think." Margaret broke off and looked at her father.

"Dad, to tell you the truth, at that point I thought Mr. Ellis was a little off. But then he said, 'Margaret allow me to show you what I mean with your own example.'

"I was shocked! Instinctively I moved to the edge of my chair and focused on him. At that moment, I stopped being snobby, I wanted to learn how to think in the way Mr. Ellis was saying. Looking straight into my eyes, as if reading my soul, and in a professor's tone of voice, he told me: 'According to the file on my desk, you graduated Magna Cum Laude. That was the first prerequisite you met to be here. Second, the Assistant Inspector General selected you to be in my Fellowship without you knowing it. I assigned all the work you are doing, consistently you deliver your assignments on time and better than I expected. When you ask questions, you show relevance and discretion, and in each report, you cite your sources and indicate the basis for your judgment. Case specific, I assigned you three banks that had consistently been of interest to The Inspector General because of complaints filed by people with disabilities, the elderly and college students. Out of these reports in a few months, you rendered a memorandum pointing that the "Louisville Midtown Bank should be given individual attention.""

Harry looked very interested in this part. "What lead you to signal that attention?" he asked.

"My task was to read the reports filed by these three banks, identify any issue on the bank's reports that seemed unusual, analyze the data and report my findings," Margaret responded. "Dad to tell you the truth, after three months of doing this reading, day in and day out. I was getting sick of looking at numbers. I was about to quit! Then on a Monday morning last summer when I was ready to hand my report to Mr. Ellis, I realized that all new real estate guaranteed mortgage loans reported by the Louisville Midtown Bank on their last three reports were issued to people over 55 years of age. On top of that, all the loans were processed by same mortgage and title companies this coincidence made me very interested in what else could be going on."

"That's interesting, tell me more," Harry said.

"In preparing my memorandum of what I found, I researched the relevant federal and state of Kentucky regulations. Results lead me to read the U.S. Consumer Protection Bureau final ruling that required mortgage lenders to consider a buyer's ability to repay home loans before extending them credit. Then, I turned around, picked up a report, and delivered to Mr. Ellis and said, 'Check this out, Mr. Ellis!' His eyes got real wide, and he asked, 'Were all the buyers over 55?'

'Yes. Sir!' I responded."

Margaret noted that her father was completely focused on her words. "The main reason for this ruling was the failed home loans made during the 2006-2007 recession. There was also loose underwriting practices by some creditors, including failure to verify the buyer's income or debts. Moreover, qualifying customers for home loans based on "teaser" interest rates that would cause the monthly mortgage payments to jump to unaffordable levels after the first few years.

"Dad, I must confess at that moment I became angry. I hated the Louisville Midtown Bank. I hated the people running the bank; I hated the fact that they were taking advantage and robbing the people of Kentucky of their homes by placing them in jeopardy of repossession. Then I realized that other issues at that bank needed attention."

"What happened when you found out Mr. Ellis was the decision maker in your cases?" Harry inquired.

"I was so happy because I knew then something was going to take place and the people from that bank and the others would face judgment in court!" Margaret bubbled excitedly.

"Then, Mr. Ellis dropped the bombshell!" He said, "Margaret, today I am recommending you to go to the FBI Academy for training as Special Agent. Your first assignment will be to go after the people of this bank. You are to immerse yourself in learning all you can about the people running the bank." Margaret paused.

"Dad, are you sworn to secrecy?" she asked suddenly.

"Yes, I am." Harry looked at her for a second, then Margaret reluctantly continued; "Remember last summer, when I asked you guys' for permission to go on the special trip to Kenya?"

"Yes I do," Harry said. "I never bought the idea, nor the journey, and after checking with my friends in Nairobi, and checking with a media person, I knew you were never there. However, knowing that you were working with the Inspector General's Office, your destination was not a big deal to me. But your mother! That was a different story. You managed her like a professional, with the gifts, the postcards, and the photos." Margaret nodded, thinking back to that time.

"I was on special agent training at the FBI Academy in Quantico, Virginia. When I graduated, my assignment was to supporting the successful prosecution of the Louisville Midtown Bank and to fully immerse myself in the bank business and its people. However, Dad, I must confess, academic training is one thing, the real life is another, and I'm really scared."

"Sweetheart, it's good you're afraid! The most dangerous situation for someone doing the work you're doing is to be overconfident. Overconfidence is a sure path to failure and even being hurt. I'd like you to learn this tonight. Whatever you're doing remember God is with you, and there is someone better than you at the same task or assignment. By embodying this teaching, you'll have His protection and remain on this earth for as long as I have." He took her hand tenderly. "My golfing queen, let's call it a night. Sleep in late and enjoy the weekend. I still have some stuff to do down here."

Wow! Is it three o'clock in the morning? Good night, I mean hi, Dad." She stood up and walked to the door.

Sweet dreams!" her father called as she shut the door softly behind her.

Chapter 13
HEIGHTENED FEELINGS

On Monday, all appeared to go smoothly at the Louisville Midtown Bank until three in the afternoon. While passing by the main conference room, Margaret suddenly heard someone shout "Look here you Son Of Be#**! She recognized Mr. Lubec, the Chief Financial Officer, screaming at someone who must have been Mr. Jordan. She moved closer to the door, pretending to be looking at something on the floor. "I told you six months ago; we need to move some of that money back to the reserve account and earmark it for the initial capitalization transaction of the Caribbean Bank!" Mr. Lubec continued yelling. "But instead, you kept it in the discretionary fund like a F***ing idiot! This fund is swelling like beached whale and even a blind man is going to be able to tell there's something fishy going on there!"

Margaret's phone began ringing loudly, and she rushed back to her desk. "This is Margaret speaking, how can I help you?" she said with perfect composure.

"Margaret this is Larry," her boss said sternly from the other line. "Go find Mr. Jones and tell him to get over here as fast as possible."

"Yes. Sir, I'll get him for you." She found Keith's office door locked, so she rapped on three times in quick succession.

"One moment please," Keith's voice said faintly from the other side.

The door opened, revealing a dirty man with a dirty shirt and the stink of alcohol. For a second Margaret thought someone had gotten into his office, but after the initial shock had passed, she could tell it was indeed Keith.

"Margaret, what can I do for you?" he croaked.

"Mr. Jordan and Mr. Lubec want you in the conference room right away," she said primly. "And you look pretty bad. You should probably clean up a little. Here, I'll help you." She entered his office.

"Do I look that bad?" Keith slurred.

"No! You don't look bad at all. You look terrible!" Keith looked downcast. "I'll call Mr. Jordan and buy you some time," Margaret offered quickly. "And see how I can help you look presentable." Margaret whipped out her cell phone and called the conference room, and Keith began to clean himself up. "Hello? Is this Mr. Jordan? This is Margaret. Mr. Jones has gone to the Public Protection Cabinet, Department of Financial Institutions responding to a recently filed complaint and is expected to return within an hour," she lied smoothly.

"Okay, you stay there until he turns up and bring him up here with you!"

"Yes sir, I will."

Margaret turned towards Keith, "Now we have 45 minutes. What size shirt are you wearing?"

"Size 16, sleeve 37."

"Okay. I'm going to go across the street to the Charles Shop and get you a shirt and tie while you go and wash up to look presentable." Margaret, with a sense that she was acting in a mission impossible movie rushed to the men's shop and bought a light blue shirt and a coordinating yellow and blue tie. She also stopped by the gift shop on the ground floor of the bank and purchased a shaving kit and mouthwash, and then returned to Keith's office. He was nowhere to be found. Discretely, she asked several people on the floor if they had seen Mr. Jones. No one seemed to know, except Janes, a secretary who told Margaret—"I saw him entering the men's restroom when I was coming out of the women's room, and that was about a half-hour ago."

Margaret thanked her and walked away, feeling frustrated and tense. "Now what do I do?" she muttered to herself. Margaret looked around to make sure everyone was busy working and not paying attention. She walked towards the end of the corridor holding the Charles Shop bag under her arm. Margaret slowly passed the men's restroom, and briefly stopped to detect any noise, but heard nothing. Then she walked a little further and returned for the second time to verify that was no one was coming. She couldn't listen to a sound in the bathroom.

In a moment of desperation to find Keith, she entered the men's room. She found Keith sitting on the floor, trying to button his shirt, which was smeared with a brownish substance. "What's happening to you, Mr. Jones?" She whispered.

Keith looked up. "Who are you?" he asked, his voice slurred and incoherent.

"I am Margaret, here to help you," she said, grabbing his arm. "Let's get out of here before there is more trouble. Quick, hold on, one, two and three! Up we go!" She pulled him to his feet and supported him as he could barely stand by himself.

"Where are we?"

"We're in the men's room, stop talking and start walking, and don't make any noise. Stand still while I check outside the door, when I signal you to come out, you move, and we'll go to your office and finish putting you together. The welcoming committee in the lobby is waiting for you, and we have less than 30 minutes before your hanging time is up!"

With a surprised look and blurry eyes, Keith asked, "Did you mean hanging?"

Trying to give him a sense of urgency she yelled; "Yes. Sir, hanging! Mr. Jordan is mad, Mr. Lubec is fuming, and Nancy is hysterical on the phone. And your head looks perfect for hanging on Mr. Jordan's trophy wall!"

Margaret was carrying the Charles Shop bag on the right shoulder and holding Keith's right arm over her left shoulder. Both were walking towards his office, when turning the corner a few more steps before Keith's office door, Margaret saw Nancy coming in the opposite direction and nearly collided with her.

Surprised and alarmed, Nancy exclaimed; "What is happening!?"

"Mr. Jones fell by in the hallway, and I am helping him to recover," Margaret lied quickly. "Mr. Jordan and Mr. Lubec are expecting us in less than thirty minutes in the main conference room."

For a second Nancy seemed nonplused. Then her face hardened in the decision. "Okay take care of him! I go up and find out what's happening with Mr. Jordan."

Keith remained silent, still hanging onto Margaret's shoulder and looking down at the floor as if nothing was happening. Once at his office, Margaret put the bag down on the receiving sofa. She dropped his full arm from her shoulder so he could stand by himself. "Take off that dirty shirt, go to the sink of your bar and shave with this lady's razor, while I remove the pins from your new shirt," she ordered him.

Margret handed Keith a small bottle of mouthwash. "Rinse your mouth with this mouthwash, don't drink it, or you'll be meeting the welcoming committee in hell."

Keith did what Margaret commanded, docile as a lamb. After a few minutes, he came up to Margaret with his face torn with nicks and cuts from his effort to shave.

"How do I look?" he asked shyly.

"You look better! Here put this shirt on and let me help you to fasten it in place." She helped him dress, but when she got to the tie, she looked up at him, crestfallen. "I can't tie a tie!" She exclaimed. "You'll have to do it."

"Okay."

"Are you ready?" inquired Margaret as she took an up-down look to Keith. "You need to be ready for what's coming. Smile now, because it might be the last time you can."

"What do you mean my last?"

"Yes, it may be the last smile before we are both deep-fried, in the main conference room. Whatever you say, you stopped by the Department of Financial Institutions regarding a response to the recently filed complaint, but you forgot your passcode and had to return to the bank."

With a soft look in his face, Keith said; "Okay."

Margaret and Keith arrived at the main conference room hallway. However, before entering the room, they heard the loud voices of Nancy and Larry. Both were yelling at the top of their lungs. "Why didn't you notify me that you ordered Roy to transfer three million to the discretionary account all at once?!" Larry yelled. "You're going to hell, Nancy!"

In rebuttal Nancy shouted; "You said, we'd need cash on hand to purchase the property in the Islands before closing the bank deal!"

"Have we closed the bank deal?" Larry asked gratingly.

"No! But an hour ago I was on my way to the airport as you suggested to be in George Town before your arrival on Tuesday. You asked me to sweet talk those guys in the Caribbean   Bank, meet the realtor and have all papers are drawn and ready when you arrive. Instead, you call me here. You screwed up my departure, wasted my time and humiliated me in front of Roy."

They were suddenly interrupted by a loud knocking on the door. Roy opened and signaled Keith and Margaret to go and sit quietly at the conference table while Larry and Nancy stood by the NE window, now speaking in a small voice but animated with their hand gestures and body language. All of a sudden, Larry turned around and acknowledged Margaret and Keith's presence. He signaled Nancy to follow him to the conference table. Margaret looked up. "Here is Mr. Jones as you asked Mr. Jordan," she said charmingly. "May I be excused?"

"No! Nobody is leaving this room!" he yelled. "Until we determine the situation and have the plan to handle the government inspectors that will be here tomorrow at ten in the morning."

Margaret quietly returned to her chair and silently stared at Keith. He responded in silence with a quick up and down of his eyebrows as if confirming they were both in the lobby of hell. Then, Keith stood up and started walking towards the courtesy bar located at the far end of the 16 seat conference table, and announced, "I am going to pour myself a drink to gain the courage I need to hear what is coming down and to say what I need to say."

Margaret, quickly said, "Mr. Jones let me take care of the drinks, and you relax. Would anyone like a drink?"

Larry responded quickly. "Margaret, bring a new bottle of Larceny Bourbon 92 proof and glasses for everyone."

"Yes, Sir!" She brought the new bottle of Larceny Bourbon and on a tray glasses and napkins. She also included a pitcher of cold water, and then proceeded to serve drinks to everyone excluding herself.

Chapter 14
CONSCIENCE-STRICKEN

As Margaret poured a glass of water, Keith stood up. Without hesitation he said. "Thank you, Margaret, for bringing me to the lobby of hell. I thank you for the opportunity to tell off this bunch of lying predators planning to ambush me; I'm sick of being forced to do what I know is wrong!"

Margaret, discretely with her left hand pulled down on Keith's coat while raising her index finger vertically over her mouth telling him to shut up and sit down.

Instead, Nancy walked up to Keith and stood directly in front of him. "Look it's just a question of airing out the situation, so we can understand what to do tomorrow. Please relax, sit down and let Larry speak," she cajoled him.

"Keith, let Larry talk!" Keith mimicked Nancy in an exaggerated falsetto. "What the hell is this? Are you attempting to patronize me while screwing with people's money? What's your game? Am I to ruin my twenty-five-year auditing career just to sit down and listen to the "Big Game" railroad me to sign reviews that are manicured to make the packet look pristine?"

"Shut up Keith!" Larry shouted

Roy Lubec was watching Keith Jones as if he had lost his mind.

"Nancy, Gentlemen, the walls of this room are not sound proof!" Margaret said evenly. "They can hear, and some of this lively conversations can be misconstrued by anyone passing by, may I suggest that everyone sit for a moment have a drink and let me say something?" Her statement was met with absolute silence.

Finally, Keith sat down, sipping on his drink. Larry, Roy, and Nancy followed suit.

Margaret moved from where she was sitting towards the head of the conference table, standing as Larry would at conferences. "My father told me to pray when in danger. This is a dangerous moment. Therefore, everyone closes your eyes and hears these words, 'Father God we need your help now. Help Mr. Jordan, help Nancy, help Mr. Lubec, help Mr. Jones, and give me a hand. Please don't let me say anything that may cost me my job. Amen!"

The next sound in the room was Amen! The room's atmosphere had been transformed changed from a combat zone to a solemn silence. Margaret seized the moment and with a trembling voice said—"I read the following statement from a manuscript of a book my father is writing. 'The power to impact others is not so much of what we do, but in who we are.'" After this statement, she walked away from the conference table, and on her way to the door asked, "May I be excused please, I need to step out for a few minutes." She was fearful of having made a grave mistake, and intentionally took much longer than necessary to calm down and return. When Margaret opened the door on her come back to the conference room, Larry stood up. So did Roy and Keith. Nancy hurried to meet Margaret on her way to her seat.

Nancy hugged her. "Margaret you are a jewel," she said kindly. "You brought everyone to reflect on what is, not in what should be. We thank you."

"So, do I still have a job?"

Larry was lost for words. He remained standing looked at Margaret and turned to Roy and Keith, "You see fellows, and this young woman saved us from engaging in a battle with no winner. She has a gift that's hard to put into words. We should take this experience and use our time to solve problems, not bicker and blame. If we're in this boat together, we can't sink. As Margaret said a few minutes ago, this was a dangerous moment for the bank if we fail to develop a plan to respond to the government auditors coming to see us tomorrow."

Nancy signaled Margaret to the side, "Please go to go the dining room and arrange with Mario for a light dinner in forty minutes."

"Right." Suddenly she turned and asked, "Nancy, should I stay or go home?"

"After dinner, you may go," said Nancy.

Larry had just noticed that Margaret was walking out of the room. "Wait a minute!" he called out after her. "Where are you going?"

"I'm going to the dining room to arrange for dinner," Margaret responded coolly.

That is an excellent idea! Please plan to stay for dinner until we have a plan for tomorrow."

As Margaret was departing, she turned back and said: "Yes, Sir I will."

Once Margaret had left the room, Nancy turned towards Larry. "I sent Margaret away because she's too smart and we do not want her to know what's really going on. She's too young and inexperienced to understand the complexities of playing with real money, especially large amounts of money."

"I disagree," said Keith, "Margaret is the kind of woman one can trust. However, given my personal experiences with her, she has a strong belief system, which I think it matters a great deal to her."

"Today she was showing us with that prayer is the foundation of her character, conduct and incredible decision- making capabilities," Roy added.

"I'm going to put Margaret to the test," Larry revealed quietly. "Nancy and I will depart tonight for the Cayman Islands. I will have her cater to the government auditors and capitalize on the fact that all she will know is to deliver the reports we will discuss after dinner. Since she has no knowledge of the investment plans we have been using, she presents no risk, and the government auditors will welcome a new face on the scene."

Everyone nodded.

Larry continued; "The government inspectors will be expecting Nancy to attempt to persuade them to go to coffee and lunch. However, when they notice Margaret, they will be busy trying to figure out why Margaret is on the scene, and the nature of their questions will need adjustment. This will distract them from the search and maybe they will pick up the reports and set a new appointment for next quarter."

Margaret returned and announced; "Dinner will be ready in ten minutes! Please leave the glasses where they are, I will pick them up and place blank notepads for the meeting after dinner." Everyone except Margaret put on their jackets and departed for the dining room.

Mario welcomed everyone to the dining room. "Ms. Margaret ordered no wine and a light dinner," he told them and began to recite the menu. "We are in a bit of a hurry," Larry cut him off. "Please, Mario make sure we will be out of here in one hour. I'm leaving tonight and have a business to conduct after dinner."

Mario, without a word, moved quickly to the kitchen, and on his way saw Margaret coming. He winked at her.

Dinner was served, and, as usual, Larry suggested they relax so they could discuss after the meal with clear heads.

Margaret was eating, but her mind was already planning ahead for the recording session at home. She was trying to figure out how she was going to condense the events of the last four hours, plus God knows how much more after dinner. She was thinking about Harry's instructions, rehearsing in her mind what exactly she was to do when leaving the bank, and what situations to avoid when she got home.

Dinner finally ended. Nancy asked Margaret to follow her to the end of the dining room. While standing by the north-east window looking at the city lights, Nancy said, "Margaret, do you remember, I told you you'd be my shadow?"

"Oh my, yes… I do."

"Well, tomorrow is your day to be in charge of the executive office. Mr. Jordan and I are flying to George Town in the Cayman Islands tonight."

Margaret's legs began to shake a bit, but with some effort, she kept her voice completely even. "So tomorrow I'm going to be facing those government guys?"

"Yes, Margaret, you are demonstrating in action the talent of discretion and ability to defuse even the "Big Game," Nancy said emphatically.

"Wow, Nancy! I don't think I can take charge of such event without even knowing what they will want or be asking." Margaret began to tap her right foot nervously.

From a distance, Larry signaled both Nancy and Margaret with a helicopter blade upward signal, and Keith exclaimed, "Time to go back!" Upon returning to the conference room, Keith noticed that Margaret had placed blank notepads in front of each person's seat, and the previous notes were neatly arranged in front of each pad. Roy signaled Margaret to change her seat and sit next to him. Margaret ignored the gesture and instead asked in her normal voice. "Mr. Jordan, am I to accept the responsibility to handle the government guys tomorrow? Do I have the option to opt-out?"

"No, Margaret!" Larry exclaimed. "This is not an opt-in nor an opt-out option. While you were taking care of managing our delicious dinner, we agreed that you have the talent and ability to handle almost anything you set your mind to. I have seen you in action and feel confident you can handle the government, auditors."

"I believe that together we can do it," Roy offered.

Keith turned towards Margaret and in a friendly tone of voice told her "Margaret the fact that you are now in the lobby of hell with me, we need to come to an agreement. Time is running out! The auditing issues need to be on the table now! You brought me here against my will, and now I'm asking you to rescue me from the hanging by cooperating with the situation." He paused and then said, "Also, to make things worse, tomorrow is my 30th wedding anniversary, and if I'm not home by six in the afternoon, my wife will castrate me!"

"Oh no, Mr. Jones!" Margaret cried out in false horror. "That can't happen to a beautiful person like you. I met your wife last month at the fundraising dinner and believe me after spending some time talking with her I feel that if anyone has the guts to perform major surgery without anesthesia, it's your wife! You just relax and tell me what I'm supposed to do, and I'll do it!"

Larry, Roy, and Nancy began to laugh with gusto.

Nancy was standing near Margaret and began to describe her last experiences with the government inspectors. "They'll show up at my office at ten o'clock sharp. You'll see them coming from your desk. When that happens, you call, Roy and Keith. Then walk up to them and greet them. They most likely will ask, 'Where is Ms. McArthur?' You will announce that I'm out of the office. However, you are my assistant and have the authority to serve on my behalf. Offer to assist them in any way they need. Point to your desk and give them your telephone extension should they need anything. By then, Roy and Keith should have arrived. Ask where they would prefer to work. Would they like to work in the small conference room near Mr. Lubec and Mr. Jones' offices, or would they prefer more space in the main conference room?"

Nancy turned to Roy and asked for the investment reports as of last Wednesday. He produced a stack of neatly related papers with colored post-its sticking out. Roy opened the main report, "This tag is similar to the three offshore bank accounts in the Cayman Islands. One is under the name of this bank with Larry as the sole signatory; the second is under Nancy's name as the Registered Securities Dealer. The other account is the trust account for the initial cash payment to the seller's account. Signatories to this account are jointly Larry and Nancy. Here I'm justifying their existence as separate packets of capitalization for the bank under acquisition."

He continued, "Now this tag is the one that has me concerned. The

$9 million payments made are for investments in artworks and other collectibles including a candelabra, 19th Century paintings, and antique furniture. My concern is that Nancy made the purchase at Christie's 2014 Spring Auction in Hong Kong."

Keith turned toward Margaret. "You see here these accounting entries at the margin have Larry's initials." He said earnestly. "Therefore, should they ask any question regarding whether you know anything about these? Or, where in the bank are these artworks. You just respond. "I have no direct or indirect knowledge of whereabouts of any these artworks or collectibles. Then point to Larry's initials at the margin of the respective column showing Larry's initials authorizing the transaction."

With the sense of equal concern, Margaret said, "What if they ask me about the cast bronze sculptures in Nancy's office?"

"They belong to "The Roger's Family Trust!" Nancy interjected. "They're allowing the bank to display them and keep them stored. They're worth over $1.3 million. They are my joy to admire every day I'm in the office, I love the artist, and I love his work. I love the power they represent. I have two small sculptures by the same artist in my house."

"Should I say that?" Say Margaret.

"No Margaret!" Larry said impassively. "Don't engage in any explanation or discussion with the government inspectors. The discussion here tonight is for your benefit if they may intentionally ask what would appear an innocent question. Remember there is nothing honest about these fellows, they are like Keith, sharp and shrewd. If they open their mouths they have an agenda, so do not volunteer any information. If they press on, only say—I'm to give you the papers you need not the answers you seek. I have no knowledge or reason to know about the subject you are inquiring. I'm just standing for Ms. McArthur, who is at the moment out of the office."

Keith leaned towards the center of the conference table. "The fact remains ladies and gentlemen that The Special Inspector General for the Trouble Asset Program is responsible among other things, to conduct audits and investigate the management of all assets under the Trouble Asset Relief Program. This includes evaluating the characteristics of goods bought and the disposition of property acquired during the audits of this bank's financial statements and internal controls. This, my friends, is why I have not been able to sleep. This is why my conscience is bothering me. This is why Margaret found me in my office in a despicable state of disarray!"

Keith, you are becoming dramatic at the end of the show when in reality you have signed the audited reports for the last three years," Nancy reprimanded him. "Where was your conscience then?

"No, Nancy! I'm not becoming dramatic. That would be too late. I'm presenting you with the facts. So you can stop playing the daring prima donna and unscripted role! Moreover, start thinking about the unavoidable consequences to persuade the "Big Game," the good old Larry to let you keep in your office the cast bronze sculptures worth well over a million bucks! That Ms. McArthur is the auditor's translation of the meaning of auditing the management of assets under the Trouble Asset Relief Program.' How do you expect me to feel about the obvious Ms. McArthur?"

Chapter 15
STIRRING ANGER

"Look Keith! Don't Ms. McArthur me! Let me remind you that as the principal investments producer for this bank, I deserve the sculptures, the house on the beach, the apartment in Honk Kong, and more!"

"Yes Nancy, you deserve that and much more," Keith said in a modulated tone. "However, it is not a matter of deserving; it is a matter of managing the assets that ultimately are taxpayer's money. That is the issue!"

"Mr. Jordan, I believe I now know what I need to know to handle the government guys tomorrow," Margaret spoke over Nancy. "If it's all right with you, I'd like to go home. It's already ten in the evening, and I'll also need to call Carlos and Mr. Oliver if you and Nancy are leaving tonight. He's the standby pilot, and I need to let them know to file the new flight plan to depart to George Town tonight. At what time do you plan to go Mr. Jordan?"

"Thanks, Margaret," Larry responded gratefully. "Please tell Carlos first we want to be at the airport at 11:15 so we can take off tonight at 11:45."

"I will be sir, good night everyone!" She returned to her desk, called Carlos and the pilot, and gave them Larry's time instructions for his departure to George Town. Then Margaret called the security supervisor on duty and asked for an escort to her car in the parking garage.

Margaret's thoughts were on the six minutes recording. She was trying to figure out how to condense all the clues and issues she had captured from the preparation meeting and most significantly the sarcasm and disclosures resulting from the arguments between those present. Thirty-five minutes later, Margaret arrived home. She quietly checked if the lights were still on in the bedrooms upstairs. This would determine whether or not she should go to Harry's office to do the recording or wait.

"Ah… great…! All the lights are off." She murmured.

Margaret proceeded to go to her bedroom and changed into her pajamas just in case she ran into someone on her way to the basement. In silence, she checked all the rooms of the house, and after making sure no one was around Margaret entered Harry's office and reached for the recorder, and began to speak into it. The events of the day and the profundity of what Margaret was doing made her so nervous Margaret had trouble keeping herself calm and coherent. So she stopped and closed her eyes and started inhaling and exhaling slowly until her heart stopped racing. Then, went back to her recorder and pressed "replay."

"Oh, Lord!" she cried out in disgust upon hearing her voice. "Is that me? No, no, I need to do that again." She erased the record and redid it twice more before she felt satisfied with the result. She tiptoed upstairs and went to bed, but found that she could not sleep. She kept going over what had happened during the day. Finally, she got up and knelt by her bed to say a short prayer; "Father, You are in charge, I believe in You. I trust in You, I know You will protect my family and me. Good night. Amen!" After that, she fell asleep.

After Margaret had left the bank, Larry stood up and ended the meeting without much ceremony. "Good luck to you both tomorrow. I will call from George Town about three in the afternoon." He picked up his coat and signaled Nancy to gather their notepads and papers and follow him. Nancy was a little worried about what had happened and losing her temper with Keith, and she did everything in silence. She called out goodnight as she left the room.

Roy and Keith remained in the conference room as if they wanted to speak privately. They sat silently for a second before Keith suddenly said; "How would you like a drink before going home?"

"Make it a double because my son Jerry is picking me up," Roy responded.

"My daughter Jennifer is getting out of class now. Let me call her and ask if she wants me to pick her up." Keith pressed his speed dial. "Jennifer?" he said after a few rings. "This is Dad. Are you on your way home or are you already there?"

"I'm still on campus finishing some paperwork," she responded.

"When you're done with your work, would you stop by the bank and take me home?"

"Sure Dad. I will call you when I'm ready to leave."

"Thanks, I'll see you when you get here." Keith turned towards Roy and said, "Now what the hell! Bring the bottle and pour my guts out!"

"All right, let's do this together, we're in the same boat." The two men sat side by side as youngsters would normally do to talk about an upcoming event. They started to shuffle financial statements, working papers, and notes.

"You know Keith," said, Roy. "You have more guts that I ever thought you did. You are always so proper and dignified that tonight you surprised the hell out of me by putting Nancy on notice and by default placing Larry square against the prison wall. Please, pour me another!"

He continued, "I'm in worse shape than you are, my friend. I let the Big Game and his sweet talking Nancy draw me into manicuring the financial statements. However, I know the time will come when the inspectors will need to call a magician to open this bank packet. Moreover, when that happens, my dear Keith, I'll be in hell!"

Roy's words were so slurred he was almost incomprehensible. However, Keith apparently heard, and responded; "I want to make sure that you are willing to visit me wherever they will send me!" And holy cow! That means you knowingly manicured the financial statements, which I audited for the last three years?"

Roy nodded miserably.

"Holy Mosses! I'm on my way to hell, both here and at home." Keith shouted despairingly.

At that moment, Keith's phone began ringing. He promptly signaled Roy with his left hand vertically over his lips to keep silence. "Hello, are you on your way?"

"No Dad, I'll be a little late and just want to let you know, so you won't be worried." She said.

"That is okay honey take your time, Roy and I are having an interesting work discussion free of interruptions, and we've got plenty of food and water over here."

"That's great dad! I'll call you when ready."

"Okay."

Keith stood up walked to the courtesy bar and poured himself a large glass of cold water. His hand was shaking so vigorously that he spilled water on the plush carpet. His face was turning red and was sweating prodigiously. He finished the glass of water, then another and a third after that. He turned to Roy and said sternly; "You, Vice-Chair of the Society of Chief Financial Officers, are you going crazy? Are you out of your mind? What in the hell got into you that you compromised twenty-five years of prime service to the financial services industry?"

Roy stood up and went towards the bar, and in a trembling voice asked Keith to pour him a drink. "I need the courage to confess, and I can't do it in cold blood."

Instead, Keith brought Roy a tall glass of water. "Here you hypocrite! Drink this water to clear your stinking head and tell me exactly what, when, and where the manicuring has been taking place.

And more importantly, why did you do it?"

At that moment, Keith noticed Roy's face was turning white, losing its natural living color, and he suddenly dropped to the floor, shattering the glass he had been holding. "Holy Moses don't do this to me!" Keith yelled, and rapidly dialed the bank's emergency response team and asked for help. "Mr. Lubec has just had a heart attack! Please hurry to the main conference room."

The banks' emergency response team appeared on the site within a minute, and the attending nurse attempted to revive him. He came to in a few seconds, and the nurse began asking him questions while recording on his shoulder microphone. "Mr. Lubec how are you feeling?"

"I'm having chest pain," he croaked, indicating with his right hand in the center of his chest. "The pain is moving down, to my left arm and up to my neck. I feel it also in my upper back."

The nurse began dictating his findings, "The patient is anxious, sweating, exhibiting shortness of breath, and nauseating. He has an uneven heartbeat." Suddenly, Roy vomited all over the plush Syrian hand woven white carpet while rolling to his left side over the vomit. He began screaming and clutched at his stomach.

Keith was standing about four feet away to the left side of Roy's head. He rushed to his side and began yelling into his face. "You hypocrite! You don't do this to me; you screwed my career. You messed up my life! In God's name don't die on me! I'm finished. You must testify, I had nothing to do with your shenanigans."

The assistant on the scene ran up to Keith, trying to pull him back.

"Sir, stop this, or I'll have security remove you!" The emergency worker yelled at Keith.

The bank's emergency response nurse could not figure out if Mr. Lubec had acute food poisoning or a heart attack. He quickly called 911 and asked for the emergency medical team (EMT) person in charge, and gave Mr. Lubec's symptoms. The nurse and the EMT agreed on the phone for the nurse to give the subject an oral aspirin, and wait one minute. Then they placed the oxygen mask over his mouth and nose.

At 11:30 p.m., the fire department; the police, and ambulance arrived on the scene! Upon initial exam, they found the 59 years old, five foot eight, approximately 175 pounds Mr. Roy Lubec had low blood pressure, and the clinical signs of inadequate blood supply to the heart. Everything indicated a heart attack.

Chapter 16
THE UNKNOWN

Roy has rushed in the ambulance to Mercy Hospital a mile away. The emergency room physician confirmed the paramedic's initial diagnosis and immediately ordered lab tests. The tests showed a breakdown of the heart muscle, resulting in a heart attack. The treatment options were thrombolytic therapy (the use of drugs to break up, or dissolve blood clots) or coronary angioplasty (threading a thin tube through a small puncture in a leg or arm artery to the heart) to restore vessel patency. However, Roy's level of alcohol was very high, and on top of that, the episode occurred less than two hours before his arrival to the ER. The attending physician decided that pharmacological treatment was less invasive and more feasible. As soon as the medication was initiated Roy was transferred to the Intensive Care Unit for close monitoring. He was followed for signs of bleeding, changes in neurologic status, and any variation from the normal rhythm of the heart.

At 1:10 a.m. on Tuesday, Keith was sitting alone drinking bitter black coffee in the waiting room outside the ER. He remembers that Roy had said his son Jerry would be picking him up. However, Keith did not have any contact information to let him know what was taking place. Then a young physician accompanied by a nurse came out from the

ER double doors. The nurse asked, "Is anyone from the Lubec family here?"

"Here I'm," said Keith, quickly standing up. "I'm the one who called the paramedics. How is he?"

"Are you a member of his family?"

"No, I'm his associate, we work together in the bank. How is he?"

"I can't discuss that with you. Can you contact Mr. Lubec's family?"

"Doctor. "Keith pleaded, "it's one-thirty in the morning, I have known him for over twenty years. I work with him. This morning at ten, we had the government inspectors coming to talk to him and me. Please, doc, have mercy and tell me if he's alright?"

"Sir, I'm sincerely sorry for your situation. The law limits to who I can disclose Mr. Lubec's medical condition. Does Mr. Lubec has a wife?"

"Yes!"

"Please get in touch with his wife and ask her to come immediately to the ER. I will talk to her, and if it is okay with her, I will speak to you at the same time."

"Thank you, doctor, I understand!" At that moment Keith's phone began to ring as Jennifer called him.

"Dad, are you all right?" she asked, sounding scared. "I went to the bank, and no one could tell me where you were until a little while ago when I requested to speak to the person in charge of security. He told me what happened and that you went with Roy in the ambulance to the hospital. Where are you?"

"I'm in the ER lobby at Mercy," Keith responded. "I just spoke to the attending physician about Roy's condition. However, I couldn't get any information. I'm in trouble; would you come over here, please?"

"I will be there in a few minutes."

"Okay, honey, thank you so much. I'll see you soon."

Suddenly, Jennifer appeared,

"Honey, thank you for coming," Keith said gratefully. "I need to call Roy's wife and ask her to come here to speak with the doctor about

Roy's condition."

"Now I understand why you're in trouble! Bertha has the reputation of a walking hyena. Once she wakes up, all she does is howl. Bertha seems to detest everybody who disagrees with her ways. She acts as if the world owes her the courtesy of life. However, the way to tame a hyena is to show no fear. Dad, you just relax and let me call her how."

Jennifer called Bertha's phone. The phone rang three times, and then a deep voice answered, "What do you want? This better be important."

"Bertha, this is Jennifer, Keith's daughter."

"Who?"

"Hey! This is Jennifer Jones, Keith Jones daughter. Please get dressed now and head over to Mercy Hospital, Emergency Room. Roy, your husband, is here, and my Dad and I are in the Emergency Room waiting room."

"Oh…! Sh*3#*. I'm on my way!" There was a pause. "This better be real, or I'm going to get real mad."

"Yes, Bertha, I understand; don't worry it's very real."

Thirty minutes later Bertha appeared in her comfortable pajamas. She still had pink beauty rollers hanging all over her shoulder—length blond and gray hair. In a harsh tone of voice, she demanded; "What in the hell happened to Roy?"

Keith quickly related the bank incident and the doctor's request to speak with her.

"I want to see that doctor now!" she yelled

A few minutes later, the young physician and same nurse reappeared. "Are you the Lubec family?" the doctor asked seriously.

"I'm his wife!" Bertha exclaimed, but now there was a slight tremble in her harsh tone.

"Mrs. Lubec, I'm Doctor Richardson," he introduced himself. Your husband suffered a heart attack, and he's now in intensive care. His condition is guarded. We are doing all we can so he can stay in ICU and improve."

"Can I see him now?"

"I don't recommend it at this moment," Doctor Richardson said. "The ICU team is monitoring him closely, and anyone's presence outside the medical personnel would cause unnecessary anxiety. The fact is that he just had a major heart attack. Because of this, any emotional upset could be fatal."

"Holy Moses!" Keith swore. "That means Roy could die?" The doctor ignored Keith. "May I advise that everyone go home, get some rest and if there is any news my nurse will call you. You should go back, there is nothing you could do here so rest and be available when she calls. Please give her your contact numbers."

After the doctor and nurse disappeared through the ER double doors, Bertha suddenly sat down and began to cry, shocking Keith who was accustomed to her almost barbaric personality. "Roy had it all planned out for us to retire this winter to the Caymans," she sobbed. "Roy already surprised me with paying over a million dollars for our three bedroom beach home there."

"Describe the house to us," Jennifer asked her kindly, putting an arm around Bertha.

"The house is all white and blue Dutch architecture, beautiful." Bertha stuttered out through tears. "Just imagine from our master bedroom, smelling the fresh ocean air! From our porch you could see the Caribbean, big and blue out to the horizon, then you could walk to the beach, all that white sand under your toes . . ."

She began to moan and rock herself back and forth. "Why is Roy abandoning me now?"

"Bertha, there is nothing we can do here. Please come with me," Jennifer soothed her. "I'll drive you to your house. My Dad can drive my car because he rode in the ambulance with Roy, and his car is in the bank. We're all upset but need to rest and be available when the nurse calls you with an update on Roy's condition,"

"I need to get home and be ready for the government inspectors that will be at the bank at ten today," Keith added sleepily.

"Go now dad," Jennifer handed her father her car keys. "I'll take

Bertha home. You can meet me there."

Bertha stood up and shook her head. "No. I'm going to stay."

"Look, Bertha, you can't stay here in your pajamas and be of good cheer to Roy!" Jennifer said sternly. "Please try to understand and come with me."

"Do I look that bad?"

Ignoring her question, Keith signaled to the exit. "Let's go now. Time is running out, and I have to take over Roy's responsibilities."

Walking together to the parking lot and while in the car with Jennifer, Bertha continued repeating what she had said to all of us regarding their beach house and retirement plans.

Upon arrival, Bertha exited the car without saying a word. She went inside and, slammed the front door. Keith arrived, and Jennifer and Keith drove home.

Keith commented, "I need to sleep a few hours to be in good shape for the auditors."

"Dad, at what time do you want me to take you to the bank?"

"I must be there before ten."

"Okay, don't worry," Jennifer reassured him. "You just go to sleep, and I will make sure you will be there on time."

Chapter 17
UNEXPECTED HERO

At eight in the morning, Margaret arrived at the bank and proceeded directly to the main conference room. Her plan was to ensure that everything was ready for the government inspectors. "Oh, Lord! What has happened here?" she exclaimed upon entering the conference room. She first noticed the financial statements, working papers, and notes for the inspectors strewn all over the table. The carpet was a mess, with mysterious stains and rotten food all over. There were two partially emptied bottles of bourbon, and the potent smell of alcohol permeated the room. The smell was so bad Margaret felt herself becoming sick. However, she picked up the phone and called the banks' security office.

"Hello, this is Margaret Gianelli, I need to know if there is an incident report regarding events last evening in the main conference room?"

"Ms. Gianelli, a few minutes ago the nurse on duty last night delivered an emergency response incident report," the officer on the other line told her. "The time was ten forty-two in the evening. It named Mr. Lubec as the victim. He is now at Mercy Hospital."

"Thank you."

She began to panic but kept outwardly calm. 'Lord, please help me!' She thought to herself. 'What do I do? Who do I call? What's going to happen in the next hour and fifteen minutes? Where's Keith?' Then she remembered her dad's explanation of the tactical and strategic worker.

"Now is time to be both!" Margaret said aloud to the empty conference room.

She stood up and began gathering and ordering the financial statements in one pile and separating working papers into another stack. She collected all the documents, and then, as she was departing from the conference room, she placed a "Do Not Disturb," sign over the door. Back in her office, she called Mercy Hospital to ask about Roy's medical condition. The ICU nurse only told her that Mr. Lubec's "state remains guarded."

Immediately, Margaret called Keith's cell phone, but to her dismay, the call went straight to voicemail, and she had no recourse but to leave a message. "Mr. Jones, this is Margaret, it is nine o'clock on Tuesday morning, and in one hour the government inspectors will be here. Please call me. I'm at the bank." She took the business statements to the conference room near Roy and Keith's offices. This meeting room was known as 'The Money Room.' Margaret removed from view all documents not related to the inspection and neatly arranged the financial accounts in the same way as she had presented her past reports to Mr. Ellis at the Inspector General's Office. She called the dining room and ordered two pots of coffee, one natural hazelnut and one decaffeinated. She also explicitly instructed for them to be brought hot to the "The Money Room" along with freshly assorted Danish pastries.

The clock was ticking, and Margaret became increasingly anxious. She called Keith again, but her calls kept going to voicemail. Margaret stood and began to pace, feeling the anxiety well up within her. The only way she could see to calm down was to pray.

She knelt down and began; "Lord you know I'm in trouble! My time is running out! No one is here, and I don't know what to do. Please hear me and do something! I'm going to stand here waiting to be fried alive when those guys from the government show up. I can already smell my flesh. Just look at me, my makeup is looking like I'm walking the golf course on a hot summer day." She glanced once more at the wall clock, "Oh my God! Where are you? Please, Lord, help me!"

As she knelt there with her hands clenched against her chest, she suddenly heard; "Good morning Margaret! What are you doing?"

"Thank God you're here!" Margaret cried, leaping to her feet.

"Come on, we only have a few minute to prepare," Keith said, looking around the room.

"All is in order in "The Money Room," Margaret told him, already feeling completely calm. "Please go there and double check while I wait here for the inspectors."

"Thanks, Margaret. When they arrive, buy me a little time. I need to mentally adjust to Roy's absence. Once they depart we'll talk about the shenanigans that my friend Roy pulled on me last night."

"You go ahead, and I will take care of those guys when they show up!"

As anticipated at ten o'clock, the elevator bell rang, and three men with briefcases emerged. "Good morning, I'm Mr. Smith," the front one introduced himself and shook Margaret's hand. "These are Mr. Gomez and Mr. Stevenson. We're from The Special Inspector's General Office. Is Ms. Nancy McArthur available?"

"Ms. McArthur is out of the office," Margaret said politely. "I'm Margaret Gianelli, her assistant and have the authority to serve on her behalf. I'm here to assist you in any way I can. This is my desk, should you need anything, please pick up any telephone within the bank and dial seven to reach me." Then, she continued, "Please know that last night Mr. Lubec was taken to Mercy Hospital, and he is there in Intensive Care. When I spoke to the hospital a few minutes ago to inquire about his health, the supervising nurse told me his condition was "guarded." Therefore, you will be meeting with Mr. Jones only. Allow me to call him to see if he is in his office now." She excused herself and went back to her office to call him.

Margaret waited for a few moments, buying Keith time, and then walked back outside. "May I offer you some coffee while Mr. Jones joins us from the parking lot?" she asked sweetly.

"That'd be nice," said Smith. "What about you gentlemen?"

The other two agreed.

"Ms. Gianelli, how long have you been with the bank?" Gomez inquired while they were waiting for their coffee. "This is the first time we've seen you here."

"I've been with the bank for a little over a year, working in the investor relations department and most recently promoted to be the assistant to Ms. McArthur." She said innocently. "I'm still in training on administrative policy and procedures, and I'm still finding my way around." She gave a friendly giggle.

Everyone was enjoying the hazelnut aroma of their piping hot coffee and having a casual conversation about the upcoming Kentucky Derby. Then Keith appeared on the scene. "Good morning gentlemen, please excuse my tardiness, but we had an eventful evening that kept me up until three this morning."

"What happened?" asked Smith.

"Well, we had a meeting preparing for your visit today. Then about eight in the evening we all had dinner together before Mr. Jordan and Ms. McArthur departed for George Town. Mr. Lubec and I came up to the conference room to arrange the documents you'll be inspecting today. We sat for maybe half hour, then Mr. Lubec stood up to get a glass of water. Then, like a rock, he hit the ground. He looked bad, so I called the bank nurse, and she came up immediately and called 911. In a few minutes, Mr., Lubec and I were in the ambulance on route to the Mercy Hospital. There he was diagnosed as having a heart attack. I called this morning, and he still there in the ICU."

"We are very sorry for Mr. Lubec," Stevenson said solemnly. "We're sorry for his family and the people of this bank."

"Mr. Jones, are you prepared to take the place of Mr. Lubec, should we have any questions today?" Smith asked.

"Yes, I am. Shall we go to the conference room near my office and work from there?"

"Thanks for the coffee," Gomez said to Margaret with a smile as they left the room.

Margaret called the housekeeper as soon as they were out of the room. "Good morning, this is Ms. Gianelli from the executive office, may I speak to James, the daytime supervisor?"

"He'll be with you in a moment," said the female voice answering the phone.

Within seconds he was on the phone. "This is James, may I help you?"

"James, this is Margaret Gianelli. As soon as you are available, please come up here to the executive office, I need to assign a job that requires your experience to determine the best solution to a problem."

Without hesitation, James responded, "I will be up there within 30 minutes, I'm completing the supplies purchase order that must be placed this morning for delivery tomorrow."

"Thank you, James I'll see you when you get here."

Almost as soon as she put her phone down, it began ringing again. She picked up. "This is Keith, please Margaret brings us the file labeled "Caribbean Bank Escrow."

"Right away, Sir." She collected the full file and carried it to "The Money Room."

"Do you need anything else?" she asked after she placed it on the table.

"Not for now, thank you," Keith said somberly. Margaret returned to her office and found James standing at the door waiting. "Hello, James. Thank you for coming. Last night, we had an incident in the main conference room. I placed on the door a "Do Not Disturb" sign to avoid any alarm, but it's a pretty big mess in there. Please go there assess the situation, come back and let me know your recommendations."

"Right away," he said with a nod.

Within minutes, James returned. "Ms. Gianelli, this needs to be resolved by experts," he reported grimly. "The plush white carpet is badly stained with what looks like spilled food residue and alcohol. It requires specialized treatment. If it's okay with you, I'll go down and start researching the best companies. In the meantime, to avoid gossip, I'll change the door lock and instruct my people to cancel that room from their daily tasks. They'll be happy to hear that!" he added with a laugh. "In the past, the cleaning crew has complained of the delicate details needed to take care of that place."

"Let me know the results, and please keep this matter confidential. We don't know what happened. Therefore, it may cost us our jobs if we let this situation out of this office."

"Understood."

Margaret was feeling in control of the situation and began to link the arguments of the night before with Keith's explanation to the inspectors. She had a hundred questions about what happened there. However, she would not speculate until she got the facts from Keith during their next face-to-face conversation.

At 1:15 p.m., Margaret tapped twice at the door of the money room, "May I come in, please?" she called out.

"Yes, Margaret, what do you need?" Keith's voice sounded faint from the other side."

"Well it's about lunch time, and it's pouring rain outside. May I arrange to bring you lunch here?" Margaret offered. "We have delicious choices from "Transactions," our dining room. Alternatively, if you prefer, I could arrange a large table there so you gentlemen can have working lunch in a relaxed atmosphere. What would you prefer?" Keith looked to Smith for a response, he, in turn, looked to Gomez and then Stevenson.

"Let us see what "Transactions" has to offer us," Gomez said mysteriously.

"I can go for that," Smith gave his assent.

"Ms. Gianelli, for a newcomer you're a genius," Stevenson said to Margaret as he stood up. "Thank you, we accept to have lunch there and return to work here where all our documents are in order."

"Please give me thirty minutes to arrange a good meal, and I will be back with you." On her way to the dining room, she began silently to plan her strategy to sit at lunch with the inspectors and collect additional information for her recording session in the evening. Once there, she immediately sought out Mario.

"Mario I have three government guests, Mr. Jones and me for lunch in thirty minutes. No alcohol is to be offered, but plenty of food for them to relax and be happy," she instructed him once she had tracked him down in the kitchen. Mario smiled.

"Ms. Margaret, you go ahead and bring your guests, I will make them relax and send them back to work feeling happy."

The government inspectors, Keith, and Margaret arrived at the dining room.

"Wow," Smith whistled as he walked in. "This is a five-star restaurant." Mario welcomed the guests and escorted them to a table with the full view of the city and rainy sky. "I have prepared for you a light meal consisting of the cream of tomato, veal with capers, pasta with white sauce, and Caesar salad."

"That sounds exquisite," Smith said.

"Please, Margaret join us!" Keith called over to Margaret.

Gomez looked at Margaret and smiled as she sat down. "I was expecting our host to be with us for lunch," he said smoothly.

"Thank you, I'm glad to be here so I can learn more about what you gentlemen do," Margaret told him coyly, meeting his stare.

Gomez, charmed by Margaret's apparently naïve comment promptly began explaining; "We are concerned with a broad range of possible violations of the law. These include bank fraud, conspiracy to commit fraud or to defraud the United States, wire fraud, and making false statements to the Government."

"Wow!" Margaret gave him a look of wide-eyed wonder. "Is that why you're here? For an investigation?"

"Oh no, Ms. Gianelli," Smith interjected. "We're here for a routine verification of the bank financial statements and internal controls in managing the bailout funds given to this bank to stay in operation during the financial crisis."

Margaret wanted to get inside information to determine the situation while appearing as stupid and ignorant as possible. "What's going to happen now that Mr. Lubec is in the hospital?"

"Well, there is no problem because Mr. Jones has audited the statements in the past," Smith responded, businesslike. "And he will be in an equal position to answer our questions if we have any. In the past inspections, for the most part, Ms. MacArthur assisted with providing additional documents we requested. Mr. Lubec as Chief Financial Officer provided the responses to our inquiry." However, continued Smith, "This unfortunate event of Mr. Lubec's absence can be used constructively to get a fresh view of any new or developing issues."

"Should we need any additional documents not aligned with the financial statements or working papers, would you be able to help us, Ms. Gianelli?" Stevenson added.

Margaret remembered the discussion with Larry and Nancy the night before. "I have access to the files by name, so if you need any document, I can find it for you by name."

"That's excellent Margaret" Keith quickly interrupted.

Lunch ended. "Delicious and satisfying," Smith described it to Mario.

"So shall we return to work?" Keith asked, tapping the table.

"Thanks, Ms. Gianelli, for an exquisite lunch, we appreciate the special treatment," Smith said over Keith.

"Gentlemen, please do what you have to do," Margaret smiled. "I have some other dinner events I need to work on here. If you need anything at all, please ask Mr. Jones to reach me. I'm normally in my office, and if I'm not responding, please ask Mr. Jones to send me a text message, and I'll be ready to help." The lunch had confirmed her suspicion that the Government inspectors were not just auditing the bank. They were conducting the investigation Mr. Ellis had recommended to Ms. Crystal Reyes, The Special Inspector General.

MONEY & GREED

JORGE RIVERA

Chapter 18
INTERNATIONAL SCOPE

At 3:30 p.m., Margaret's desk phone began to ring. It was Larry. "Hello! Margaret!" he said. "I'm calling from George Town. I need you to make plans to come here tomorrow morning and participate in a celebration golf challenge that the Caribbean Bank and the Chamber of Commerce have scheduled for Saturday. We've already accepted, and there is a cash prize for the winning team. Our team will consist of Nancy, the new bank president, Ms. Harrington, you, and me." Margaret listened and made mental notes.

Larry continued; "We made a good deal and ended up making a little over two million to go back to the discretionary fund to acquire additional assets." He paused. "Ah…!" he groaned. "I almost forgot since this is an out of the country travel you need a valid passport. Do you have one?"

"Yes, I do."

"Good!" Larry's went on about his accomplishments and never asked about the audit. Finally; "Should your parents need confirmation of my request, please connect them with me at any time. I want to make sure that they are informed that you are representing the new bank. Travel and medical insurance will be provided for you, everything's already arranged for you. Also, don't worry about tropical clothing. We'll buy you anything you need. The weather is hot and at times and very humid. All you need to bring is personal items and your best golf clubs."

"Yes sir, I understand."

"So, tell me did the Government inspectors show up as Nancy predicted? " Larry finally got to the issue.

"Well Mr. Jordan, are you sitting or standing where you are?"

"Oh! Hell did they arrest Keith and Roy?"

"No. Mr. Jordan nothing like that," Margaret said evenly, taking note of his reaction. "It's much worse. Mr. Lubec had a heart attack last night. He's in intensive care at Mercy Hospital."

"That's horrible!" Larry exclaimed, but Margaret could not help but notice a tangible sense of relief, even over the phone. "Earlier this afternoon I had three calls from Jennifer, Mr. Jones' daughter. She told me that she went to the hospital to assist Mr. Jones and Mrs. Lubec. Jennifer said that Mrs. Lubec had lost her mind. She's hysterical, and since she went to the hospital, all she's been able to talk about is the beach house Roy bought in the Caymans and their retirement plans." Margaret paused, but Larry did not offer any comment.

"Mr. Jordan, that's not all there is," continued Margaret, "About twenty minutes ago, the Government inspectors called me and asked to bring all of Nancy's files! They told me to empty the entire cabinet and bring the contents to "The Money Room" where they are meeting and probably tearing Mr. Jones to pieces and eating him alive!"

"Margaret," Larry stopped her calmly. "First, call the hospital and speak to the head nurse and find out how Roy's doing. Second, call Mrs. Lubec and determine what her real situation is. Third, don't worry about Mr. Jones, he'll survive. The government inspectors are doing their job. An audit is what they are doing, attempting to determine if there are possible violations of law, for example, any type of fraud or impropriety in the bank's business. So, there is nothing to worry about. Fourth, when the government inspectors leave, have Keith call me. Fifth, after you complete your assignment call me back and brief me on the real situation as you see it."

"Yes sir, leave it to me."

"Make sure you bring your golfing gear and be here tomorrow. I want you to meet Ms. Allison Harrington, the bank president, and her new management team. Also, we want to schedule a couple of games to familiarize ourselves with the golf course. I've heard it's similar to San Andrews Links in Scotland, the ocean, changing winds directions and the degree of difficulty."

"Mr. Jordan, please know that representing the bank and playing at a dream golf course would be my honor," Margaret said. "However, how do you propose that I get there tomorrow? I do not have the kind of cash available to purchase the last minute airfare. Besides, I need to consult with my boyfriend. I hope you understand. He's important to me."

"No need to worry. I already called Mr. Oliver the pilot that brought Nancy and me here. He is ready to carry you and if you would like, you to have my authorization to invite your boyfriend or your parents. We have room for eight people here and on the plane, and there are plenty of accommodations available here. All are welcome. This will be a special round-trip flight, with accommodations, meals, and all incidental expenses paid."

Despite herself, Margaret could not hold back her excitement, and for a second she forgot the dark drama of the whole situation. "Thank you Mr. Jordan!" she blurted out. Then more seriously; "I'll get on it, there's a lot to do." As soon as she hung up the phone, it began to ring again. "That's been happening a lot today," she muttered to herself. She checked the wall clock, it was four-fifty in the afternoon. She sighed and answered the phone. "This is Margaret, may I be of service?"

"Could you please come over, please?" It was Keith.

Margaret excitement over her trip to the Caymans evaporated.

What do these guys want from me? She thought to herself, anxious. On the way to the conference room, her mind mulled over a thousand possibilities. 'I really don't know anything about anything they may want. Besides, I'm following Carlos employment safety motto. I have eyes but can't see. Ears but can't hear. Mouth but can't speak.'

She rapped on the door, and Smith opened. "Ms. Gianelli, we are finished for today, and we all wanted to thank you for your courteous arrangements for coffee, lunch and the effort to bring all the files here," he thanked her graciously. "Also, in advance thank you for putting them away." He shook her hand.

Margaret's heartbeat began to return to normal. "Thank you, gentlemen, for the education about your assignment and for the opportunity of being allowed to have lunch with you. When will you be back?"

"This could be our last visit," Stevenson said flatly, a sharp contrast to Smith's gentlemanly air. "We'll let Ms. McArthur know if we'll be visiting again."

Margaret glanced at Keith, who got the message and quickly offered to escort the auditors out of the building. Within twelve minutes, Keith returned to 'The Money Room,' and found Margaret putting together Nancy's files.

Keith signaled to Margaret to leave the documents on the table and sit down.

"How did the inspection end?" Margaret asked him.

"To tell you the truth, these people had a different type of review in mind. They looked over the financial statements Roy prepared, and I audited like passing pages of an easy-read book. They didn't talk at all most of the time, except when they asked me to call you to bring Nancy's files. Then, in the last twenty-five minutes of their visit, they focused their questions on the assets purchased by Nancy in Hong Kong." Margaret nodded, and Keith continued on with his description of the audit.

"Then, Stevenson found the real estate appraisal for the Cayman Islands home for a cool $3.8 Million. "This assessment is recorded in the name of Ms. Nancy Mc Arthur, a single woman. Why not the bank? He asked me. I quickly responded that her intent was to secure an additional appraising without disclosing that the bank was behind all of it. Then this strange thing happened. Gomez looked at Smith and said "That makes sense," and lifted his eyebrows in this really suspicious way."

"Then what happened?" Margaret asked, intrigued. Keith cleared his throat and went on.

"Smith turned and asked, How long Mr. Lubec and I have been with this bank. Feeling the weight of my responsibility and the heaviness of my conscience as the Bank Auditor, I told them Roy has been here twenty-one years, and I've had my position for fifteen. Stevenson asked if I had worked in auditing before and after that, they left."

"Did his statement mean anything to you other than the obvious?" Margaret asked, now a little alarmed. "The fact that they say nothing outside the ordinary should it interpret a matter of concern or just government guys doing their jobs?"

Keith wrinkled his brow and looked down. "Well, let's say for now that this inspection does not sit well with me. A situation such as an advance of scheduled review, nothing out of the ordinary, was asked, and they just took the financial statements audited by the outside auditors. I'm clear that the inspectors had a hidden agenda. Besides, the papers from Nancy were cursorily reviewed with a single annotation without an apparent objection as to the appraisal that was performed and paid in the name of the bank. However, the report was issued on behalf of Nancy and that triggered my deepest fear." Keith suddenly slapped his forehead Oh S#*&*! Margaret, today is my wedding anniversary," he gasped. "And 'You know who' is waiting for me at six this evening. If I'm late you know, I will be castrated, and my life will be over!"

"Ah! No, that shouldn't happen to you. Please go, go," Margaret told him. "I'll take care of the cleanup, and if you are walking tomorrow, we will finish our conversation. No! I can't talk to you tomorrow because I have to go to George Town to play golf."

"Play golf in George Town, tomorrow?" repeated Keith, as he got his things together to rush out of the room. Margaret did not respond, and he did not wait for her too.

Margaret remained sitting. "Now I'm left holding the bag," she said aloud to herself. "Roy's in intensive care. His wife is acting as she has lost her mind. Keith is about to lose his manhood if he is late for the renewing of the wedding vows. Larry is expecting Keith to call him upon the departure of the Government inspectors. Nancy's papers are scattered on the table. And then there's my unfaithful boyfriend. Tomorrow at the same time I will be in the Cayman Islands. To top it all off, Mr. Jordan is expecting me the report on the issues he entrusted me and to give him confirmation that I will be in George Town on time for the golf practice rounds."

She buried her face in her hands. "What am I to do Lord?" she cried. "Please talk to me, there is no one here except You and me. I'm going to shut up and listen to You! Every minute was longer and longer." She turned off the lights as if the darkness would be a better environment to hear what the Lord had to say. Her heart was pounding in her chest. She sat there for a few minutes, and just when she felt she was truly beginning to panic, her cell phone began to ring. She picked up and could not help but start crying into the other line.

"Hi Honey, it's Dad!" she heard her father's voice exclaim. "What's wrong?"

"I'm in deep trouble I must see you and talk to you as promptly as possible," Margaret pleaded while trying to find the light switch.

"How soon would you like to see me?" Harry said calmly.

"Now!" Margaret said without hesitation.

"Well, I came to a meeting at the University. Since it is nearly six, the evening rush traffic is terrible, I called to ask if you would like to have dinner while the traffic dies down."

"Wow! Thank You, God! Yes, come over, and I will meet you in the lobby in thirty minutes. I have to put away some stuff here in the office. Thank you, thank you!"

Margaret began to collect the files and calm herself. In no time at all the documents were neatly returned to their original locations. With a sense of urgency, she checked and removed all papers on her desk, and ran to the elevator as fast as she could. The elevator ride felt like it took forever, and while waiting she began to tap her right foot anxiously In the lobby, she looked at her wristwatch and found that thirty minutes passed since she last spoke to Harry. He was nowhere in sight.

The loud sound of an ambulance siren suddenly broke the silence in the lobby. She began to panic again and at lightning speed a dozen scenarios of what could have happened to her father raced through her mind. Her heart began to pound painfully when suddenly she felt a gentle tap on her right shoulder. She spun around and saw her father. She hugged him tightly immediately, and her feelings of fear turned to joy. "Ah! Dad, I'm glad to see you!"

"I called your mom and told her we won't be in for dinner," he crooned. "The weather's bad, and the traffic's terrible, I was going to call you to bring some dinner home. Your mother's not feeling well. She has a headache, and not too excited to eat, nor start cooking. Besides, Bobby is at Johnny's, and his mother will feed them before bringing him home."

"That's good, so we don't have to rush, and we'll be able to talk freely. Where's your car parked?"

"At the public parking next to the bank."

"Good so let's eat at the Chinese place around the corner," Margaret suggested. "Afterward, we can walk back here and drive home."

At the Chinese restaurant, Margaret asked Harry, "Let me order. I know the menu, and I know what you like."

"Yes please."

Margaret was ordering for both, "We'd like bird nest soup, chicken with walnuts, mixed vegetables, white rice, and tea, please." After the server had walked away, she looked around to made sure no one from the bank was nearby so they could overhear what is about to take place.

"Dad let's eat first, and during tea, we can talk."

"That sounds right," Harry agreed. "I'm hungry."

The bird's nest soup was hot and tasty, the sweet smell of spicy walnuts and sesame seeds over the chicken made the meal most satisfying for Harry and Margaret. Then, she called the server and ordered sweet red bean cakes, and a pot of the piping hot jasmine tea to go with them.

Chapter 19
FACTS AND OBSERVATIONS

Immediately after the server had left, Margaret began to tell her father, in summary, what had happened the day before. First, unexpectedly being part of a situation briefing with the people at the bank, Mr. Larry Jordan, the Chief Executive Officer; Ms. Nancy McArthur, Executive Assistant to Mr. Jordan and her new boss; Mr. Roy Lubec the Chief Financial Officer; and Mr. Keith Jones the bank's Internal Auditor. Margaret described to Harry a few facts worth noting, with specific details. She focused on her recent observations, like the tension she had felt coming from the participants about the announcement of the surprise visit by the government inspectors two weeks ahead of the previously scheduled time, and her surprise of being asked for her opinion on a matter with which she had no experience. She talked about the mention by Lubec of his wishes for the government inspectors of 'removing the bank packet and closing the books,' and his casual reference to taking a permanent vacation in the Caymans.

Margaret also discussed the body language and verbal friction between Larry and Nancy. Nancy's instructions to Lubec to transfer three million dollars to the discretionary fund's account, and Nancy's explanation of being under the wrong assumption that Larry needed that kind of cash to purchase the new property in the Cayman Islands before the acquisition of the Caribbean Bank. Margaret also described the confrontation between Keith and Nancy.

She told Harry how Keith expressed openly there was something wrong, but that he could not identify it. Moreover, Nancy's perception of her producing business for the bank as a deserving economic right versus Keith's definition of, 'appropriate use of government funds, ultimately the taxpayer's money!' And the sarcasm that ensued. She related Nancy's indirect confessions of possible wrongdoings, and she needs to exhibit over a million dollars' worth of art in her office, buying an apartment, and artworks at an auction in Honk Kong.

Then, Margaret put the icing on the cake by telling Harry what had happened that day. She began with her arrival at the bank and the mess in the conference room. Then there was Roy's heart attack and what she learned from the government inspectors during the lunch, and Keith's comments about the silent glances between the government inspectors made during the documents inspection.

Based on the lessons learned with Mr. Ellis she suspected the federal government inspectors' visit was a segment of the formal investigation of the Louisville Midtown Bank. Then Margaret announced to Harry the details of the Bank's golf tournament in the Cayman Islands, and her directives to George Town the following day. Moreover, she told her father of the approval from Larry to invite her boyfriend, Jonathan and asked if the family would want to go.

Harry, was attentive, but did not ask any questions, nor make any comments until Margaret asked, "Dad—what are your thoughts?"

"Well, first I don't believe Jonathan or us should be invited to go. However, you should notify Jonathan that the bank is sending you to take part in a bank function that includes golf in George Town. His new employer is a large law firm. Therefore, these events are not a rare situation. He's mature and trusts you. He'll understand and encourage you to play your best."

Harry continued, "Your mom, well that's a different story. Tell her that we spoke tonight and that in my opinion, this is an official event and part of your new job. Inform her that tomorrow you are going to George Town to represent the bank at a golf tournament. Let her know you will call upon departure and arrival and during your time there. She'll be happy and encourage you, but try to keep details to a minimum. You know how much she worries. Now, based solely on your description of the facts, and the sequence and timing of the events, I have no question in my mind that the government is chasing the whereabouts of the government money for at least three years. Your placement in the bank and promotion is a common strategy to secure key access to the exact location and facilitate the collection of evidence. However, the government's interest is in understanding why these people at the bank may have turned to crime. The inspectors would rely on the facts they learned during their periodic audits, what witnesses told them in the relevant interviews, facts they read in documents both obtained from the routine inspections and records, they would seize in future searches and trial testimony."

Harry tilted his head towards Margaret, and looking upward, began a monolog as if no one was near. "These constant battles of greed and the love of money are at the center of the unjustifiable desires of men and women to acquire land, houses, cars, yachts, planes, artworks and other luxuries. These uncontrollable cravings are trigging these people, unethical conduct that is impacting all sound financial decision-making. Also, anger, envy, and jealousy are apparently the dominating passions of once perfectly respectable men and women pushing them to make wrong decisions in their relationships and personal choices, ruining their lives and the lives of many others. Their actions are destroying the lives of the elderly who entrusted their life savings and retirement funds to the financial institution lead by the felons in this case. They're ruining the dreams and lives of students who placed their college education funds in this bank. Devastating the lives of sick people who put their survival money in the trust of this bank, whereby, you, my golfing queen, are liable to be withdrawn at the will of any of the players if you fail to keep your focus on your government assignment."

"Thank you, Dad. I understand more about the complexity of the situation at the bank and the importance of my prosecuting facilitator role. From now on I'll focus on minimizing any comments that may give away my knowledge of the magnitude of the problem these people are facing."

"That's my golfing queen: smart and cautious," he said emotionally. Then he added, "Let's go home, so you will have enough time to talk with Jonathan and be ready to depart for George Town on time. Remember to take the phone I lend to you and deactivate the "location" feature. This is set up for international calls as local calls. Forward all calls from your phone to that one, and use it to phone Johnathan and us. All calls will show as dialed from your own phone without disclosing your actual location."

After paying the dinner bill, Harry and Margaret departed, each to get their car from the respective garages. The traffic going in the direction of Woodland Hills was now normal, and there was no more rain. On the way home, Margaret called Johnathan.

"Hi, this is me, can you come over? I have something important I need to tell you in person."

"Alright," Johnathan answered. "You caught me just in time. My mother and I were just finishing dinner, and we were going to go to a book presentation at the library. I'll change my plan and see you in an hour."

"Great! I love you, see you in an hour."

Harry arrived home a few minutes ahead of Margaret and was advancing to Janet, some of the news regarding the golf tournament.

"Great! She's a good player and will make an excellent representative," was Janet's reaction.

Shortly after her father Margaret arrived. "Mom, I'm home where are you?"

"Honey, I'm here in the kitchen," Janet called. "Dad just told me the good news of your playing golf tomorrow in some tropical paradise!"

"Hi. Yeah, the bank is sending me to represent it at a business event. The trip includes playing in a golf tournament and paying for the private flight. They're going to cover all my expenses, including any new clothes I might need for the hot weather. Not a bad deal for a few rounds of golf! I've missed playing!" Janet smiled at her daughter.

"Speaking of that, Jonathan will be here in forty-five minutes," Margaret notified her. So I'm going to go upstairs to refresh and be ready, I need to let him know what is going on with my trip tomorrow."

"Sounds good honey."

Margaret's phone rang, but she was in the shower. She picked it up after getting out to hear a voice mail message from Johnathan. "Sweetie, I'm sorry I'm not able to go tonight. My mother didn't tell me that she was planning to have me as a chaperone. The fact that my father is out of town and the library list of guest for this book discussion is filled with single men." I'll call you later tonight, and we can talk on the phone. I love you."

"Ah, that is okay," she told herself. Jonathan's cancellation will allow me more time to prepare and get ready."

At nine that evening, her phone rang again. It was Jonathan. "Hello, Margaret, we just returned. The book presentation was most impressive. It dealt with how emotions drive our financial decisions. My mother bought the book, and I'll have a chance to read it for free. How was your day at the bank?"

In a loving tone in her voice, "My love I'm happy that you are calling. My time at the bank was right. As a matter of fact, that is the important subject I want to tell you about. Today, our bank acquired a small bank in George Town, in the Cayman Islands.

Margaret continued, "My boss, Ms. McArthur and the Chief Executive Officer, Mr. Jordan are there closing the transaction and filing all regulatory documents. This is an important business event for the George Town Chamber of Commerce, and next Saturday they are holding their Annual Golf Challenge. Earlier today I was asked by Mr.

Jordan to go George Town, tomorrow, meet the new bank President and her management team. Then, play a couple of practice rounds and participate in the Golf Challenge with our bank team consisting of my boss Nancy, Mr. Jordan, Ms. Harrington, the president of the bank and me! What are your thoughts, my love?"

"That's fantastic! You are going to make a killing. You'll make their team shine. When are you leaving?"

"Tomorrow before lunch, I will be traveling in the chartered plane of the bank. Ah…, I almost forgot, guess what?"

"What!"

"The bank is paying me extra, I believe the bonus is for being out of the country. However, that's not all. The bank will pay for my food, lodging and any clothes I may need for the tropical weather. How about that?"

"Sweet Margaret, my heart, and mind are with you. I know you will make a significant contribution to the winning team. Remember, to keep your eyes on the target and don't forget the challenging trade winds near the ocean are traitors! As for my thoughts? This is an excellent opportunity, and being part of the executive team of this bank is something to enjoy and learn. We are learning every day. My best wishes for a safe trip, a good time, and a winning return."

"Thank you, my love, I will call you tomorrow when ready to depart, and after my arrival in George Town. Good night."

"Good evening, my dear Margaret, we will talk tomorrow before you go. I'll be in the office all day."

Chapter 20
CALLING INTO QUESTION

After talking with Jonathan, Margaret could not sleep, she recalled the time she found Jonathan at Starbucks, having coffee with his ex. She was busy rehearsing in her mind the events of the day. She was thinking about the government inspectors' friendliness and their undercover investigation. Margaret was concerned for Keith's celebration and his late arrival to face their judgment. Her mind was going so fast that before she knew it, it was morning. At seven o'clock her phone began ringing. She checked the caller ID but could not recognize the caller. However, aware that any number of people could be calling her, she answered anyways.

"Hello?"

"Margaret, Hi, this is Larry, sorry I wasn't able to contact you earlier. Last night, we had a massive storm, and there were no communications on the islands until this morning. So fill me in on what's happening."

Margaret realized no one had called Larry as he had expected, due to the excitement of the past day. Without missing a beat, she said,

"Yes sir, we're okay. Mr. Lubec's condition remains stable but guarded. The government inspectors worked in the Money Room with Mr. Jones. I arranged for them to have lunch served in the dining room, so they were happy. At four forty-five in the afternoon, they went home without telling us when they'd come back. Then, as you may remember from your invitation, Mr. Jones had a ceremony at six in his home to renew his wedding pledge or "Woe" as he called it. I'm not sure what happened because he left the bank late. You know Mr. Jordan, Mrs. Jones is not the soft and kind hearted blond as she makes people believe. She could be a hazard to Mr. Jones' health if he fails to do what she wants. As you can tell Mr. Jordan, time was not in our favor either, you had a storm, and we had our fill of unexpected events."

Without any comment on Margaret's report, Larry asked, "How is your travel itinerary coming? Are you bringing your boyfriend or your parents? What time are you departing?"

"I'll be leaving home in two hours to Louisville Airport. I'm coming alone with my golf clubs. The flight plan is set to depart at 10:00 a.m. to Miami. The pilot informed me we would have thirty minutes stop there, and then to Owen Roberts International Airport in Grand Cayman. Our total flying time including the short stop in Miami will be five hours and forty- eight minutes."

"That's good! Nancy, Ms. Harrington and I will be waiting for you at the airport. Then, we'll take you to your room at The Ritz-Carlton, Grand Cayman. We'll have dinner and a business briefing. After a good night's sleep, we hope you would be awakened by the beautiful sounds of the ocean and the fresh smell of newly cut grass. The view of the Blue Tip Golf Course, designed by Greg Norman, is just outside your window. It embraces the island's beautiful natural elements: water, mangroves, and fresh challenging trade winds."

"Wow!" Margaret was getting excited thinking about the bright Blue Ocean and green golf course. Mr. Jordan, I can't wait to get there and meet the challenges ahead."

"Have a safe trip, we'll be waiting for you."

After Margaret hung up. She could smell coffee brewing downstairs, and heard the upbeat sound of 'Happy,' the song by the Grammy Award winner, Pharrell Williams. The combination of the smell of brewing coffee and the upbeat music began to lift her spirits. Adding to her sense of excitement was the crisp feel of her white poplin dress. These reminded her of her tropical destination, and at the same time added a new twist to her excitement, and she began to hum along with 'Happy.'

"Mom! Are we having breakfast soon?" she yelled down the stairs. "Carlos will be here to pick me up, and we're leaving for the airport in an hour and twenty minutes. I just finished speaking with Mr. Jordan, and all is well. My boss Nancy, Mr. Jordan, and Ms. Harrington, the new bank president in George Town will be meeting me there."

Forty-five minutes later, Margaret, quietly walked down to the kitchen wanting to surprise her mother. She stood in silence by the door, posing like a model on the front cover of Vogue magazine. Her bright brown eyes were the frame of her shoulder-length golden wavy sandy hair. Margaret was wearing a white wide brimmed "Panama" hat. She was standing in her white and black, fitted above the knee floral skirt, and double breasted yellow blazer. Margaret had on her left hand a matching yellow tote bag. She was standing in white Gladiator sandals with white and yellow stripes mid-calf. The distinct and subtle smell of her Italian "Givenchy" cologne alerted her mother to her presence.

"Oh… my goodness…, you're beautiful!" Janet exclaimed upon seeing her. "Don't move. Let me get my phone to take a picture. I want to capture the essence of seeing you shining happy just like the song."

Margaret stayed like that, frozen. Janet got her phone and begins to take pictures, without noting the increasing smell of cooking bacon. Then, Margaret came out of her freeze like a stage actor and yelled, "Mom, mom, mom! The bacon is burning!"

"Here honey, hold my phone! I'll take care of that, and you and I will have breakfast."

"After all mom, this crispy, bacon smells delicious. I'll skip the waffles because I'll be in flight for more than five hours and want to feel comfortable."

"Of course, honey that's a smart move,"

Someone began knocking on the door. "Hello, Mrs. Gianelli!"

Carlos' voice called faintly from beyond the door. "I'm here to drive Ms. Margaret to the airport."

"Carlos, please go to the garage and load my golf clubs and the carry on the bag next to them," Margaret called out in response.

"Yes, Madam." Janet went out back and showed Carlos the way into the garage.

"Mom, I'll call you before departing from the airport." Margaret gave her mother a kiss on the cheek and walked out with Carlos. While standing in front of the house, Janet waved her goodbye.

"Have a safe trip, and a good time, I love you!" Margaret waved back and then turned to Carlos. "

Good morning Ms. Margaret," he greeted her politely. "A few minutes ago I spoke to Mr. Jordan. He instructed me to take you Bowman Field Airport. There, Captain Roger and his co-pilot are waiting for you to take you to the Cayman Islands, via Miami. Other than the golf clubs and the small bag, do you have anything else I should load?"

"Thank you, Carlos. This is all I'm taking with me."

At Bowman Field Airport, Carlos stopped and parked the car at the level one parking garage. He opened the right rear door for Margaret and indicated for her to follow him to the "Bistro Le Relais" Restaurant situated in the airport terminal where Captain Roger and the co-pilot were waiting for her.

"Thanks, Carlos, what about my golf bag?"

"I'll take your luggage to the terminal before you go through security after we know which hangar the plane is and what departure gate will be assigned for your flight."

They found their way to the restaurant, where Carlos recognized the captain.

"Good day, Captain Roger, this is Ms. Margaret Gianelli, your passenger to the Cayman Islands. Mr. Jordan and Ms. McArthur will be waiting for your arrival at the Caymans with further instructions."

"Thanks, Carlos," said Captain Roger. "Nice meeting you Ms.

Gianelli, this is my co-pilot, Mr. Burton. He's one of the best. Our plan is to fly to the Cayman Islands via Miami. There, we will go to security inspection for both the aircraft and the onboard loads. That'll take 30 to 45 minutes depending on the traffic on landing. Once we get flight clearance to take off, we will go directly to the Grand Cayman. The entire flying time would be five hours and fifty-five minutes. The weather is good, and we will have tailwinds which could help improve our time."

Margaret nodded.

So let me explain what's going to happen now. Mr. Burton and I will go to the Airport Authority, confirm our flight plan and announce our readiness to work. In turn, we will be assigned a departure gate. Mr. Burton will return here and give you that information so Carlos can bring your bags to the charter checking desk. Then, you can proceed with Mr. Burton to the security checkpoint. I will be waiting for you both at the assigned gate. This preparation to take off will take approximately thirty minutes. Do you have any questions?"

"No Captain, I have no questions."

Twenty minutes later, Burton returned. "Ms. Gianelli, we've been assigned to depart from Gate Four, located in the main terminal."

"I will meet you both in front of the charter departure desk," Carlos said. "It's located just to the right side of the main entrance, so Ms. Margaret can check the golf bag."

Both Burton and Margaret were standing by the charter desk, situated near the last security area. Carlos arrived and handed over the golf equipment and a small carry-on bag to Margaret. In turn, Burton approached the female attendant behind the charter desk and gave her the passenger manifest. She read it and signaled to Margaret to place the golf bag on the weight scale. The attendant printed out a boarding pass and put a claim tag in the golf bag. Then, a skycap appears bringing a plastic liner. He covered the entire golf bag and sealed it with tape, placed a label saying, 'Charter number 137' on it, and then put the golf bag on the conveyor belt. He returned and asked, "Are there any more passengers?"

"No. Thank you," responded Burton and gave Margaret a quick two thumbs up.

Burton and Margaret proceeded to the Transportation Security Agency (TSA) documents checkpoint. There Margaret handed the TSA officer her boarding pass and U.S. Passport. The TSA agent completed the document verification and signaled for Margaret to proceed to the screening line with the rest of the passengers from all the commercial airlines departing at that time. In the meantime, Burton had cleared passage through the Crew line. He was waiting for Margaret in the hallway near Gate Four. Upon reaching the hall, Margaret told Burton, "I'll see you in a few minutes in front of Gate Four. I want to buy something from this shop, and make a few calls."

"I'll be there waiting for you, take your time."

A few minutes later, Margaret arrived and handed her boarding pass to the flight dispatcher. Margaret and Burton walked down the corridor leading to the small path to the parked plane to begin boarding. "Wow!" Margaret exclaimed upon climbing into the aircraft. "This is beautiful, there are only four seats!"

"Yes, we were anticipating four passengers," Burton told her.

Without delay, he continued, "Please Ms. Gianelli go ahead choose your seat and fasten the seat belt. We'll be departing in a few minutes."

He closed the cabin door and showing Margaret where everything was.

"The Captain has turned on the "fasten seat belt." The intercom suddenly turned on, and Roger's voice issued out from it; "Ms. Gianelli, this is Captain Roger speaking, welcome aboard Charter flight 137 non-stop service e to Miami then continuing on to the Grand Cayman in the Cayman Islands. Our flight time to Miami will be two hours and thirty-five minutes. We will be flying an altitude of 30,000 feet at a ground speed of 380 mph. Mr. Burton, please prepare for gate departure."

"Doors on automatic, cross-check, and report. Thank you."

A few moments later, the plane began to move slowly forward. "Ms. Gianelli," Burton said over the speaker, "may I request your attention to the video monitor located to the side of your seat. We will be showing you our safety demonstration and would like the next few minutes of your complete attention. Thank you."

Margaret was in her first private plane flight experience. Curious about the differences between a charter and a routine commercial flight, she pulled out a notepad and turned her complete attention to the video screen. She took notes as an opportunity to refresh the facts that she has given limited attention in the past. She wrote:

"The female presenter on display begins. "Welcome aboard this charter flight. We are required by law to provide you with this pre-flight safety information. This aircraft is a Cessna Citation, M2 Business Jet."

"The following electronic devices (laptop computers, CD players) may be used when the seat belt sign is off." Margaret underlined segments of her notes and added, 'My cellular phone must be off during the entire time of the flight. I'm glad I'm not a smoker, it's forbidden onboard. Ah! There are detailed pictures in the safety information card.'

Suddenly the voice of Captain Roger announced, "Ms. Gianelli and Mr. Burton, please prepare for takeoff."

The ascension of the private jet plane was a new experience for Margaret. It gave the sensation of climbing much faster than a commercial airline. After they had settled into altitude and during the rest of the flight, Margaret made notes summarizing the facts, and her impressions of the events of the day before at the Louisville Midtown Bank in preparation for the meetings in George Town.

The flying time to her initial destination was quiet and, passed almost without notice. "Ms. Gianelli," the captain spoke again, completely breaking her concentration, "the local time in Miami is 3:23 p.m. The temperature is 83 degrees, with light showers. We'll be arriving in twenty minutes. Please make sure your seat back and table are in the upright position, and your carry-on luggage is stowed underneath the seat in front of you. We have begun our descent. Please fasten your seat belt." Margaret complied and enjoyed the impressive sight of Miami from the descending aircraft. Captain Roger announced, "We are clear to land." After touchdown, and as the plane was turning off the runway and taxing to the assigned charter gate, Burton made one last announcement. "Ms. Gianelli, welcome to Miami, the local time is 3:42 p.m. For your safety and comfort, please remain seated with your seatbelt fastened until the Captain turns off the Fasten Seat Belt Sign. Please wait to use your cell phone until we are inside the terminal. Thank you."

The plane is parked, and the engines turned off. Burton opened the cabin door and invited Margaret to disembark. Outside the arriving gate, Captain Roger instructed Margaret and Burton to follow him to the International Departure Gates. He explained that the aircraft would undergo a refueling and clearance inspection by the Airport Authority and TSA, and that could take up to forty-five minutes. He indicated to Margaret to take this time to go somewhere not too far from the gate and return in thirty minutes, to be issued a new boarding pass to the Grand Cayman. "Thank you, the Captain, and Mr. Burton for the excellent flight here," Margaret said. "I'll see you both here in thirty minutes." She walked off ways and dialed her mother.

"Mom? This is Margaret, we just landed in Miami. The flight was great. I enjoyed the attention from the pilot Mr. Roger and co-pilot Mr. Burton. Both are nice guys. They are treating me like royalty. The plane is beautiful, the interior seats are full and comfortable, cream color leather. During the entire flight, I was busy preparing my notes for the meetings with Mr. Jordan, my boss Nancy and the other people from the bank. How are you?"

"Thanks for calling honey, I was worried about your flight," Janet responded.

"Mom, there's no need to worry. The pilot is a thirty-year veteran. The co-pilot is an eagle. The aircraft is two years old. I'm 23 years old and happy to travel in style.—How about that answer to calm your nerves?—Tell me how is your music project is going?"

"Good that you ask honey, I'm so happy to be alone today and work a little on my music. Your Dad is out until late tonight. After school, Bobby took Rome to Johnny's house to play, and they'll stay there for dinner. I'm listening to "Happy" and dancing away until I get my inspiration to write music. How about that answer for calming my worries and for a little vacation time?"

"That's great, Mom! You work so hard all day for all of us that you deserve to enjoy any free time you get. Ah...! Mom, sorry to cut this call short, but I need to call Johnathan. I only have another ten minutes before boarding for the Grand Cayman. I will call you when I get there. I love you!" She hung up and immediately called Johnathan. The phone rang five times, then went to voicemail. "Jonathan, it is me. Margaret, I'm calling you from Miami, ten minutes before boarding for the Cayman Islands. I'll call you when I get there."

At the international charter gate, Margaret received a new boarding pass to the Grand Cayman. This time, she followed Captain Roger and Mr. Burton down the stairs to the shuttle that would take them to the ground transport 700 feet away from where the private jet was parked. On board, the aircraft Burton repeated same pre-flight routine as in Louisville.

Margaret remembered some of her notes. "Ah, yes! Fasten your seat belts, there is the emergency exit, no mobile phone in use while flying, of course, no smoking." Then, the voice of Captain Roger said, "Our flight time to Owen Roberts International Airport in the Grand Cayman will be one hour and thirty minutes. Margaret took out her notes and followed the safety demonstration. She did not realize how fast the time was passing until she heard Captain Roger announcing "We are in our final descend to Owen Roberts International Airport, the local time is four fifteen in the afternoon."

Margaret was surprised to hear the time. She checked the time on her wristwatch which she had re-set upon arrival in Miami. She was puzzled that after flying for an hour and thirty minutes, would be landing at same time as Louisville or an hour behind Miami, but Margaret did not say anything nor express any surprise. She waited until she saw a clock at the arriving terminal to explain her doubt. However, her question about the time difference remained, until she heard Burton announcing "Ms. Gianelli, welcome to Owen Roberts International Airport, the Grand Cayman Island. The local time is 4:33 p.m., the temperature is 84 degrees with a clear sky. On behalf of Captain Roger and me, we thank you for the opportunity of serving you on this trip, and we are looking forward to seeing you on board again shortly. Have a lovely stay!"

Chapter 21
THE GRAND CAYMAN ISLAND

Margaret was fascinated looking out the window to the foreground, on one side the azure ocean, white sand beach, palm trees, and on the other beautiful green grass. The plane was on the runway and taxiing towards the front of the airport building. She noticed a pyramid-shaped brick structure on the upper floor. This was an observation deck with people standing to look towards the incoming planes. On the ground floor of the building centered on the pyramid shape was a sign reading "Welcome to the Cayman Islands. Owen Roberts International Airport." Margaret was surprised how close the plane came to the terminal before it finally stopped. The plane was parked, and the engines turned off. Burton opened the cabin door and invited Margaret to disembark.

Margaret exited the plane and jumped down from the steps onto the runway. "Oh… my goodness…, the heat feels like an oven!" Margaret exclaimed as she rushed towards the entrance of the building to go through Customs. While inspecting Margaret's passport, the immigration officer said, "Welcome to the Grand Cayman. What is the purpose of your trip?"

"Thank you. I'm here to play in a golf tournament and meet the people of the island."

"Have a pleasant stay and enjoy our hospitality," said the officer while returning to Margaret her passport.

Outside the arrival door, Nancy was waiting with another woman, who turned out to be Ms. Harrington. "Hello Margaret, please meet our Bank President, Ms. Allison Harrington. How was your flight?"

"How do you do, is a pleasure meeting you, Ms. Harrington, and good afternoon, Ms. McArthur. My trip was excellent, it was a new experience for me. It was my first flight where I was the only passenger."

In a thick British accent Ms. Harrington said: "Welcome, I hope you will enjoy our tropical weather, the friendly people of the Cayman, our food, and hospitality."

"Thank you, Ms. Harrington, I'm sure I will," Margaret responded politely.

"I have an excellent report from both Mr. Jordan and Nancy, as to how well you are doing as their assistant, and that you are the new member of the executive team. Please call me Allison."

"Thank you, Ms. Harrington," Margaret gasped and covered her mouth. "Oops! I mean Allison."

Ms. Allison Harrington, the president of the Caribbean Bank, was fifty-two years old, Creole, five-foot-nine, 140 pounds, with short black hair and dark green eyes, a modulated voice with a light British accent, and a well-shaped body. On this day, she was wearing a body-fitted short sleeve white dress, green shoes, and complimentary green handbag. She was married and had no children. Allison was a member of the Board of Directors of the local Chamber of Commerce and active in other business associations. She had a Masters in Banking and Finance from the University of London. She was a golfer and an avid reader of nonfiction.

Margaret turned to Nancy. "Wow! Ms. McArthur, you look so beautiful. That pastel yellow dress and mandarin shoes and bag fit you to perfection."

"Thank you, Margaret, I would also appreciate it if you just call me

Nancy."

"Thank you, Nancy. How is Mr. Jordan?"

"He's meeting with the pilots that brought you here, and discussing our return schedule. He'll be joining us this evening at seven at the hotel, where we will be meeting with the bank's CFO, Ms. Springmyer, and the manager Mr. Garten. We'll have dinner and a meeting to review the schedule of events for the remainder of the time we're here. Now, let's go to the arrival luggage area to your golf equipment," said Nancy.

Fifteen minutes later, a porter carrying on his shoulder a golf bag, and on his hand sign, that read 'Ms. Gianelli' appeared from a door at the rear of the Lost and Found desk.

"I'm her," Margaret said, waving her hand.

"Where's your transport?" the porter asked courteously. "I'll take your bag there."

"Our transport will arrive in ten minutes to the front of the building near the "Departures" door," Allison told him. "Let's go there, and wait inside the building until I see him, so we can stay calm."

The Porter signaled his delight with two thumbs up and hitched the bag back up his shoulder and followed the three ladies to the departure area.

As they are walking, Margaret said, "When I deplaned, the temperature was so intense that it felt like being near a furnace."

"Today, we have had high humidity, and we are expecting rain at any moment," said Allison.

Margaret thoughts focused on how to handle the moisture, as her clothes were already soaking wet. When should she ask Nancy where she could buy fresh tropical clothing to change? Margaret's wardrobe, as directed by Larry, consisted of the clothes she was wearing, personal items, and golfing clothes.

A white Ford van arrived, and Allison signaled the driver. The vehicle stopped, and a black man dress in all white clothing emerged from the car and promptly opened both the front and the rear doors, and without delay loaded the golf equipment.

Meanwhile, Margaret was tipping the porter, who was most pleased with the gratuity in American currency. The passage between the building and the van was another hot experience for Margaret. Immediately upon boarding, she noticed the driver was seated on the right side of the vehicle, not on the left. To establish rapport and distract her attention from the clothing issue she noted; "I'm glad I'm not driving. It must be a challenge to drive on the left side of the road especially for one who is accustomed to driving on the right side."

Once inside the van with the air conditioner at the maximum Allison instructed the driver; "Milton, please take the Easterly Tibbets Highway to The Ritz-Carlton Grand Cayman Hotel."

"Madam, I'm not familiar with the route. Should I ask for directions, or could you guide me?"

"No problem," said Allison, gesturing to a close-by exit sign. "Exit the airport terminal and turn left. Take the first right and follow the road until reaching a stop sign. Turn left at the halt and follow the path to the first roundabout. At the roundabout, follow the signs to Seven Mile Beach. I will tell you more when near the first roundabout."

They drove on for ten minutes until they began approaching the roundabout. "Milton, when you reach the roundabout, continue straight until the second roundabout. Continue straight ahead until the third roundabout, and turn left. Then continue straight until the fourth roundabout and turn right onto West Bay Road. Continue along that road until you find the entrance to the Ritz-Carlton on you right. We should be there in five minutes."

Allison's last instructions to Milton gave Margaret some sense of relief that soon she would know when to ask Nancy about the clothing issue. Upon arrival at the entrance to the Ritz-Carlton, for a moment, Margaret forgot about heat and humidity. Her expression of admiration for the surroundings represented her spirit full of life. She brought both hands to her Panama hat, and exclaimed, "My God! This is beautiful. It is like walking in April, through the multicolored and delicious smells found only in the Butchart Gardens in Brentwood Bay, British

Columbia, Canada. These gardens are just as beautiful!"

Margaret's candor made an impact on Allison forming a distinct mental image of her perception, communication skills, and imagination. Allison had no knowledge that such gardens existed. However, Margaret painted a picture that sparked Allison's curiosity.

Milton stopped the Suburban in front of the hotel entrance. Within seconds, two porters simultaneously opened the vehicle's front and rear doors and helped Allison, Nancy, and Margaret disembark. At the same time, a bell boy unloaded the golf bag, placed it on a kart, and disappeared into the building. In the meantime, the chief porter dressed in white and gold military-style uniform approached, "Welcome to the Ritz-Carlton Grand Cayman. Are you staying with us?"

"Yes, my friends are the guests," said Allison.

"Please, this way," said the chief porter, indicating towards the registration desk.

"Thank you," responded Nancy as she led the way.

"Good afternoon Ms. McArthur and Ms. Harrington!" the man behind the desk greeted them. "My name is Chayton, and I'm at your service."

"Thank you, Chayton. This is Ms. Margaret Gianelli, she is one of the guests of the Louisville Midtown Bank. She just arrived from Miami, and will be staying on the floor facing the Blue Tip Golf Course."

"Yes, Madam. We have selected a beautiful room for Ms. Gianelli."

Allison and Nancy stepped to the side and started talking together while Margaret registered.

"Ms. Gianelli, may I have your passport and credit card, please?" Chayton asked. He proceeded to process and complete the hotel guest registration. A couple of minutes later, courteously presented the documents back to Margaret including a registration card for her signature. "According to our records," he told her, "all purchases in the hotel, including any items from any of the shops in the hotel, are pre-approved. All you need to do is to present this room key as a form of payment, and sign the receipt."

Chayton rang a bell, and handed Margaret's room key to a young woman, "This is Kathy, and she will accompany you to your room, and make sure the location, and room amenities, are to your satisfaction. Kathy will be your personal assistant during your entire stay."

"Wow! This is great, thank you, Chayton." She turned to Kathy and shook her hand.

"Hello Kathy, I'm glad to meet you." Margaret was most uncomfortable with the humidity and dampness of her clothing, and silently considered her need for fresh clothes.

"Hey! Margaret, I see you already have your personal assistant with you," Nancy remarked.

"Yes, she's Kathy. I'm going talk to her about my tropical clothing requirements."

"She'll be a great asset, use her knowledge. Allison and I will be conducting some minor business to complete the talking points for tonight. Consult with your personal assistant about where to buy and what you need and plan to be at the Blue Restaurant, five minutes before seven tonight."

"I look forward to our time together," added Allison kindly.

"I'll be with Kathy to find and buy what I need," Margaret said. "I'll see you both at six fifty-five this evening." They departed, and Margaret and Kathy began walking towards Margaret's room.

"Ms. Gianelli, as we walk to your room, please tell me what you need so I can figure out where to go right away. Getting to "the Blue" at five before seven is going to be a challenge!"

"The proper attire for this evening is our first priority. Then, if time permits, a couple of long pants and blouses," Margaret responded.

"This is your room," Kathy said upon arriving at and open the door. "I'll check the details when we return. Please, take a few minutes if you need and then let's go right back to the store where you'll find all you need." Kathy then went to the room's telephone and punched in a number. "Hi Wendy, this is Kathy, may I bring Ms. Gianelli, a VIP guest, that needs an evening dress and shoes for dinner at the "Blue." We have an hour to get her ready and at the restaurant, can you do it?"

"Have I ever disappointed you?" Wendy responded. "Bring her right away. Ask her pants size, and I will take it from there."

"Okay, hold the line." After a minute, "Wendy, size six long."

"Tell Ms. Gianelli a new shipment arrived from London yesterday and have pants to her heart's content. Does she need closed shoes, if so what is her size?"

"One moment . . . American seven and one-half."

"We have a good assortment of Italian shoes she can choose."

"We are on our way!" Kathy continued, "Ms. Gianelli, all is in order, all you need is to relax, and we'll have time to spare."

"Thank God."

Upon entering the clothing store, Wendy locked the door and placed a sign on the window that read; "Returning in 30 minutes, please call back. Thank You."

"Welcome Ms. Gianelli," she greeted Margaret courteously as she walked back into the store. "I understand time is of the essence, so let's focus on you. Based on Kathy's brief description, I have prepared the first of the new collection of pantsuits that arrived from London last Friday, and also, the new Italian shoes and evening handbags from Milan. These came two weeks ago. Please open that white door, and you will find what I have selected. Standing here with me is Sarah, our seamstress, and she will make any adjustments you may want in a few minutes."

"Wow! This is wonderful, thank you so much," Margaret said. In the dressing room, three beautiful evening dresses and three pant suits, matching shoes and evening bags were lined up on the counter and on hangers to both sides of the beautiful dressing area.

There was a small platform with three-way mirrors. Ten minutes later. Margaret emerged from the dressing room with her hair up in braids. Her long neck was adorned with a three-inch silk band beautifully decorated in the front with a brocade carved figure of a unicorn. The band was sustaining from her front only, the pastel blue, Sleeveless, bare back flowing pantsuit. She was wearing royal blue, continental style soft leather, four inches high heel shoes. Over her right shoulder, she was carrying a silk, long sleeve jacket. Her attire was complimented by soft silk matching Royal blue color evening bag.

Wendy, Kathy, and Sarah, were looking at her and in unison exclaimed, "You are beautiful!"

"My Lady, you are so tall," Sarah gushed, "let me feel the fit of the pantsuit to your body. She is stunning! Her selection matches perfectly. She doesn't need anything else to make heads turn, wherever she goes!"

"Thank you all for your kindness. I'll take this with me and tomorrow I'll come back and may buy the other pieces you selected. Please set those to the side. Once I know the schedule of activities I'll know what is most appropriate."

"Ms. Gianelli, while you get ready, Sarah will inspect the garments to ensure all is in perfect condition, and she'll bring these to your room within ten minutes,"

Immediately, Kathy handed Wendy Margaret's room key. "Please charge it."

"Ms. Gianelli, please sign here," Wendy told Margaret, handing her a form. "Thank you for accepting my selection, I'm saying this because I personally selected these garments in London and the shoes and handbag at a Milan fashion show."

"Thank You, Wendy," Kathy said politely.

"We'll see you tomorrow."

"Sarah, is Ms. Gianelli's room 1206?"

"We'll see you there in a few minutes." Kathy and Margaret departed and moved swiftly towards 1206. Upon arriving at the room, Kathy said; "Please go ahead get ready, I'll wait for Sarah and stay here to check everything and take you to the "Blue" on time."

"Great, thank you so much. I'll be ready in a flash!"

Twenty minutes later, Margaret came out of the shower while Sarah and Kathy were lining up her new clothing in the dressing room area.

Margaret's hair was shining and arranged on top of her head secured with a simple silver fish-shaped pin. The warm color of her hair and soft white skin made her brown eyes reflect the light wherever she turned. While she was putting on the finishing touches and dressing, Kathy and Sarah, were standing to the side waiting to see Margaret fully dressed in the new garments.

Margaret appeared from the dressing room area. She looked taller than six feet, her long legs, well-shaped arms, and walk completed the fashion model look. Sarah could not contain her emotion. "My Lady! You are so beautiful and look so elegant, that I would love to have a picture with you. Tomorrow, I will show it to my daughter and some of her young friends. It will show what a model looks like in real life, without the illumination of commercial lights. Is that okay?" Margaret nodded happily.

"Kathy, please use my phone and take a picture of Sarah and me," she said. "Tomorrow, when we return to the store, I'll give it to you or have a paper copy made."

"Camera, and Action!" Kathy said as she took the photo. "Now, before we go would you like a glass of mandarin juice to refresh you? We have time to spare."

"No thanks, before my shower, I drank a large bottle of mineral water."

"Good night Ms. Gianelli, enjoy the evening and keep that friendly smile. We Caymanians love to see others happy and smiling!" Sarah said as she left the room.

"Have a lovely evening, Sarah."

"Good, so we can start walking calmly towards the "Blue," Kathy said once Sarah was gone. "On the way there, I'll show you some of the hotel amenities, local paintings, and other culture so you can enjoy the hospitality of our people." While walking Kathy spoke of the British heritage of the Islands. "The unique influences on the culture of the Cayman Islands—have come from North America and Jamaica. There are 113 nationalities on the three islands that compose our country. Lastly, the traditional Caymanian dishes are made from turtle meat."

"Turtle meat?" Exclaimed Margaret. "That reminds me of my first trip to China. At a celebration dinner, I was served little turtle soup. I couldn't muster enough cultural or social savvy to eat those peaceful creatures. I had a pet turtle then! The thought of eating hot turtle soup made me feel I was betraying my best friend."

Kathy could not help but laugh while realizing it was 6:55 and they were in front of the restaurant. "Here you are, on time and ready to enjoy the evening, and make heads turn. Should you need me, you have my card with my mobile number. I'm here at the hotel until ten this evening. Tomorrow, I'll be here at ten in the morning, please call me then and let me know how I may make your stay as pleasant as possible. Good night, Ms. Gianelli."

"Good evening, Kathy and thank you for all your help," Margaret responded warmly.

Chapter 22
BANKING IN THE CAYMAN ISLANDS

Within a few minutes Allison, Nancy, and another lady and gentleman appeared approaching the Blue. "Good evening Margaret," Allison said when she saw Margaret waiting. "This is Karla Springmyer and Arthur Garten, the management team leaders of the bank here in the Cayman,"

Karla Springmyer was forty-nine years old, black skin, five-foot-four, 120 pounds, short black hair, and brown eyes, with a soprano voice, and a robust body. On this evening, Karla, adhered to the dress code etiquette in the Cayman Islands, as it remained a British crown colony. So she was conservative and wore a mid-length, flowing floral short-sleeve dress, white, continental style soft leather shoes with four inches heels, and a white handbag, and was carrying a long sleeve all white linen jacket. She was married and had a seven-year-old boy. Karla had a Bachelor Degree in Accounting and Finance from the University College in the Cayman Islands. She was active in the business association and led a group of entrepreneurial women seeking to start their own business. She was also involved in family oriented water sports.

Arthur Garten, the Operations Manager of the Caribbean Bank, was 52 years old, Creole, five-foot-ten, 150 pounds black shiny hair and deep brown eyes with a modulated voice and a slender build. On this evening, Arthur was wearing a formal all white, high collar, long sleeve, mid-body length shirt, tailored pants, and white shoes. He was married and had a sixteen-year-old son. Arthur had a Master Degree in Business Administration from University College in the Cayman Islands. He was active in the local business owners Association and coached the island soccer team. Margaret turned and said, "Hello, Allison, you look beautiful." Allison's hair was exceptionally shiny. Her green eyes were sparkling and she wearing emerald marquise earrings and dressed in a sleeveless pastel green color flowing pantsuit, dark green continental style soft leather shoes with four inches heels and a matching green color handbag. She was carrying a long sleeve white silk jacket.

In introducing Margaret, Allison showed a friendly smile, and then she said in a warm voice, "Ms. Gianelli is the assistant to the Executive Office and will cover many of the functions in Nancy's absence."

"Thank you, Allison," Margaret said. "May I just clarify a small but significant detail? Nancy is my direct supervisor, and we both report to Mr. Jordan."

Karla responded in a soft tone of voice; "This is good that we know the organization structure. In our case here on the Island, Arthur and I are accountable to Allison on both policy and bank operating procedures."

"Shall we go in while waiting for Mr. Jordan? He will be here at any moment," said Nancy. On this evening Nancy's beautiful olive skin shone; her straight black hair was up with a twist. Her green, cat-like eyes were outlined in black, and her ears were adorned with ruby red earrings. She was wearing white continental style pants, a red belt, and a long sleeve linen jacket, red four-inch heel shoes, and a soft leather red envelope-style bag. Then, she signaled the host, announcing that, "The Kentucky-Caribbean Bank party is here."

Immediately the attentive host greeted everyone and escorted the party to a table located al fresco on the southwest corner, where the open air balcony gave a panoramic view of the white sand beach, palm trees, and the emerald green ocean, regardless of where one was sitting.

At seven fifteen, Larry arrived to find the party having a lively conversation about the beauty of the site. On this evening, Larry was wearing a formal all white, high collar, long sleeve, mid-length shirt, tailored pants, and white shoes. Everyone was talking. The theme was centered on the spectacular view of the setting sun. Everyone was commenting on the changing images of the palm trees—moved by the evening winds that were adorning the hypnotizing view of the Caribbean Sea!

Once Larry was seated Nancy made a formal announcement. "Hello, everyone. Thank you for coming to enjoy a good meal and productive evening." Larry looked at Nancy and asked, what's on the menu?"

"Earlier this afternoon I spoke to Eric, the chef, and he recommended two of his signature seafood dishes, as the evening temperature is ideal. These are, seared red wine cobia, beluga lentils, bock choi with a citrus mustard emulsion; and striped bass, pan seared, calamari, palette pepper jam, with Basquiat sauce. Ah! I almost forgot Eric recommended that we taste the honeycombed, port cherries and pineapple cheese, with a small glass of chilled Moscato."

As she was finishing, Chef Eric appears alongside a server. He introduced himself and welcomed every person by name. Then he signaled the server to place a sample of his famous cheese on each plate. Then, he bowed his head and said as he departed, "Please enjoy it, and let me know how can I make your evening one to remember."

"Thank you so much," responded Nancy as she looked at the delectable treat.

In a friendly voice, Larry said, "May I propose that everyone make their choice of the main course while we are enjoying this cheese along with a bottle of Moscato Rocca Cerrina?"

Everyone complimented Larry for his own choosing. "My purpose in asking my executive team to this dinner tonight is to enjoy a good local meal and to us an opportunity to know each other. After the food, we'll talk about the Board of Directors approval of this acquisition. Also, I want to share my goals and objectives, and how together we will provide our clients the best service, for a fair return on their investments." The apéritif wine was served, and Larry proposed a toast, "I'm offering this evening to celebrate the beginning of good relations between our banks." Larry continued, "To celebrate good personal communications and interpersonal relationships with each other, and our clients. Then he added, I'm offering this evening to celebrate in advance the victory of the Louisville Midtown-Caribbean Bank team at the golf tournament, this coming Saturday. Cheers!"

Dinner was delivered, and the comments began to flow. "This seared cobia is delicious," Larry said with gusto.

Nancy followed with, "this bass, is just right for me, I'm happy!"

"I'm in agreement with Mr. Jordan, and Karla, the cobia is fantastic," added Allison.

"I'm glad Eric brought us the sample of delicious cheese," Margaret said. It made my seared bass taste delicious. But the company is what really makes this an evening to remember."

"May I recommend a local desert that has become famous at this hotel," Allison offered. "This is made of passion fruit with white chocolate, sesame seeds, and raspberry sorbet."

"A dinner like this one cannot miss a local choice of Costa Rican Terrazu coffee," said Karla.

"I'll pass on the coffee and as a Cayman," Arthur said. "I'm going to order a cup of wild Himalayan lavender tea."

"I'll go with Allison's and Karla's recommendations," interjected Larry.

The same here," said Nancy.

"I will take Allison's and Arthur's choices," said Margaret.

Dinner was over. After twenty minutes of real talk about the weather and the beauty of the site, Larry called for the server to remove the dinnerware from the table, and leave the coffee and tea services. Then he announced, "We are going to have a small business and planning meeting, then rest—so tomorrow morning we can play a practice round of golf—to become familiar with the challenges Greg Norman, 'The Shark,' envisioned when he designed this golf course."

"May I take a moment with Margaret? I need to get a folder for our meeting," asked Nancy.

"Yes, by all means," said Larry.

Nancy and Margaret excused themselves and walked away from the table. On the way out of the "Blue," Nancy handed Margaret a room card key and asked, "Would you please go to my room, the number is 703. On the desk, there is a black folder that contains the talking points for this evening. Please bring it to the front desk, ask them to make a copy for each of us, while I set the tone of our first join executive team meeting."

"I'll be back in a flash with the copies! I'm ready to hear the plans for our golf practice, and the schedule events for the rest of the week."

At room 703, when she opened the door, to locate the black folder on the desk, the first thing she noticed was the Dalton and Barnes book bag on top of the nightstand!

Margaret slowly walked towards the nightstand and looked around—as if there may be someone in the room. An overwhelming sense of curiosity made her heart jump in her chest. As she moved towards the bag, she felt like an intruder. The feeling of curiosity was overwhelming. All she wanted to do was to glance at the content and verify if indeed, it was the same package she had brought from Victoria Secret and had placed in Larry's office.

Margaret stopped before looking inside the bag.

All of the sudden someone began knocking on the door. Margaret quickly called; "Who is it?"

"The night service, may I come in?" She heard a female voice say from the other side.

"Please come in." The maid entered.

"Good evening Madam, all I'm to do tonight is to turn over the bed covers and place these chocolates." As she was showing the little box of chocolates, the woman accidentally tilted the book bag from the night stand.

The package was no longer wrapped in the branded Victoria Secret box that Margaret had placed inside the Dalton and Barnes book bag at her house. The content was free and fell to the floor.

Margaret immediately picks up the lingerie. Her emotional reaction was exuberant, and her comment was vivacious in tone and in the gesture of her hands. This was beautiful black lingerie, so soft and silky to the touch, and most provocative and enticing to the eye. Then, holding, looking, and feeling the underwear in her hands, she told the maid calmly; "Don't worry, this happens to me all the time." She placed the garments back in the book bag, and moved to the desk and picked up the black folder. Then, along with the woman she left room 703, with a myriad of questions and her imagination running wild. She remembered Mr. Ellis famous exclamation "I knew it…!"

We are putting a piece of the puzzle together!

Margaret began mulling over the way Larry and Nancy were so familiar. The "Friday" evenings a usual time to presumably review the week's unfinished business. The heated argument between Larry and Nancy and her outburst the night before the government inspectors visit, All of these facts begin to resonate in Margaret's mind.

The time it took her to walk between room 703 and the front desk to the hotel seemed so short that Margaret realized she must put aside her hypothesis formulation and focus on having copies of the talking points made and delivered for the meeting.

"Hello, would you please make me seven copies of this document?" She asked the receptionist. A few minutes passed, and the receptionist said, "Here you are, is there anything else I may do for you?"

"No, thank you. Please charge these to my room." Margaret handed her room card key.

"Oh, no charge! This is a courtesy of the hotel."

Margaret now had difficulty focusing on the meeting. She was struggling to put aside her thoughts about the findings in 703.

In the "Blue" she gently tapped Nancy on her shoulder, "Here is what you need."

"Please, give one to Mr. Jordan and pass them around." She told Margaret.

"Here are the talking points Mr. Jordan wants to discuss with us tonight," said Margaret while distributing a copy to each person.

Larry was reading the agenda in an authoritative tone of voice. "Let us begin!" he said upon finishing the plan. "We are united in the philosophy that a good banking relationship starts with a mutual acceptance of each other, and the understanding of our goals and objectives. We come from two different cultures, the American influenced by the Southern way of life, and the British influence on the Caribbean culture and language. Adopting a standard banking terminology that is mutually acceptable in its meaning and practice are the first order of business."—Larry paused and asked Allison to appoint a person from her management team to formalize the first draft for discussion in thirty days. Then, without much preamble he added,— "Margaret will be handling the project from the American side."

Larry concluded, "Thank you for being here tonight. As you all know, we have a golf tournament on Saturday. Allison, Nancy, Margaret and I are the team representing our new banking presence in the Islands. To place the names of both the Caribbean Bank and its partner the Louisville Midtown Bank on the main scoreboard for the attending public to see, we are donating five thousand American dollars. In return for our investment, and to motivate more businesses to participate in the event, the Chamber of Commerce is earmarking two thousand dollars and the winning trophy with the name of our banks engraved along with the top five business donors for the team with the lowest score."

"What if we are the winning team?" asked Margaret, looking surprised.

"Good question!" Promptly without hesitation, Nancy interjected, "We have not allocated personal profits to the discretionary investment fund. If we are the winning team, this account will be the best source of funds to reward our team with a "Promotional Bonus."

"Tomorrow I will call Keith, and ask him if that will be the best way to manage a potential conflict of interest," added Larry.

"That is a right decision," Karla said agreeably, "as far as the Caribbean side, we never had a situation like the one Nancy is indicating. Therefore, tomorrow before our afternoon meeting, I will verify our local banking regulations and have a response for our position on this issue."

The temperature was 70 degrees, the winds were calming down, the night flood lights from the hotel were shining on the white sand beach and far off these lights are creating dancing shadows of the palm trees. The lights were dimly glowing on the waterfront.

At nine-thirty, and without much ceremony or additional comments, Larry said, "Thank you all for a delightful evening!" As he was walking away from the table he added; "My team, I will meet you tomorrow morning at eight-fifteen at the golf shop. We start at nine o'clock. Good night everyone!"

In unison, "Good night Mr. Jordan!"

Once Larry left the restaurant, Allison said, "Please give me a minute, I have a surprise for our team, I'll be right back!"

Meanwhile, the conversation turned to the Caribbean music being played by the dynamic group at the end of the patio.

Margaret's attention was distracted by her concern with the discovery made in 703.

Karla, noticed her momentary distraction and asked, "Are you a good player?"

"Well, I'm a player that plays to win!" Margaret responded thoughtfully.

"That means you are excellent," Karla laughed.

"Ah, no far from good, golf is the game that one can't conquer; it's played one shot at a time, and one game at a time. I played for my university team for four years, and learned not to let my emotions be carried away before or during the competition!" Her own statement was serving as an awakening to Margaret. At that moment, she realized that she needed to take control of her curiosity about the findings in 703. Otherwise, she would be compromising what she held dear, her golf game, and possibly the investigation of the Louisville Midtown Bank.

Immediately to remove her focus from her idle curiosity, she asked Nancy, "Have you played here before?"

"Yes, in the last three months while conducting negotiations, we stayed at this hotel and had the opportunity to play a few rounds of this golf course," Nancy replied.

"What are the course challenges?" Margaret inquired, back to her usual involved self.

"The trade winds are treacherous. When you're playing and feeling in control, suddenly the wind changes direction and speed, forcing you to rethink each shot as a new strategy for playing the fairway or the green at that moment."

"Your comments are helpful, for when playing any course for the first time, the unknown is a killer," Margaret noted.

At that moment Allison returned with six gift-wrapped packages. She gave one to Nancy, Arthur, Karla, and Margaret.

Then, she handed the last one to Nancy and said, "Please, Nancy, give this to Mr. Jordan."

"Thank you so much, I'll give it to him in the morning at breakfast." Margaret made a mental note of Nancy's response, as no one has mentioned a breakfast meeting.

Then, Karla asked, "May we open the package or should we do it in private?"

"Please, take it with you. Since it's already nearly ten in the evening, and I'm to return tomorrow morning by eight-fifteen, I would like to excuse myself and go home." Allison said.

"I'm with Allison, let's all go back and get some rest," Nancy said, and Margaret noted she seemed a little nervous. "I'll see you and

Margaret in the morning at the golf shop, and in the afternoon at four o'clock, we'll meet with Arthur and Karla in the bank."

"Thank you so much for a splendid time tonight. Good night everyone." As Nancy departed, Margaret said, "Thank you, Karla and Arthur, for a real time. I'm excited to learn the Cayman bank business and to enjoy the local culture and hospitality. We'll have a good time in the process, I'll see you both tomorrow at the bank. Good night." Margaret went to her room and realized it was after ten in the evening, so she decided not to call her parents nor Jonathan until it was morning. In the meantime, she opened the gift. It was a lemon butter color golf shirt with her initials embroidered in purple and silver color thread.

Margaret normally had no problem falling asleep. However, on this night, she was experiencing some difficulty in reconciling her rest. This might be due in part to the mounting excitement of playing again, and in part from the multiple questions emerging from her earlier findings in 703.

Soon it was six-thirty in the morning, her mind and emotions were alert and focused on the new opportunity to play golf once more. She jumped out of bed, opened the blinds and saw the spectacular view of the golf course, and behind that the Caribbean Sea. She opened the window and felt the fresh, crisp morning air, and the gentle wind that was bringing the unmistakable smell of fresh cut grass of this Par 36 nine-hole course. The view from her room was inspiring, the sun was slightly shining, still wet grass and palm tree lined one side of the nine fairway and on the other were water hazards, and white sand bunkers.

The ninth hole was within her view, it called for a dramatic finish over water to a challenging island green. Out loud in an enthused voice she exclaimed, "Wow… I'm going to get ready, have an early breakfast, and go to the practice range to warm up before going to the golf shop."

At eight-thirty, Larry, Allison, Nancy, and Margaret met in the golf shop. After the morning greetings, they focused on the practice game plan. Larry and Nancy had already checked the players in, and the starting time was confirmed as nine o'clock.

"Who would like to keep the score card?" asked Larry. No one responded, so he proposed seven holes on the putting practice green. The lowest score would select the record keeper and the order of play.

"That's a good idea," commented Nancy.

"I'm in agreement," said Allison.

"Let's go do it," Margaret said.

On the putting practice green, Margaret noticed in silence that the speed of the rolling ball on the ground was slow. Then Allison commented, "The morning dew is affecting the ball's speed."

"Don't let that fool you," Nancy said. "In less than an hour, the ball will move faster than anticipated because the heat is increasing."

Larry was making his best effort to maintain impartiality. The contest was over. Margaret, Allison, and Nancy finished even par or seven puts. Larry ended with eleven sets total score.

Allison took the initiative and appointed Nancy as the game score keeper. Larry nodded and agreed. "We'll let Nancy keep score and buy lunch for the team."

At nine o'clock, on the first Blue Tip tee, Nancy announced, "The order of play is, Allison, Margaret, Larry, and me. This is a par four, 340 yards. Allison, you're up to play."

There was total silence, and the focus was on Allison's ball gliding slightly left and returning to the center of the fairway for a safe landing 220 yards away.

Margaret pulled out her driver club and hit a shot gliding slightly left and correcting itself to the center-left parallel to the sand bunker 250 yards away.

Larry played with his driver club and landed next to Margaret, except in the sand bunker.

Last, Nancy a little nervous, played her driver club and fell slightly behind Allison's ball 215 yards away.

In the order of the game, Nancy was next to play. She felt the wind on her face, took a five iron club and hit the ball, which landed on the green twelve inches away from the flag.

Allison played and fell on the front of the green, and so did Larry. Margaret tested the wind direction by lightly tossing a few leaves of grass and pulled a seven iron club and hit a perfect shot falling eight inches from the first hole on the opposite side of Nancy's ball. While playing no one spoke, as everyone focused on their game.

In the order of putting, Larry being the farther away from the hole played first, and his third shot landed 30 inches from the flag. Allison put next, and her ball stopped just eight inches from the hole. Margaret and Nancy sank their own putts, placing them tie for the one under par score on the first hole.

Allison played with a par, and Larry scored two over par.

The spirit of competition was ignited in Margaret's silent behavior.

Nancy walked to the next tee, without a word to anyone.

While walking next to Larry in a light tone of voice Allison said, "From the way, we start to play, we have a right team, what's your opinion?"

"I've played with Nancy many times, however, judging from Margaret's performance, I'm in agreement, we might have a winning team."

Allison nodded. "The next eight holes defined the nickname for this Blue Tip golf course, "The nine-hole Caribbean Monster." It is carved along a natural saltwater lagoon. The five long par fours into the Caribbean trade winds, make a 470-yard hole play like 600 yards."

At the end of the first nine holes, a dramatic finish over the water to the island green made the statement by Allison become a strange reality. Margaret and Nancy were tied, at two over par. Allison was next with five over par, and Larry was last with six over par.

"Let's take a short break, eat some fruit and drink some water," Nancy suggested. "The temperature is rising, and the next nine holes will be played by strong trade winds." For the next nine holes, the order of the game was changing, Margaret was shooting first, and then Nancy, Allison and Larry last. He was not talking and was showing some frustration.

What was bothering Larry?

Shortly after refreshments, Margaret commented, "We are going to play to win this tournament. The course is in perfect condition, other than the trade winds, I see no greater challenge to overcome, the fairways are flat with plenty of water on the sides, and sand bunkers to contend for the first prize, therefore, demands precision in each shot."

"I know we can do it," said Allison.

With a light sarcastic tone Nancy said, "The way Larry is playing today, and his long face, I'm worried about building high expectations."

"Well, let's you and me, put a little money where your words are," proposed Larry.

"Listen, ladies, this is a side bet between Larry and me," Said Nancy. "You, Larry, call the price."

"Okay, then, let's play fifty a hole for the last nine, and at the end, it will be a gift for the lowest score of the 18 holes, and what do you think?" Nancy agreed.

"Then you're on Ms. McArthur!" Larry said coldly.

The balance of this game was atrocious, the sarcasm between Larry and Nancy was almost unending. The pressure was almost uncomfortable, and it indirectly affected Allison and Margaret.

The final hole was the crown for Margaret. It was an island green par three, paying 156 yards from the Blue Tip Tees. She would generally play a seven iron for this distance, however, left to right high winds mandated this club selection be the trademark of a professional golf player. In her mind were images of previous tournament challenges at the university, and she was taking longer than anticipated focusing on the target while observing the palm trees left-to-right moving direction to select her playing club. She picked a four iron club and hit a perfect shot. She was aiming to the left of the flag, and the ball appeared so slow that it seemed stationary. However, upon the ball landing, the ball stopped. Then, the wind pushes it gently to the edge of the hole, Margaret yelled, "Go, go, go in the cup!" There was suspense, and the wind kept pushing the ball very slowly a little closer, a bit closer to the hole. Then, with one last blow of the wind, the ball disappeared from view, for a grand finale, hole-in-one.

After seeing this spectacular finale, Margret yelled, "Praise the Lord!" and hugged Allison and Nancy.

Larry pointed to the sky, which was showing at a distance some upcoming lightning. "Let's pick up and end our practice round now with an image that we can win the tournament."

"I agree, there is nothing we can gain by playing this hole and much we can lose by lightning, let's hurry to the clubhouse," agreed on Allison.

"I agree, with Allison. Let's go now, the rain is pouring!" Nancy added.

"I must walk to the green and retrieve my ball from the cup. Otherwise, I will forfeit the score," Margaret said, a little dejectedly.

With a laugh Larry said, "I already bet with Nancy, to double the fifty on this hole, that you would not go and pick up your ball because it's pouring rain."

"Oh no, Sir! That will never happen, I'm on my way to the green and need to ask Allison to come with me, to witness the extraction of the ball from the cup, so it is an official "Hole-in- One. Because you disclosed your bet, you and Nancy are not required to verify my moving the flag and taking the ball out."

Soaking wet, the foursome were briskly walking towards the clubhouse and talking enthusiastically about the unique experience of playing this practice round. Margaret was feeling the sense of achievement she used to feel playing at the University. Larry's face had changed from a distressed look too friendly and happy. Nancy was a little reserved, she might have been a bit jealous of Margaret's play, or concerned about Larry's behavior during the entire game.

However, Nancy kept talking about the flight path of Margaret's ball. "It moved slowly as if suspended in the air. Straight into the wind and almost floating in the air," she gestured, the memory still vivid in her mind. "Then it stopped on the green, move a little, stop a little, a bit more….and then disappear from sight into the cup!"

As the foursome approached the bridge to the island, Larry said, "You two go ahead, and pick up that ball, while Nancy and I wait here."

"Okay, Mr. Jordan," Margaret said.

With a happy tone of voice, Allison said, "Margaret, you are a good player, and you know what to do in cases like this, I never had this experience, I never had a hole-in-one."

"Here we are. Please, Allison, hold the flag. Here is my ball…!"

"Congratulations, well played, I was amazed when I saw you selecting a four iron club to play. At the most, I would have played with a five iron. Now I know you experienced this before."

"Yes, this is my fourth hole-in-one. However, it feels like my first!"

As they were walking away from the green, Margaret extended her right arm upward and shows the ball to Larry and Nancy, and yelled, "It is official."

As the foursome was arriving at the clubhouse, Allison suggested, "We are all soaking wet, I have my dry clothes here in the locker room. May I recommend that you people go to your rooms and change, then we can have lunch here, and then go to the bank for our four o'clock meeting?"

"Great idea, we will see you at the restaurant in forty-five minutes," said Nancy as she was giving her golf equipment to the locker room keeper. At the same time, Margaret and Larry were placing their equipment in line to be cleaned and stored for the next game.

"I will see you in forty-five minutes," said Margaret as she promptly departed for her room.

Larry was waiting for Nancy to sign the receipt equipment key, then the two of them disappeared into the main hotel building.

Upon arriving at her room, Margaret called her mother "Hi mom, how are you feeling today?"

"I'm well honey, how's your trip going?"

"Excellent, I just finished playing a practice game, under a pouring rain and wild winds. I scored a hole-in-one!" Margaret said excitedly.

"Congratulations honey, you sound a bit in a hurry, are you?"

"Yes, mom, I'm just calling before taking a shower, showing up for lunch in forty minutes, and a meeting at the local bank, I'll call tonight for more details. I love you, mom."

"I love you too."

As Margaret was putting down the phone on top of the dressing table, she noticed a note from Kathy, "Hello, Ms. Gianelli, earlier this morning, while you were playing, I saw the ending time of your game and the incoming weather. This tight schedule will not afford us enough time to go shopping for clothes. In anticipation of your clothing needs for your activities of this afternoon, I had your white and yellow outfit, clean and pressed. Also, on a trial basis, I took the initiative to bring you one of the three outfits you had chosen last night, both are hanging in the closet. At your convenience, please call me and let me know how I might be of service, I'm in the hotel until ten this evening. Kathy."

Margaret looked at the time, and by now she only had twenty minutes left before lunch. In a few moments, she was ready to get dressed, and she opened the closet in the dressing area.

"Wow!" she exclaimed.

There she found hanging the outfit she selected the night before, consisting of new white cotton tailored pants, a four-inch wide green belt, cotton, light green and yellow flowered blouse with mid-length sleeves, a pair of dark-green leather striped open flat shoes, and a matching flowered carrying bag.

"This is perfect! I'll wear this new one."

She was briskly walking away from room 1206, feeling victorious and looking forward to what was ahead for lunch, and the upcoming meeting with Arthur and Karla in the Caribbean Bank. As she turned the corner in the lobby towards the restaurant near the clubhouse, she noticed Larry and Nancy coming from the opposite end. She stopped and waited for them.

At the same time, Allison approached from behind Margaret and said, "Well, this is right timing, we're all here. Given our schedules for today, I took the liberty to select a light lunch and it will be served in ten minutes."

"That's a good, let's go to our table," said Larry.

I'll be with you for a couple of minutes, I need to go to the front desk, to take care of some business," announced Nancy.

"Okay, I'm hungry and excited about going to the bank and seeing how it looks, and how I'll fit to bring about my first assignment in the islands."

Lunch was served, and at the same time, Nancy approached the table. While standing she said, "Here Mr. Jordan, please do the honors," and handed Larry an envelope.

With a thumbs up gesture, Larry delivered his signature statement before meals; "Let's eat before we plan our meeting for this afternoon."

Soon the light lunch of fresh green salad, various cheeses, fruits, and passion tea was over. "Today, our talking points are open to responding to Arthur and Karla's questions and discuss any matter Allison might have that needs clarification," Nancy said.

"Well, Margaret, my only point before we go to meet the people at the bank," Larry said, "is that according to the score, you are the winner of bets between Nancy and me. For the last nine holes, we bet fifty a hole, plus an additional fifty for picking the ball out of the hole in the pouring rain. On all counts, you have the lowest score, and you retrieved the ball from the cup. Therefore, Nancy won these bets, and as agreed, you are the winner. Here're five hundred dollars."

"Oh, my goodness! I'm overwhelmed, I thought you were betting fifty cents a hole, not fifty dollars! Thank you, so much." At three-fifteen, Allison said, "Our playing time over, and we should be going, no need to worry about the bill, it is courtesy of the Caribbean Bank. Should we go now, so we can negotiate the rain, and be on time? Milton, our driver, is already at the front waiting for us."

Indeed, for the next thirty minutes, the rain was slowing the traffic a bit. "Observing the local people, especially women, they walk with a unique gait, like a dancing rhythm, going about their business, and acting as if rain is nothing out of the ordinary," said Margaret.

"Ah… yes. "This is typical of the locals, they move with the Caribbean rhythm," responded Allison.

"The way men walk here is exciting to me," Nancy said suddenly.

"That's interesting, I've not noticed this pattern, however, now that you ladies are mentioning it make sense," commented Larry.

A few minutes before arriving at the bank, the rain was subsiding, and Milton, the driver, announced, "We are at the bank on time."

"Thank you, I will call you when ready to leave," said Allison.

Chapter 23
CARIBBEAN BANK MEETING

A security guard opened the door for the arriving party and announced its presence to the public relations officer, a young man in a business suit. "Welcome everyone, my name is Joshua," he introduced himself. "I'll let Mr. Garten and Ms. Springmyer know you are here."

In an admiring tone of voice, Margaret said, "Wow! This building has a beautiful simplicity in its form and design; its modern architecture, and a high technology environment."

At that moment Arthur and Karla arrived. They courteously greeted the party, and without delay invited them to the conference room for the 4:00 p.m. tea and the scheduled meeting.

During the tea service, Allison said casually, "Since Margaret is going to be working closely with Karla for the next thirty days, it's important for her to know some of the facts, and benefits a partnership between our banks will offer to our new clients."

While opening her notebook, Margaret responded; "That is most appreciated."

"These are a few examples," Allison continued, "the Cayman Islands has the highest income per capita in the Caribbean Region, and ranks 14 in the world, in Gross Domestic Product per capita. Also, the Cayman Islands have no corporate tax, no capital gains tax, no sales tax, and no payroll tax. These facts have partially allowed the Cayman to become the sixth largest financial center and the epicenter of hedge funds worldwide. As a result of these unique benefits, eighty percent of the world's top banks have branches in the Islands, including now the Louisville Midtown Bank."

"That is, in a nutshell, is why we are here," Larry commented.

"May I ask a question?" asked Margaret. Allison nodded. "Why are the Cayman Islands, and no other Caribbean nations enjoy these tax benefits?"

"As a native, from lessons in history, this is what I learned," said Karla. "On February 8, 1794, the people of the Cayman Islands rescued the crews of a group of ten merchant ships. The ships had struck a reef and run aground during rough seas."

Arthur interjected, "Legend has it that King George III of Great Britain rewarded the Caymanians with a promise never to introduce taxes as compensation for their generosity, as one of the ships carried a member of the King's own family. Whether this legend is true or not, the Cayman Islands have a rich history of relying on indirect taxes, making it one of the best places in the world to do business."

"Those are compelling reasons to continue developing our client's portfolio of investments," concluded Nancy.

"Speaking of investments," said Allison, "this morning, the realtor called to let me know that the closing documents in the new house will be ready for final acceptance and signature tomorrow at four o'clock and that the seller will also be here in my office. With this matter out of the way, may we start on the agenda for this meeting?" She looked around and then went on. "The first item is the Caribbean Bank response to the potential for conflict of interest, in the event, we win the golf tournament. Karla checked with our regulatory authority and the bank's bylaws. There is a dark line of interpretation that could render unacceptable the receipt of compensation by the executives or staff of this bank for non-banking related activities. Thus prize money is subject to erroneous interpretation. Therefore, the Caribbean Bank position is to exclude itself from accepting any money in the event of the join team winning the tournament".

"If we win this match," said Larry. "That is the position of the Louisville Midtown Bank. Last night, I called Keith and asked for his advice on the same issue. He also advises that since we are the investors in the publicity with our names on the scoreboard, winning and paying the team any money from the same proceeds could be open to criticism by the local people, and instead of attracting new business, we could create the wrong impression and drive it away. Further, he could not consult with Roy, because he is now undergoing post-cardiac rehabilitation, and will be out of the office for the next eight to ten weeks. This is the major issue that has occupied my mind since speaking with Keith."

In a sympathetic tone, Nancy said, "Now I understand your preoccupation, and it justifies your game score."

The score, the winning, and the money distribution issues ended with Nancy's commentary. The time remaining was used in discussing and formalizing a memorandum of instructions to the legal department on how to transmit the Board of Directors approval of the partnership between the two banks. They also used the time to instruct the chief legal counsel, to prepare the mandatory regulatory disclosures for the public announcement of the new business relationship.

"This relationship of activity and our local asset acquisitions will serve well to promote new investments in the Islands," said Nancy.

"How can we at the local level, be of assistance to bring about your concept?" asked Arthur.

"You see," Nancy said, "for example, we are purchasing this exclusive beach home. It's one of only a handful of houses located along the Seven Mile Beach which, as we all know, is one of the most beautiful stretches of white sand in the Caribbean, and which enjoys spectacular sunset views across the clear waters of the Caribbean. The house will be professionally refurbished upgraded to high technology, and well decorated and furnished. It will be staffed with a resident housekeeper, an on-call driver, and a grounds keeper. The property is classified in our investor chart of accounts as an income producing asset. Therefore, it may be used to show pre-qualified investor, the type of property acquisitions they might contemplate adding to their individual portfolios."

"How would the legal ownership be defined, in the event several investors are interested in participating in the same asset purchase when it is not listed as a commercial property?" Karla asked, intrigued.

"Well, that is a real question," said Larry. "Let me illustrate the answer with a real example, Nancy has some investors who have placed large sums of money in her 'Agent' discretionary investment fund. She uses this pool of money to purchase private assets, such as the new house we are closing the deal on tomorrow. Immediately, after the acquisition and ownership title are cleared, she'll coordinate and manage the hire of architects, IT workers, and interior designers, with their single assignment being to bring the property to the right level of exclusivity. Regarding luxury and cash value that includes furnishings, works of art, and other technologies which, upon completion of the project and sale of the property, in some cases, will bring the participating investors profits substantially above average."

"What happens with these benefits?" asked Margaret.

In a matter-of-fact tone of voice, Nancy said, "Upon closing each project, I report the results to my clients and give them the option to take out some, or all their share of profits in direct relationship to the amount of money invested by each person in the discretionary fund. In some cases, an investor elects to roll over the new profits to their account, for new investments, and in some other situations, they move the profits to another investment vehicle of their choosing."

"Thank you, Nancy, for this useful example," said Margaret.

"I need to check with our legal people," Allison said slowly. "To find if we are allowed by regulation to promote your concept here in the Islands since we are not per se licensed real estate agents. I will add this item to our agenda for tomorrow's meeting after closing the deal on the house purchase. We thank you for the valuable time of our discussions today." Allison picked up the telephone and called Joshua. "This is Ms. Harrington, please call Milton, let him know we are finished with our meeting and will be ready to return to the hotel as soon as he arrives."

With a friendly voice, Larry said, "Thank you all for your input. This was a good and productive meeting. Allison, are you returning with us to the hotel?"

"No, I'm not able to go with you today, because at six this evening the Chamber of Commerce is having a board meeting. Based on current discussions and mutual agreements in this session, I will announce to the chamber, that if we are the winners of the tournament, we are donating the two thousand dollars award to the committee's operating fund. However, if we are fortunate enough to win then, we'll keep the trophy as a reminder of our participation and support of the Chamber business promotion effort."

There was a knock on the door, and Joshua entered the room. "Good afternoon, Ms. Harrington, Milton is here and at your service when needed," he announced.

"May we excused?" Arthur asked. "Karla and I need to finish some other bank business before going home for the day."

"Yes, please go ahead, the team needs to discuss the next practice round, and determine the strategy of play for Saturday," Allison said.

This part of the statement, "The strategy of the game," was a reminder to Margaret on the order of business for the rest of the afternoon and possible the early evening. Meanwhile, she was thinking of the main reason of her duties; to facilitate the prosecution of the Louisville Midtown Bank. Furthermore, at the same time Margaret was evaluating the words she heard; Nancy saying at the Blue the night before "… we have not allocated personal profits." Also, Larry's example… "Nancy has some investors who have placed large sums of money in her "Agent" discretionary investment fund." Margaret's mind, ears and communication skills were focusing on discovering more information about the operational details of Nancy's discretionary fund while planning the golf practice for the next day, and tournament play on Saturday.

"Hey, Margret are you dreaming again?" Nancy asked, interrupting Margaret's thoughts.

Margaret's reaction was calm. "I'm just thinking about how I believe we will win this tournament, and make a name for our banks."

"That is what I want to hear," said Larry. "Tomorrow we'll practice at the same starting time. My proposal is to play the round as a dry run to win the tournament."

"Does anyone know the game's format?" asked Margaret.

"It's a modified Team Stroke Play," Allison replied. "The Chamber has signed fifteen teams to play, and to give each team a good chance to win, we'll be playing the net score. It involves counting the total number of strokes taken on each hole by the foursome, divided by four, the result being the score for the team for that particular hole. The winner of the game is the team who has taken the fewest number of strokes over the eighteen holes."

Larry nodded, "Good, now we'll have a better idea on how to develop a winning strategy. For our practice game, Nancy will keep the score, Allison will dictate the order of play regardless of the score, and Margaret will analyze and propose the rule of the game. And I, at the end of the practice, will be the one suggesting the strategy for winning Saturday's tournament."

"That sounds good to me," Allison said with a nod.

"I'm in agreement, I like my assignment," Margaret agreed.

Nancy leaned towards Larry and told him; "I'll keep the score and propose to be the one who will break the tie, in the event of disagreement on the strategy of play for the tournament."

"You are on Ms. McArthur!" Larry exclaimed. Then he turned to Allison and said more softly; "Thank you, Allison, for the tea, and a good meeting. We'll see you at eight-fifteen tomorrow morning."

The business meeting was over, and Larry, Nancy, and Margaret were on the way back to the hotel. Margaret still could not stop thinking about her government assignment. To distract herself a bit, she began talking. "It was interesting to me to learn how Nancy operates from Louisville, and from there finds investment opportunities in other countries. When do you present the new investment prospects to the clients that are participating in your discretionary fund?"

"That is an excellent question," Nancy began. "I maintain close communications with our banking partners located in the countries where local regulations on investment banking offer unique benefits. For example, here in the Cayman, there are no taxes; in Honk Kong, and Singapore there are no taxes on dividends either."

"I'm most pleased with the attention you are giving to the main reason for our business here in the Islands, and how well you are articulating your question," Larry said approvingly.

"Thank you, Mr. Jordan. What are the plans for this evening?"

"I'd like you to call Roy's wife and find out how Roy is doing, and what the bank might do to help to facilitate his quick recovery. I'll call Keith, and get his personal opinion on Roy's condition and state of mind. And Nancy, please call his rehab facility and talk to the nurse on duty, to get an additional perspective. Then, let's meet at seven this evening at Andiamo, the Italian restaurant by the pool, to have a casual dinner, and discuss our findings on Roy's health condition."

By now, Milton was approaching the hotel entrance. He drove up to them and rolled down his window and, asked: "Would there be any need for me to remain here, or should I return to the bank?"

"Thank you, Milton, you may get back to the bank, we'll see you tomorrow," Nancy said.

"Thank you, everyone, have a good evening."

Without much delay, and given the time constraints to make the assigned calls, and get ready for dinner, Larry, Nancy and Margaret exited the van and rushed in the direction of their respective rooms.

Upon arrival to her room, Margaret noticed a red blinking light on the nightstand telephone. She followed the instruction to retrieve a voice mail message and found it was a call from Jonathan. "My sweetheart, I called your cell, but no circuits were available. This message is to let you know that I'm leaving this evening at 6:00 p.m. to New York, to assist on a case my boss is handling there. If convenient, please call me after nine this evening. I love you!"

Lamenting for a moment with a sigh, Margaret felt relieved and proceeded to call Roy's wife. The phone rang thrice, then a voice said; "Hello?"

"Bertha, this is Margaret Gianelli how are you and Roy doing?"

In reply, Bertha promptly began to cry. "He's in rehabilitation," she sobbed. Roy had it all planned out for this winter to be the beginning of our permanent retirement on the Cayman Islands."

"Is it there anything you need that I can communicate to Mr. Jordan?" Margaret asked.

"Where is he?" Bertha asked, no longer crying.

"He is not available at the moment, but I will be seeing him soon and will be pleased to give him any message," responded Margaret.

"Please tell him that last night, his wife, Barbara, his son Ralph, and daughter Megan came to visit Roy at the rehabilitation facility. Also, let him know that the people from the bank have shown real concern. Keith and Jennifer also visited Roy. He had so many visitors that the hospital asked not to have more than three people in the room at once."

"That's good to hear. Thank you, Bertha, for the update on Roy's progress," Margaret said kindly. "I'll give Mr. Jordan your message and let him know how much we, the people of the bank care for your family."

The assignment on Roy's condition was successful, so she had time to call her mother. The telephone rang and rang until Janet's voice mail answered.

"Mom, this is me," Margaret spoke to the machine. "I'm calling to tell you guys I love you all, and that I'm okay and super busy. Tomorrow morning between seven and eight, I'll call you again." Thankful for the extra time to get ready for dinner, Margaret's thoughts were focusing on Bertha's responses to Roy's condition, especially on her continuing comment on the Cayman Islands home acquisition. She was moving swiftly to get ready for dinner at Andiamo.

JORGE RIVERA

Chapter 24
THINKING CELEBRATION

At seven o'clock Larry, Nancy, and Margaret arrived at Andiamo. "Hello again," said Larry. "Let's find a table on the terrace, away from the noise and with a view of the golf course and the waterways."

Nancy pointed at an empty table past Larry. "Look, there at the far end to your left, is a table, and no other people are sitting close."

Thinking quickly Margaret said; "I'll go ahead and get that table before anyone takes it."

Larry signaled Nancy with a slightly left to right eye movement and said, "That is a good move Margaret, you go, and we'll follow in a few moments."

As Margaret was ready to sit down, she noticed Larry and Nancy standing and facing each other by the bar, as if they were discussing placing an order for drinks. To avoid the obvious observation, Margaret turned around towards the waterways and remained to stand, looking at the beautiful sight of the golf course.

"Are you dreaming again?" said Nancy.

"Ah yes, I'm imagining winning this tournament, so I can tell my boyfriend I'm still a good player."

"That is good news, let's order our dinner and then we can talk about Roy's condition," said Larry as they all sat down.

183

At that moment, the waiter arrived. "Welcome to Andiamo," he said with a friendly smile. "Tonight the temperature is 79 degrees, perfect weather for a bottle of cold white sparkling wine, and a basket of hot oven parmesan and Mediterranean herbs bruschetta to share while deciding what to order for dinner."

"That sounds good, please bring us a bottle of Verdicchio, and a basket of bruschetta," Larry ordered. "By the time you return, we'll be ready to place the dinner order."

"Wait, wait, hang on a moment," said Nancy. "Tonight, I suggest that we "Think Celebration—think Champagne!" Please bring first a bottle of Pol Roger Sir Winston Churchill, and the wine along with the dinner."

With both thumbs up Larry said, "That one is an exquisite British champagne."

"Wow! Nancy, this is exciting," Margaret said with a sparkling smile. "From the first, champagne has been the choice for celebrations of all kinds. Royal, diplomatic, political, national, fashionable, or sporting— like celebrating the planning on making a name for our banks by winning a golf tournament on Saturday—whatever the occasion, it has to be champagne!"

After a few minutes, the server returned and presented the bottle of champagne to Nancy. She inspected the front and back of the bottle and indicated him to offer the bottle to Larry. The server gave the bottle to Larry. Larry lowered his head to signal the waiter his approval to open the bottle.

"This prestigious Cuvee was introduced in 1984 by Pol Roger in honor of his most prestigious and loyal customer, Sir Wilson Churchill," the waiter said in a distinctly British accent. "From the time he ordered the first case of 1895 vintage in 1944 until his death in 1965, he insisted on drinking what you are about to experience..." There was a discreet popping noise as the bottle was opened, then a crackling, fizzing sound as the wine was poured and the effervescent whoosh into the glass—a sound like the stirring of leaves in the breeze or the rustling of silk

taffeta lace. The bubbles burst, hissed, chattered, babbled, whispered…
, and then faded. Then another waiter brought a basket of bruschetta,
and presented it to Nancy, "My goodness! It looks so artistic in the
basket that I just want to look at the bread. I'm sensing the delicate
smells of basil, oregano, rosemary and thyme, those are so subtle that
one intends to taste this bruschetta right away!"

"Um-huh! I love the taste and texture of this Parmigiano Reggiano
cheese, my favorite," exclaimed Margaret.

"Cheers!" said Larry, lifting his glass. Then, he suggested that Nancy
starts off their dinner order.

"For him and me, the fettuccini in white wine with clams and grilled
vegetables. What about you Margaret?"

"I would like a vegetable pizza and Cesar salad."

"Thank you, I'll bring dinner in fifteen minutes."

In a bright tone of voice, Nancy asked, "Apart from being dreaming
about playing golf for real money, what are your impressions of this
trip?"

Margaret was looking upward as if seeking the answer from above.
"Well, first my arrival was a shock," she began cautiously. "The
temperature change from the plane to the ground was as like I'd jumped
into a furnace, but the gifts were extraordinary, and I'll put them to
good use, now and in the future. I say in the future because I'm
anticipating my return to fine tune the banking terminology assignment
before I'm to present it for approval and adoption. Also, I'm learning
about the bank's decision to operate here in the Cayman, because of
the many tax benefits to your investors. Of course, I have a lot more
to learn. I'm delighted to be a member of the golf team and have
unexpectedly earned $500. However, I'm most happy to be your
assistant and to be given a chance to succeed."

"We are succeeding, the champagne and wine are good, and the
bruschetta is appealing to the eye; smells fresh with its delicious herbs
and is so tasty. Dinner is here. Let's relax, eat, and then we can have our
business meeting regarding Roy's situation," proposed Larry.

There was little conversation during dinner, mostly between Larry and Nancy, talking playfully about the texture and taste of the pasta and clams. Meanwhile, Margaret was eating in silence, revisiting her earlier observation of Nancy's familiarity with Larry, and her lead in ordering his food. This thought was a remainder of her government responsibility and the need to focus her attention on the clues to advance her primary mission; facilitating the prosecution of the Louisville Midtown Bank.

The waiter returned, and asked "Would you be interested in some desert? We have gelato, fresh fruit, tiramisu, and, of course, Cuban coffee espresso!"

"I'd like tiramisu and espresso, with a wedge of lime," Larry said.

"Me too," added Nancy. "What about you Margaret?"

"I'd like a coconut and cream gelato, and also an espresso."

Dinner was over, and without much ceremony, Larry said, "I spoke to Keith, regarding Roy's condition. His heart is not stable, he is not out of the woods.

"Roy is not feeling his leg sounds complicated. Also, I spoke to the supervising nurse at the hospital, and by her indication, Roy's condition is stable, but she was not able to give me more details, because of the patient privacy laws," Nancy offered.

"Well, I called Bertha," Margaret said, "and she basically told me the same thing as Mr. Jones said to you and she kept crying over and over that Mr. Lubec had it all planned for their retirement to the Cayman Islands. She emphasized paying over a million dollars for the three bedroom beach home, but she doesn't think they'll be enjoying it unless Mr. Lubec recovers. Also, she asked me to let you know how appreciative she is that your wife and children visited Mr. Lubec. Many people from the bank continue to show real sympathy and are visiting, to the point that the hospital has asked that only three people be in the room at the same time."

"That's my wife! Caring and on top of social matters. I'm happy she was representing us and continues teaching the children how to express sympathy in action," exclaimed Larry with a calm expression and his usual thumbs up.

While he was speaking, Margaret discreetly maintained an observing eye on Nancy's reactions. Sure enough, upon hearing Larry's praise of his wife, Nancy shot him a look of annoyance. "I'm sure Barbara is maintaining her politically right skill of handling people, that makes Ralph like her so much," she said sweetly.

"Ah no, Ralph is like me and enjoys hunting. However, I don't get to see him much because he is committed to his music and studies."

Feeling the mounting tension between Nancy and Larry, Margaret asked in an inquisitive tone of voice, "Is he a composer, or a musician?"

"He is both and is working on releasing his first album, sometime this year." Responded Larry.

"That's good, my mom is a new author and composer, she is presently working on a new project, that'll be done sometime soon—although even she doesn't know—when that is!"

After that funny remark, Nancy's attitude was calm. "Now that we know Roy is not going to be in a condition to return to the office anytime soon, we need a plan. We need to figure out how we'll function while he is out of commission, as well as how to manage the on-going financials in anticipation of another surprise visit from the government inspectors."

"On Monday, I'm going to present the situation to Keith, and ask him to temporarily step into Roy's position until he recovers, or we find a solution. In the meantime, I'd like Margaret to consider befriending Tamara, Roy's assistant. She's an accountant and has worked with him for five years. We must plan immediately how to maintain the weekly trades in shape with our investment plans to proactively stop any transaction that may bring us a problem that only Roy can resolve."

"Anticipating solving a problem is a good thing, however, what is your recommendation and rationale for me to out of the blue befriend Tamara?" Margaret asked. "I have only seen her on my way to the money room and just exchange a simple greeting."

"I think that you should open the conversation with "I have been out of the office, and found out Mr. Lubec is in the hospital for the next ten weeks. Who is going to do his work while he recovers?" suggested Nancy.

"I don't think that will settle well with Tamara, she would ask who you to ask are." Larry disagreed. "I would suggest that we explore another option. Margaret on Monday morning goes to Tamara with the news that you are Nancy's assistant. And because Nancy is out of the office, say you need to find out her availability to schedule a meeting with me late in the afternoon to discuss Roy's condition and on-going work plans."

"Mr. Lubec's condition and immediate work plan feel more natural to me, and I think it will be well received by Tamara. Because her first thought under the circumstances would be, I'm up for a promotion?" Margaret said.

"Good, it is settled, I will plan to have lunch with Keith and Nancy while you prepare the terrain with Tamara. Let's schedule a brief at my office at two in the afternoon, and based on the results, I'll meet Tamara at four-fifteen in the conference room."

"Okay, I'll take care of these matters."

"That plan also sounds good to me. It's nine-thirty, and we have a starting time tomorrow morning at nine, we should get to bed soon and rest," Nancy stated in a bright tone of voice.

"Thank you for dinner and my new assignment, I will see you both at eight- fifteen by the golf shop. Nancy, and Mr. Jordan, good-night."

On the way to her room for the night, Margaret's phone rang, and Margaret responded to find it was Jonathan. "Hey, I'm glad you're calling, we just finished a dinner meeting, and I was on my way to call you. How are you doing in New York?"

"My tropical golfer, I'm doing fine, and I'm just busy helping my boss with the case scheduled to start at nine in the morning. So because I need to be sharp and ready for action, I'm calling you now instead of waiting for your call."

"That makes two of us, I have a final practice starting at nine also, and I'm on the way to my room to get a good night's sleep. However, before saying good night, I have some huge news! Do you have the time or should I hold until I see you on Sunday?"

"Ah no, I'm ready to listen now!"

"Today, I scored a hole in one!"

"Congratulations, sweetheart, that is now your fourth hole-in-one!" Jonathan exclaimed.

"That is not the huge news, the huge news is that I got $500 from a side bet between Nancy and Mr. Jordan!"

"As your dad says, you are a golfing queen. I'll be waiting to see you and talk in detail on Sunday. Please let me know your arriving schedule, for now, good night my sweet Margaret."

"Goodnight." Said Margaret, while feeling a little suspicious of Jonathan hurried attitude.

Before going to sleep, she called her mother. "Hey, mom how are you? How are Dad, Bobby, and Rome doing? I'm sorry to call this late, there is so much going on, I'm super busy with bank meetings, practicing for the tournament, and there is little time to spare. However, I have huge news!"

"What is going on?" her mother asked anxiously.

'Well, today I got a hole-in-one, and won $500 on a side bet between Nancy and Mr. Jordan."

"Honey that is wonderful let me tell your dad, he's sitting next to me, better yet, you tell him." The phone crackled as it was passed along.

"Your mom is all excited," Margaret heard her father's gruff voice say. "What's new?"

"Dad, I scored an ace during our team practice for the Golf Challenge on Saturday."

"My Golfing Queen, congratulations! Your mom wants the phone again, wait, hold on, Janet wait for a moment . . . We'll talk more when you get home."

Janet pulled the phone from Harry's hand and said, "Honey, how are you managing the wardrobe? I'm worried."

"Mom, there is nothing to worry about you'll be pleasantly surprised. How's Bobby?' "He is asleep, and so is the dog," Janet responded ruefully.

"Good, mom, it is unlikely that I will be calling you in the next couple of days because the schedule of meetings and events is super busy. Therefore, please don't be concerned and relax a little."

"Thanks for letting us know honey."

"Goodnight mom and dad, I love you guys!"

"We love you too!" From Janet's end, there was a clicking sound as Margaret hung up.

Chapter 25
GAMBLING

At six-thirty in the morning, Margaret was awakened by her phone. She stretched and said, 'Thank you, Lord, for this new day. Bless me in all I'm about to do.'

She opened the window. The sun was bright, the sky clear and the temperature already 67 degrees. It was the perfect setting for an early morning prayer while admiring the beauty of the emerald the Caribbean Sea! It was an ideal time for a warm up walk on the white sand beach while preparing her mind to play the final practice before the Golf Challenge on Saturday. Upon leaving the hotel, she noticed two young women going in the same direction towards the beach.

"Hello, I'm Margaret, are you going for a walk on the beach? May I join you and we can walk together?"

"Sure. I'm Jill, and this is Ruth. We're here for a golf tournament next Saturday."

"Ah, that's wonderful, this is my first visit to the Cayman Islands and my first walk on this beach. I'm glad to meet you both."

"We're glad as well. We arrived last night, and couldn't wait to enjoy the beauty of this place," said Jill in a friendly voice,

Ruth nodded. "I read a tour book about Seven Mile Beach, and its beautiful white sand and the blue and green colors of the ocean. But

191

actually, its beauty can't be expressed in words or writing. It's divine."

Purposefully Margaret avoided any golf talk. Instead, she told about her arrival experience and the temperature shock from the plane to the airport building. All started laughing and sharing similar stories. Suddenly Margaret turned around "My goodness, we're far from the hotel. What time is it?"

"It is seven-twenty," said Jill.

"If you don't mind I must return right away, I have work to do, and little time to get ready. Thank you so much for walking with me. Until next time," said Margaret as she returned running to the hotel.

Back at the hotel, Margaret ordered a light, fresh tropical fruit plate and lavender tea for breakfast. She got ready and was on time at the golf shop. A few minutes later Allison arrived, then Nancy and Larry.

In a jovial voice, Larry said, "Good morning everyone, I hope we are all well rested and ready for this last practice game. Last practice, because this afternoon at four we have the meeting with the seller of the house and tomorrow we have new business meetings. Besides, we need to conclude all activities by nine in the evening to rest and be ready to win the Golf Challenge. Are you ladies ready?"

With a happy voice, Nancy said: "I'm feeling glad to know we have an excellent team."

"We're on time to start at nine sharp from the back tees," Allison said, "the same tees we'll play from on Saturday. The tournament committee determined that there will not be a distinction between men and women tees, the tournament will be played from the back tees, so to level the playing field because of the scoring method. As agreed, today I'm the scoring person. The order of play for the entire practice regardless of the individual score is Larry first, then Nancy, Margaret, and me."

"What's the expected temperature and rainfall for the next four hours?" asked Margaret.

"Let me check with the starting desk." Larry went inside for a moment and then reemerged. "The temperature is supposed to go up to 88 degrees with no rain."

At nine, the team was ready, and Larry drove off with a solid hit to the right of the sand bunker 250 yards away.

Nancy followed with a 220 yards shot that fell in perfect position for a second shot.

Then Margaret drove off with a perfect center roll, the ball stopping 260 yards away.

Finally, Allison drove off with a hit 195 yards right in the middle of the fairway. There was no conversation during play, each player focused on the next shot and left all other concerns aside.

The rest of the first nine holes were reasonably balanced, and the game was played with equivalent scoring. Driving distances were steady for the team. The second and third shots, and on the green putting was competitive, bringing the team a sense of possible victory. However, at the last tee before Margaret's turn to play, all of the sudden said, "Please forgive me, I need a minute to the side. I'm a feeling a little weak, and can't concentrate on my shot."

"Oh dear, are you sick? Asked Allison.

"No, no, no, I'm having a cramp in my right leg and need to move my toes." Margaret sat, removed her shoes and stood straight with her arms extended skyward and remains like a statue, just flexing body upward on her toes. Nancy was totally oblivious to what was happening because she was having an argument with Larry, one that was being expressed mostly in body language.

"Are you okay Margaret?" asked Larry.

"Thank you, sir, I'll be ready in a minute or two. From time to time, this happens to me because I haven't been drinking enough water and today it's hot and humid." Margaret walked around the starting tee ground, picking up blades of grass, throwing them up in the air, and looking at the distance to the white flag on the green. She put her shoes back on and in an apologetic tone of voice, "I'm ready, let's play!"

The winds were getting stronger by the minute. Nonetheless, Allison made the best shot of the game and fell a few inches away from the flag. She screamed "Wow! Wow, I almost got a hole-in-one. By this time, Larry was raising his voice to Nancy and at the same time with a visual effort from Margaret's perspective, he was trying to maintain appropriate behavior. The first half of the game ended and the foursome walked to the clubhouse for fresh juice and fruit before playing the last nine holes.

After a few minutes of resting and refreshment, and the last nine holes began. From the moment Nancy and Larry drove off the tee, the rest of the game promised to be a disaster for everyone.

Allison whispered to Margaret, "Let's you and I play the game and ignore those two. Otherwise, we are going to ruin our lovely day!"

With a sound of confidence in her voice, Margaret said, "I'm okay with that and the more, the better."

"What do you mean?" asked Allison.

"You see, there is a big difference between a good round of golf with friends and associates and gambling. When betting at their level of stakes, it takes the essence of the game away, the whole thing turns into an unpleasant experience. However, for me, this is a test to calibrate my emotions and blank my mind of everything around me, except the next shot."

With an expression of joy, Allison said, "Wow! You are a professional player, I could never figure why many times I played my best but ended with a poor score. It makes sense."

From that moment onward Margaret and Allison enjoyed the remaining holes, playing for fun, while Larry and Nancy's game declined with each passing shot.

"Thank God, this is the last hole," said Larry.

Without any response but, with an "Oh Sh@&+*…! I missed again," Nancy swore.

Allison was next to shoot and again landed near the flag, while Margaret's shot missed the green and fell into the water. At this point, Larry and Nancy remain arguing and standing at the ninth tee while Margaret and Allison were walking towards the island green.

Allison turned around and yelled, "Let's go, remember the house deal is closing today, and we need to be there on time, clean up, eat lunch, and be at the bank at four!"

"Okay! You ladies go ahead and finish playing, Nancy, and I will meet you for lunch at Andiamo in forty-five minutes," Larry yelled from the tee.

With a sense of caution and friendliness in her voice, Allison said, "May I speak openly about this situation? This episode is not new. Every time I've played with them during the negotiations between our banks, the betting gets larger and larger. And at the end, as you will see, they pay one another and continue to act as civilized as you and I are working right now. Therefore, dear Margaret doesn't be discouraged and let this be a lesson in your new position of power and prestige. Nothing should disturb you or make you formulate quick impressions or judgment until you know the facts. Emotional misperceptions could ruin your banking career."

"Aha! That is how the game of big money is played!" Margaret exclaimed.

"That's about right!" Allison said.

"Did you enjoy the game?" asked Margaret.

"Yes, I did. Seeing you play is a real pleasure. You are a professional player, or better yet have you consider playing professional golf?"

"I did many times. However, the reality is that if you don't win or classify within the top fifteen players, you end up losing money, and after you are near bankruptcy, the only prestigious job is on the staff of a private golf course, or a hotel golf shop."

"I had the idea that those people I see on the TV screen playing the tour, at least most of them, were financially well off," said Allison.

"Let's use me for example, I played with the University team for four years. At the end of that time I was number three in overall scores, the team played many events with money as the carrot. However, the fact is that the most money I ever made playing golf was $500, and that was yesterday!"

"Public perception as shaped by the media, it's powerful and serves people emotional needs to be distracted from the issues of life. Broadcast news is equally compelling. Maybe that's why the 2016 U.S. presidential campaign is going wild!" exclaimed Allison.

"You hit the right target!" said Margaret. "I'm a political science major and terribly upset by the political hunger of our masses, and the irresponsibility of the political leadership. If you were to stop ten people on any city street in America and ask why you are a Democrat, Republican, or an Independent? I'm willing to gamble my $500 now that maybe one person will give you an approximately correct answer. The vast majority of people in the United States do not know that the Electoral College doesn't have a sweatshirt, a logo or a mascot. It's not a physical building. Its members never get together (except with colleagues from their own state), and it ceases to exist as soon as it's performed its function. The term electoral college doesn't even appear in the United States Constitution. Yet its 538 members are responsible for one of the most transcendental tasks in the world: choosing the president of the United States.

"This is not to say that we are limited in information. The fact is that there is no spare time during the day to learn other subjects not related to work, work, work, and more of the same. On the other hand," Margaret continued, "the Caymanians, for example, Karla and Arthur, I'm noticing are faithful to living life. That is talking about the issues of life and culture. There's no rush to do or to be or to show that you enjoy a high standard of living, and play host to the big money of the business world."

Allison completed the statement, "We Caymanians know that life in the islands is moved by money."

Margaret responded quickly, "However, emotions are the controlling factor of money. Just to prove my point, right now Mr. Jordan and Nancy are going at each other's throats because of money. You and I are indirectly affected by the quality and results of our game because of money. Politics and democracy in America are affected by who spends the most money in an election campaign. My father is writing another book title "Money controls the World—Emotions controls Money." The best foundation of this truth is a personal experience. In my family. We've experienced both ends of the money spectrum, plenty of money to travel the world and enjoy what it can buy, and the price of paying for wrong emotional decisions. So, the lesson I'm learning every day is that to be in peace and enjoy life. We must continue learning day-by-day the intelligent use of money."

With a happy face and in an admiring tone of voice Allison said, "We need to talk more about this, maybe tonight during the celebration dinner the Caribbean Bank will be hosting. However, for now, we must, as you were saying, rush to get ready for lunch and be on time for the bank to meet the seller of the house. Let's go, drop off the equipment to be ready for Saturday and you and I will focus on winning the tournament. I know we can do it!"

As Margaret was passing the hotel lobby in the direction of her room Kathy intercepted her, "Hello, Ms. Gianelli, did you have a good practice? I see you're in a hurry, I will walk with you and help you to be on time wherever you need to go."

"Good. Please come with me because I have some questions." Margaret said

Kathy, with a rushing tone in her voice, said, "Me too. I have something for you."

JORGE RIVERA

Chapter 26
INTELLIGENCE

"This morning a call from the States came in," Kathy told Margaret as they returned to Margaret's room. "The caller asked the telephone receptionist to speak to the manager. The receptionist, the reception supervisor, and the secretary to the manager all tried to screen the call, but the mysterious caller finally identifies himself only to the manager. Since I'm your personal assistant, I'm the only one who has authority to deliver the mystery caller's message. It's for you. Here is the envelope the manager gave me to give to you."

Margaret, utterly surprised, stopped. She opened the note and in silence read, 'Call me from a secure line, between five and six in the morning your time. Thank you, Ellis.'

"Is it something I can help you with?" asked Kathy.

"Thank you, not in this matter. However, I have a bunch of questions I need your help with between now and getting ready in thirty-five minutes for a luncheon meeting."

"I'm at your service."

As they walked Margaret said, "Allison, the local bank's president is hosting a dinner dance this evening at a place outside the hotel, and she is bringing a male friend to be my social partner. I'm a little concerned about how to handle the situation, because for a year and nine months, seven days and a bunch of hours, I had not held the hand of a man other than Johnathan's, my boyfriend who I'm planning to marry. Especially today, I'm feeling vulnerable; my hormones are jumping up and down as if the clock is ticking. You understand, don't you?

Kathy started laughing, and the more Margaret explained the hormonal issue, the harder she laughed.

Then at the door of room 1206, Margaret looked for her key, "I must have lost my key when I sat down to take my shoes off."

"No worries, I have the master key, and I'll order new one while you take a shower. Then I'll be right back to talk about your social partner," said Kathy.

"Okay, all good. I'm not laughing I'm a little scared because Nancy commented last night that the way men walk here excites her and of course, I'm made of flesh and bone. So, there you are; think about my problem and hurry right back."

Margaret took a shower and then called her father. She was on the phone when Kathy knocked on her door.

"Please come in Kathy. I'm on the phone with my dad…" Then, immediately adopting a natural tone and demeanor "Okay, dad, don't worry you'll fix the amplifiers. Please, dad, don't worry I will call you back late tonight, and hope by then you have them. I have a meeting in ten minutes and need to talk to Kathy on my way there. Give my love to mom and Bobby."

Margaret was ready and dressed in a pale blue above-the-knee, body-tight skirt, royal blue short-sleeve blouse and on her arm hung a white blazer. She had open white multi stripe gladiator sandals and white and blue shoulder bag.

"You look great!" Kathy exclaimed.

"Thanks to you for selecting all these beautiful clothes, I'm indebted to your assistance and our new friendship," Margaret replied.

As they started briskly walking towards Andiamo Kathy said, "The men here are friendly and by American standards sweet as honey and gentle as olive oil, hum…, hum…! They are by culture, excellent dancers. Maybe that's why Ms. McArthur feels excited. They have rhythm in the way they walk and talk. In fact," Kathy continued, "Caymanian men place a high value on cultural achievements and social position. They strive to reach the heights in these two areas because those are the dominant elements of financial stability and good paying jobs. Tonight, just go with the flow and keep your knees together."

Margaret laughed. "Well, we're here. Thank you, Kathy. I'll see you tomorrow and let you in if something hot happens!"

Larry and Nancy were already at the table talking and getting ready to order lunch.

"Hi Margaret, wow! You look sharp." Nancy said.

"So, do you Nancy. Hello Mr. Jordan, have you seen Allison?"

"No. I'm sure she's coming soon." Just as Larry finished, Allison tapped Nancy on her right shoulder, Oh la la. You look ready for a fashion show!"

"Come on, Allison you are not doing the catwalk before my turn are you?"

The exchange of compliments set a friendly tone, and as usual, Larry said, "Let's enjoy a good lunch, and I'll brief you before meeting the house seller, the realtor, the escrow agent, the seller and the barrister."

"A barrister?" exclaimed Margaret. "I thought those guys just practiced law in England in the Inns of Court with the privilege of pleading in the higher Courts."

"Excuse me," said Larry. "I intended to say, solicitor. Better yet lawyer. You would like this fellow; he's smart, handsome, and single."

"Oh Mr. Jordan, that sounds fantastic, but I'm a one-man woman, and, for now, my heart, eyes and all of me is waiting to marry Jonathan, who is also a lawyer, very handsome and still holding single."

Everyone started laughing. Meanwhile, the waiter approached and waited politely before saying, "are you folks ready to order?"

Larry looked at Nancy, and she said, "For him and me grilled tuna, broiled vegetables and a great passionfruit juice."

"What about you ladies?"

Allison, "I'll have the same, except that I would like a pineapple coconut juice."

"Ditto, for me," Margaret said closing the menu. She continued making mental notes of Nancy's familiarity with Larry on the ordering of food.

"It will be about ten minutes. May I offer you an appetizer? Again, Nancy responded, "No, thank you, we have limited time today."

"Very well. The tuna arrived this morning, it is very fresh and looks appetizing, I will be back soon with the food."

Indeed, within twelve minutes two waiters appeared. Each plate of tuna was beautifully decorated with a uniquely shaped yellow flower. The flower's aroma recalled the scent of sea salt. The tuna was lightly seared, with encrusted sesame seeds, and had no fish smell. In the mouth, it had an almost emotional feeling and a unique taste that enticed the palate to savor it gently and slowly. The broiled vegetables were arranged on a wooden leaf-shaped base. The base's plate was lined with a banana frond. The colors were sharp and appealing to the eye. The texture was crispy, and one could sense an individual and distinct smell of green onions, zucchini, yellow squash, green, and red peppers; spread lightly with virgin olive oil, and a touch of Modena balsamic vinegar, salt, and pepper.

As usual with Larry, there was little talking during the meal, mostly innuendo between him and Nancy about the oral sensation of the tuna in the mouth. However, the consensus was that the lunch experience was one to remember.

While everyone was enjoying the freshly made fruit juices, Larry turned to Allison, "Do you know who the seller is?"

"No, as a matter of fact, when we made the final offer, the accepting party was the young solicitor. At that time, I placed a demand on the escrow document that the seller must be present at closing."

"Good, we don't want any more surprises. We've had plenty, and I'm not in the mood to deal with more bad news!"

"What do you mean bad news?" asked Allison.

"Well, the day before we arrived here, the outside auditors showed up, two weeks in ahead of schedule. My CFO had a heart attack, his wife is going crazy, and my wife is on my case for not being there to help out."

At the reference to his wife Nancy shot Larry a look of annoyance.

Margaret captured Nancy's reaction in her mental notebook.

"Oh, dear," Allison said. "What a tragedy. Should I call and rescheduled the closing?"

In a confident voice, Larry said, "No, no, no. The show must go on. I'm not going to let a two million dollar profit go down the drain for anything. This is about money, and we are all in this business about the money, and to hell, with everyone, and everything else, until we get back to Louisville!

Margaret listened silently, but with attention.

"We must be very careful of last minute changes when a solicitor is acting on behalf of the seller." Nancy declared emphatically. "My experience has been that they always come up with the lame statement, 'I have limited authority.' My position, better yet, our bank position is that the deal must close as agreed on the closing document, or there is no deal, period."

"Wow! Nancy," Allison said. "Are you perhaps making a rash judgment?

"After all, at the end of the deal, my personal profits are worth the gamble," said Nancy.

Margaret in a naïve voice said, "Today, I'm going to learn a two million dollar lesson, I can't wait to experience that reality, and I'm already excited."

"Look, young lady," Larry said, "this deal is small potatoes. As you become comfortable with the term 'million' you will realize that our culture is frozen in the conception of the net present value of a million dollars. Today, in truth, buys zilch, the 'Net Present Value' is a method used to evaluate investments using the value of all cash outflows, such as the cost of the investment, and capital inflows. Returns on investment are calculated given a fixed rate of performance. An investment is acceptable if the 'Net Present Value' is positive." Then, he added, let's go and close a deal so I can take you people out to eat.

"Oh, Larry," said Allison, 'the Caribbean bank has it all planned. Our deal is tonight; then dinner, drinks, dancing and more of the same because we need to rest, and be in good spirits to win the tournament on Saturday.'

"Did you say, dancing," Larry interjected. "Who is going to dance with Margaret? I don't want to take her and exposed her beauty to the lonely wolfs waiting to devour a fresh and beautiful specimen!" Tilting his head and with admiring eyes, Larry glanced at Margaret, earning another annoyed look from Nancy.

"Ah, I'm pleased you feel that protective," Allison smiled. "So, I'm bringing her a good surprise. A handsome banker, well educated, and socially on top of the pyramid. Oh, did I say he's single? It's not just a question of protection, it's a matter of legal liability. She's performing in the capacity of a bank executive, and if anything, I mean even a small dent happens to her I will end up in court, followed by a death sentence.

"Then, Nancy will lose her walking cash register, golfing, and betting partner!" laughed Larry.

Everyone joined Larry's smile as Margaret archived her information in a mental folder.

Kathy appeared beside the table and announced that Milton, the driver was outside waiting. She could not help but notice the group's friendliness. She approached Margaret and whispered, "Will I see you tomorrow? I'm here from ten-to-ten and ready to be of service."

With a mischievous look and playful tone Margaret said, "Thank you, Kathy, I will definitely see you in the morning, what time? I don't know that yet, however, I'm planning to sleep at least until nine."

"Okay, it's all settled. Let's go and make some money!" said Larry.

Chapter 27
ROYAL MONEY

Joshua was standing by the bank's door, and promptly approached the party when they arrived. "The home seller is a Saudi Arabian man," he said, "wearing a full-length white and gold outfit, and a black and white checked headdress. He's sitting in the conference room with his solicitor. No one else is here yet."

"Okay," Larry said, "you ladies remain in Allison's office until I determine who this character Joshua is describing is. If he's a conservative Saudi, we have a dress code problem."

"Hum, I've never met a real Arab," Margaret commented.

"Allison and I have many times, and Larry is right," Nancy said. "If this buyer is old fashioned, we'll have to delay the signing, return to the hotel and change into acceptable Saudi dresses."

"Do you mean this could be a two million dollar lesson?" Margaret asked.

Allison with arms half extended, the palm of both hands open and skyward, at waist height said, "Oh, no, no. All it means is that the deal must be postponed until later today. The legal papers are dated today and must be signed today, no matter the time, as long as it takes place before midnight. Otherwise, the documents must be withdrawal and new ones issued with a different closing date. The real estate laws here are strict and unforgiving."

Meanwhile, in the second-floor conference room, Larry greeted the seller and his solicitor, "Good afternoon gentlemen, I'm Larry Jordan, chief executive of this bank."

"Good evening sir, I'm solicitor Barrington, and this is my client, the owner of the house, his Royal Highness Prince Aamir."

Larry bowed slightly at the waist. "How do you do your Royal Highness, it is a pleasure to meet you."

With a perfect Bostonian accent, the prince replied, "The pleasure is all mine. Please excuse my formal attire; once the purchase is completed, I'll be flying to Miami to meet the Royals and onward to Riyadh."

"May I have your permission to bring up my executives who are interested parties in this transaction? They are three women dressed in Western business attire."

"By all means please, I'm a Harvard graduate and have no cultural issue with dress codes or women for that matter!" said Prince Aamir.

"Thank you, I'll return in a moment."

Everyone looked up when Larry reappeared downstairs. "Ladies, the show is on, you'll be meeting the seller, his Royal Highness, Prince Aamir. One of the cardinal rules of social and business protocol is the observance of the order of precedence at all functions where officials of a government or its representatives are present. Failure to recognize the proper rank and precedence of a guest is an insult to his position and the country he represents." In a playful tone "in our case a mistake may cost us two million bucks," Larry said. "The order of precedence is Allison whom I'll introduce first; then I'll bring in Nancy and introduce her. A longer pause, then Nancy will add Margaret. Shall we, Allison?"

"Yes, Sir!"

Larry and Allison entered the conference room to find Prince Aamir standing at the head of the table. Slightly to his left and behind held the Solicitor. "Your Highness, this is Madam Allison Harrington, the bank president."

"How do you do Madam Harrington?" said the Prince.

With a slight lowering of her head, "It is an honor to meet you and conduct business in our bank Royal Highness," responded Allison.

While she remained standing, Larry returned to the holding office and brought Nancy. "Your Highness, this is Madam Nancy McArthur, the principal investment banker."

"How do you do Madam McArthur?"

It's nice to meet you Prince Aamir, May I take a moment to bring our Executive Assistant?

"Yes, please," said the Prince.

"Royal Highness, this is Miss, Margaret Gianelli, executive assistant to the president and board of directors."

"How do you do Miss Gianelli?"

"I am well, thank you Royal Highness, Prince Aamir of Saudi Arabia."

"Are you a diplomat? Asked the Prince.

"No Royal Highness, I'm a political science major. However, my father is a career diplomat."

"It is the first time while conducting private business in the United States, that a person in no official government capacity has addressed me in the appropriate order of precedence. My compliments to Mr. Jordan."

The Prince took a seat and with both arms fully extended palms open upward, indicated for everyone to sit as well. Then, after everyone was at the table, Nancy stood up and walked around to the Prince, leaned near his left ear, and in a soft voice, "may I order some lavender tea for you, Royal Highness?"

"Thank you, it is very kind of you madam McArthur."

Nancy strolled toward the far end of the table as if she were on fashion show catwalk and as she passed she left a scent of Channel 5 perfume. She opened the auxiliary door at the far end of the room and disappeared. All the time Prince's eyes had been fixed on Nancy's free flowing shining black hair and her swaying hips. Then, the Prince realized the solicitor was also enchanted. To divert the attention, he said, "Who else will be present? I have to depart in an hour."

"Royal Highness," Larry responded, "At four o'clock the realtor, the escrow agent, and the Barrister will be present."

In the meanwhile, Nancy returned via the same door. She walked slowly and seductively towards the Prince. In turn, his piercing black eyes fixed on her beautiful presence. Nancy acknowledged his look with a slight left-to-right, straight up and down semi-closed eyes and a circular head movement as if indicating the presence of the waiters following her. These servers were refined looking black men, over six feet tall, dressed in a white tailored body-tight slacks, black formal vest with a high neck, log sleeve white shirts, and white gloves. They were carrying the traditional afternoon British tea service in a Baroque style silver plate. The service included mini sandwiches and shortbread cookies.

Nancy approached the Prince, leaned near his right ear and whispered an inaudible question.

Prince Aamir, with hungry male eyes, looked up at Nancy and softly responded, "Tea only, please."

In a modulated tone of voice, Nancy said," His Royal Highness will only have tea, and we will begin business at four o'clock!" This statement clearly indicated who was in control of the agenda.

The servers ceremoniously brought the tea to the Prince first, Larry second, then Allison, Nancy, Margaret, and the solicitor last. There was no conversation during the mid- afternoon tea. As the Prince sipped, two men and a woman arrived, entering from the same door, Nancy had come from earlier.

Allison stood and in a matter- of-fact voice identified those seated around the conference table. Then she announced, "Royal Highness and solicitor, these are the realtor, the escrow officer, and the bank Barrister. We understand it is your desire to conclude this sale transaction within fifty minutes."

"Thank you, Madam Harrington, for acknowledging the time-sensitive nature of my departure."

Without further directives, the barrister said, "Royal Highness, may I have your permission to invite your solicitor and the transaction party to my office to read and formalize the documents?"

"Yes, please, proceed," said the Prince.

The Barrister, then called, "Mr. Barrington, please follow us to my office." The solicitor walked to the far end of the room where the escrow officer and the realtor, a woman, stood. The members of the transaction party disappeared.

Immediately, Prince Aamir, turned his head towards Margaret and said, "Madam Gianelli, would you please tell me a little about your business and protocol experiences, while we wait for the documents?"

Margaret turned towards Nancy and asked, "Madam McArthur, Madam Harrington, and Mr. Jordan, may I have your permissions to respond to His Royal Highness, Prince Aamir of Saudi Arabia?"

The parties present, including the Prince, were surprised and spellbound by Margaret's request. Then, Larry in a formal tone of voice said, "Madam Gianelli, please proceed."

In her natural and jovial voice, Margaret said, "your Highness, may I respectfully request your permission to shorten the protocolary formalities and speak freely and in context with your questions?"

"Please, by all means!" responded the Prince.

Now, Margaret took control of the agenda. "In response to your first question, my business experience is broad, however, limited to one year. Broad, because until a week ago I was picking up and sorting the marked "investment" mail to and from almost every department in the Louisville Midtown Bank. That job gave me broad exposure and experience to know the names of almost everyone who was important, semi-important and who waited for my arrival at their desk in expectation of a piece of "investment" mail to justify keeping their job. My money making business experience is connected with my four years of playing golf for my university team, and earning real money from being a good player. An example, yesterday, I made $500 dollars, and scored a hole-in-one."

The Prince and everyone else was exuberantly laughing at Margaret's candid response. Allison and Nancy particularly were nearly in tears. Margaret waited. Then she stood and like a soprano interpreting an aria of Elixir D'Amore with an exaggerated intonation, and body movements to match said, "As to my protocolary experience, it all began with falling off a horse. Do you want to hear about the horse accident that led to my meeting President George W. Bush? Or, shall I just tell you about my ceremonial protocolary experiences straightforward?"

The Prince was laughing with such enthusiasm as to stand and signal Larry. Both men stood, briefly facing each other. Then Larry said, "May we be excused for a moment please?"

Together, the men exited the conference room while Nancy and Allison still laughing and jovially exchanging comments about Margaret's job description.

Chapter 28
HIGH-LEVEL EXPERIENCE

Upon returning with Larry, the Prince said, "Madam Gianelli, I would appreciate hearing about your protocolary experience with President Bush. We have twenty minutes to hear your story, sign the documents, and depart for the airport."

"Royal Highness," said Margaret, "I'll get to the point, and you'll have time to spare." She stood before the Prince and began, "I was nine years old, and my mom and I were practicing for a horse show in Pasadena, California. My horse, eleven palms high, jumped the obstacle and fell to the ground, like this. . ." She stepped to the side and arms extended palms downward and head bent towards the floor mimicked her horse falling. "Then, my mom, of course, like always she was following too close, and her horse also fell on top of my horse's rear end and behind me."

As Margaret showed the event, she placed her upper body flat on the conference table. Then, with an effortless spring, she stood and continued. "This accident kept mom in the orthopedic hospital for six weeks with weights hanging from her head. During that time, my father was President Bush's special advisor. One day he asked me if I'd like to go for a western horseback ride with a friend at a place called Prairie Chapel Ranch. I said sure, dad, when are we leaving? He said, Saturday at six in the morning, and that we'd be back by six in the evening in time to visit my mom in the hospital.

"Saturday came, and at four in the morning dad began to call me to get up. But the more he tried the sleeper I got. Several times I told him I'd changed my mind but with dad, there was no negotiation, I had to go! I was pretty surprised when we drove to the airport, I asked dad why, and he told me to rest on the plane and that I'd feel better when in Waco. The next thing I remembered was landing at an airport and a black sedan with two great cowboys . . ." she showed the height of the men with her right arm fully extended upward . . . "were waiting to take us to the ranch. When we got there, there was another cowboy; he was a Secret Service special agent I learned later. With the voice of mad AIR".. ...she made a guttural sound, "gruuu . . . The officer asked for my photo ID. I told him I didn't have an ID. I'm not in school until Monday, I said."

Margaret noticed the barrister and the solicitor bringing papers for the Prince to sign. Then, with her right arm extended towards the far end of the conference room, she pointed at the incoming men and concluded, "The rest of the story, when we see you again, Royal Highness Prince Aamir of Saudi Arabia."

At that closing, the Prince stood and said, "I'm honored to be conducting business with such of pleasant and intelligent people. Madam Gianelli has demonstrated in action that industry experience is not measured by years seating at a desk, but by the precise application in the context of knowledge and communication skills. Mr. Jordan, Madam Harrington, and Madam McArthur, all of you are congratulated for your choice of executive assistant." Then, he gave his attention to the solicitor, who stood at the left side of the Prince.

The counsel presented the documents. "All is accurate and in accord with the terms and conditions of your sales offer. Therefore, may I respectfully request your signature where I indicate and initials on each page?" As the solicitor pointed, the Prince signed or initialed. Within a few minutes, the process was completed. Then, the barrister retrieved the signed documents from the solicitor, and returned to his office, to secure the signatures of the escrow officer and realtor where appropriate.

The barrister returned to the conference room and presented the documents to be signed by Mr. Jordan and countersigned by Ms. McArthur. Upon completing all documents, once more he returned to his office along with the solicitor. There all the pertinent documents were signed by the solicitor and the barrister as the authorized agents for the transaction.

The barrister then returned and handed Larry a cashier's check for three million dollars payable to Royal Highness Prince Aamir of Saudi Arabia. Larry inspected the check and handed it to Nancy. Nancy took the check and an envelope, stood and walked behind Allison and Margaret towards the far end of the conference room and made a U-turn towards the Prince, with the check in one hand and the envelope close to her chin. Then slowly and with a slight inclination of her upper body, she faced the Prince and placed the check into the envelope saying, "Royal Highness, this is a cashier's check for three million dollars, with my deepest appreciation and best wishes for a safe trip back to the Kingdom of Saudi Arabia."

Standing as Nancy approached, the Prince's eyes discretely focused on Nancy's provocative cleavage. He accepted the check and said, "Thank you for a profitable business transaction for all of us. I hope to see you again in the future." Holding the envelope in his hand, he promptly made ready to depart.

Suddenly, Nancy said, "May I have the honor of escorting you to your limousine?"

"Madam McArthur, it is a rare treat that a beautiful woman should offer to escort Prince Aamir to his awaiting car. Please lead the way."

That was an elegant put-down that Nancy missed entirely. Culturally, a woman never escorted a man, especially a Prince. He was kind as he was enchanted by Nancy.

Nancy, as before, walked ahead of the prince to the elevator where she signaled the solicitor to stay behind. The Prince and Nancy entered the elevator… Meanwhile, Larry had to descend by the stairway and was waiting on the first floor outside the elevator. Without much ceremony, he walked ahead of the Prince and stood by the open door of the waiting limousine. "Royal Highness, have a safe trip."

"Thank you, Mr. Jordan," the Prince responded.

The driver was about to close the rear door when the Prince leaned forward and added, "Madam McArthur, I look forward to our next business transaction. I will be returning in my official capacity of Finance Minister, to attend the Annual Meeting of the World Bank and the International Monetary Fund in September of this year, in Washington. I will direct my office to arrange a meeting with all of you, so we can hear the rest of the story from Madame Gianelli, and make some real money."

The last words from the Prince were a peaceful balm to Larry, who in the intense expression of his face and slightly abrupt demeanor had shown a bit of jealousy. The driver closed the car door, and within a minute, the limousine drove away while Larry and Nancy remained standing outside the Bank.

Upon their return to the conference room, Allison said, "Congratulations, the sale is completed, and the realtor has the key to delivering the property this afternoon. We should go and take possession; then we can respond to Nancy's proposal to promote the investment strategy as she has successfully been doing from Louisville."

Margaret summarized her notes, on top of the page writing, 'Three Million Real Money Deal Participation.' Silently, she connected the events that led to this transaction, the surprise visit by the Inspector General, and especially the comments made by Gomez. Also, she recalled the most recent meeting in the bank's conference room in Louisville and the heated argument between Larry and Nancy. As Margaret was making these mental notes, suddenly, she asked "Would the change of closing date have constituted a two or three million dollar lesson?"

With a peaceful expression and in a modulated voice, Larry said "Well, let's say that could have happened. We would have a loss, not two, but as Margaret put it the loss would have been three million. Why? Because this money was already withdrawal from the Discretionary Fund and a loss of that magnitude would have made Nancy unhappy, to say the least."

"I understand," said Margaret.

Immediately and without preamble, in a happy and victorious voice, Allison said "The only item pending for this meeting is related to our participation in the method used by Nancy to promote new investments in the Islands using the new house as a hook. Our legal advisors caution this promotional technique would appear as an undue influence to a third party."

"Who would be a third party in this case?" asked Margaret.

"In my example," Allison replied, "I'm picturing in my mind the wife of a potential investor who is present, but not a party to the transaction but who has considerable influence on the investment decision, as she relates to housing as representing a family asset. Therefore, according to our local regulations, we cannot use the expression, 'weekend courtesy visit' as a promotional tool to attract new investment clients."

Nancy's facial expression changed to a calm and emotionless look.

Allison continued. "I spoke to our public relations people, and they suggested that a filming location, as it is used in the movie scouting and setting business, is the best choice. It would show the property with the special effects and we save the travel and entertainment expenses of the potential client. This technique does not conflict with any of our local regulations."

In a vivacious tone of her voice, Margaret said, "Besides, the movie as a promotional tool is portable; we can easily send it via email to multiple potential investors for inspection, at their leisure, thus, eliminating the unnecessary influence stuff."

"Therefore, since you came with the 'movie' idea, I would like you to develop a conceptual plan for consideration by our joint Board of Directors and present this along with the terminology assignment," said Larry.

"Excellent, sir I will do this with pleasure," responded Margaret.

With a renewed, happy and expectant expression, Nancy said, "It's settled. Allison, please let the realtor know we are ready to go and take legal possession of this new asset to my investment fund."

Allison picks up the phone and calls Joshua, "Please bring Ms. Wellington to the conference room." After a few minutes, the phone rang again. Allison listened and then said, "very well we'll be there in thirty minutes or less, thank you." She hung up and announced to the group, "Joshua informs me the realtor is waiting for us at the location. I used the word 'location,' because I would like Margaret to refer to this assignment as a movie location under consideration."

"I like this approach," Larry said, "and it's giving us new perspectives on how we can multiply our investment capabilities, exposure and attract more potential investors. Like Margaret put it, this deal is a 'Real Money Making deal."

At the Seven Mile Beach house, Allison introduced Ms. Wellington, and the walkthrough took place as a matter-of-fact, rather than as a sales presentation effort. Since the house would be refurbished and upgraded, Nancy took the lead and said, "Ms. Wellington, thank you for the time you invested in finding this house, we like it very much. Should you get another 'unique' property within a five million range, please get in touch with me or Ms. Gianelli, who will be, returning from time to time to work with Ms. Harrington."

"Ms. Gianelli, may I have your business card please?" asked Wellington.

With her government assignment in mind, Margaret responded, "thank you for asking, I don't have one here, but on my next trip, I'll let Ms. Harrington know in advance so we can meet. I'm interested in learning about the investment properties in the islands."

Larry glanced at Nancy, and with a slight bow right-to-left tilt of his head and made a left-hand thumbs up. "I'm sure Ms. Wellington would enjoy developing a business relationship with Ms. Gianelli, she is new to real estate, but knows about real money."

"Location, location, location, and best price. That's my idea of real money," said Margaret.

In a surprise move, Nancy handed the keys to Margaret while saying, "This is your visiting residence until we proceed with our plans. You'll have the opportunity to enjoy it more often than I would because I'm going on vacations within the next few weeks."

Margaret's mouth dropped open. Her eyes got bigger than a winning horse at the Kentucky Derby, her legs visibly shook, but without any additional words and like a professional, she responded, "Thank you, Nancy."

"Thank you, everyone, I'm pleased to meet you and would be happy to learn of… excuse me what is your last name?

"Gianelli," please call me Margaret.

"Thank, you, Ms. Margaret." Ms. Wellington said. "I'm at your service, at any time that is most convenient for you. I have the honor of holding for the last seven years the record of most multi-million dollars real estate sales in the Caribbean islands."

Larry, Nancy, and Allison were pleasantly surprised by the manner and tone of Margaret's voice during the interaction with Wellington. Without much ceremony, Larry extended his hand to Wellington and said, "Thank you for the effort of selecting this excellent location and price for our purchase, we are pleased to know you, and as the time moves along, hopefully, you would seek exceptional properties for our consideration." Then, he continued, "Ladies, it is time to return to the hotel and get ready for Allison's surprise."

Chapter 29
DANCING WITH STARS

Back at the hotel, getting ready in her room, Margaret was concerned about the surprise Allison had lined up. She called Kathy. As the phone rang and rang she thought, 'Oh God! Where are you, Kathy? When the voicemail message came on Margaret said, "Oh, no, no, no! Kathy, this is Margaret Gianelli, please call me. It's very urgent, a matter of hormonal dysfunction; a matter of living or playing dead. You understand, don't you? Ah . . . Before you get a wrong idea about this message, I'm saying my hormones are jumping like crickets in a hot night in the patio of Ultra Mar, in Mexico. Of course, I don't' expect you to know Ultra Mar, but when I see you I'll tell you about the love nest of my life, I call it Matriluna. I'll tell you all about it!'

Then in a calmer but the pleading voice she exclaimed to herself, "Margaret, it is time for a surprise. Therefore, you are to put on the armor of God, and get ready, look beautiful, smell divine, and laugh all the way to the shower. When feeling the heat of the water running all over your gorgeous body, sing, sing, sing 'Happy!'"

As Margaret was coming out of the shower repeating the song 'Happy,' there was a knock on the door. It was Kathy.

"Good evening, Ms. Gianelli," she said as she came in. "I heard your hormonal message and felt compelled to return early from my break to bring you a fire extinguisher and the necessary help to get ready to go wherever you need to go. What is the plan for this evening, and where are you going? So I can be as efficient as one can be under the most remarkable circumstance of being surrounded by jumping crickets in exotic, Ultra Mar, Mexico. By the way, what is Matriluna?"

"Oh Yes! Ultra Mar is not only unusual, but it's also enchanted, and my memories of it are etched in my mind and heart,"

"Well, don't' leave me in suspense. Tell me all about this place. I love the way you pronounced the name, I'm most interested. Your eyes, they are filled with near tears of joy and longing," said Kathy as she looked at Margaret with a begging expression that moved the unmovable to spill out.

"I will, I will, I will explain later. Margaret said. "But, not now. I have a problem more serious than you can imagine."

"So, is it bad, I mean real bad? Well, then, the most important issue right now is to deal with the first impression of your surprise package. Under your critical circumstances, I would advise thinking of the most unpleasant things happening to your relationship with your boyfriend," said Kathy. Margaret's body posture was subconsciously erect as if she were walking the runway of a fashion show, balancing three books on top of her head. Her body movements looked anxious and uncertain. Then she sat at the edge of the bed and began to cry.

Surprised by the drastic change of mood, Kathy asked, "What is going on Ms. Gianelli?"

Between gentle sobs, Margaret said, "You hit the target. I'm feeling vulnerable because I'm scared. I'm afraid of cheating on Johnathan, my boyfriend, even though I am not at peace because I had seen with his ex- girlfriend, and called him on this, this twice. It's scaring me because if I'm sexually attracted to the surprise package, and he makes a bold move I may surrender without a fight. At the same time, I'm dying to experience what is like to be held by a hot Caymanian man.

However, interfering with my feeling are the memories of when I caught Johnathan, once having coffee with his ex-girlfriend at Starbucks.

While she was sipping coffee, at the table she was touching his knee, and he was acting as nothing was taking place. Except when he saw me, he almost fell out of the chair, and his face turned deathlike pale."

To break the mood, and bring the time issue into context, Kathy, asked: "At what point are you supposed to be ready to go?"

"At nine o'clock!" responded Margaret.

In a calm tone of her voice, Kathy said, "It's 8:15 and you're not even dressed. Let me help you ease your mind. If the surprise package makes a slight overture, which I doubt, you just state something like this, "I'm sorry, but I'm not used to Caymanian customs. When he hears this, two things should happen. He will apologize for the accidental bridge of social conduct, or at the end of the music, he will disappear in shame."

"Oh. Good, that eases my mind," said Margaret with a sense of relief.

All was in order, and Margaret stood in the lobby when Larry and Nancy arrived. They then went to the penthouse of the tallest building in George Town, where Allison met them.

"Hello, Larry, Nancy, and Margaret. This is my husband Thomas, and our long-time friend and investment banker with J.P Morgan, Jeff."

"Nice to meet you, Thomas, Jeff," Larry said.

Jeff shook hands. "The pleasure is mine," he said. "Please follow me to the terrace; I have reserved a table for us overlooking George Town,"

After a gourmet turtle dinner, the party moved to watch a show by a Cayman group. After the server had taken the order for drinks, Margaret excused herself from the table, and discretely approached the waiter as he was placing the order with the bartender, "Hello, would you help me, please?

Courteously and in an inquisitive tone of voice he said, "What can I do for you, madam?"

"I ordered Bacardí and Coca-Cola, but I'm allergic to alcohol. However the party I'm with has no idea, nor should they notice.

Therefore, please make sure you mention the brand when you serve me, then I'll know it's a real coca cola." Then Margaret extended her hand as if to shake the waiter's hand but, instead placed in his hand a twenty dollars bill.

"Thank you, madam. I will make sure you receive the drink you wish."

As Margaret returned, she noticed in the dim light Larry and Nancy at the far end of the dance floor, where they were silhouetted in the reflection of the city lights. They were dancing a slow dance, holding each other close, very close, so close that their bodies were tight against one another. Nancy's mouth was turned towards Larry's neck as if she were lightly kissing him on the right side of his neck at each turn while he was holding her with his right palm fully extended across her lower back, almost holding the upper quadrant of her buttocks. With that image in her mind, Margaret approached her seat.

Suddenly Jeff stood and extending his arm invited Margaret to the dance floor.

Margaret's worse nightmare began, Jeff held her so tight against his body that she started to feel sexual arouse. Then she remembered Kathy's advice, "I'm sorry Jeff, I'm not used to Caymanians customs."

Jeff instantly stopped. He led Margaret by the hand to the brightest side of the room, where she could see his eyes and he could look into hers. In a small and modulated voice, he said, "Margaret, please forgive me if inadvertently I'm holding you too close. As you can see from the people on the dance floor, we Caymanians bring the music into our hearts; we feel the music throughout our entire body to sense the lyrics and to react to the rhythm of each song. We do not dance Ballroom, nor count one, two, and three, one two and three, turn right and more of the same. We dance to feel that we are living life and that our dancing partner is as excited to be alive as we are to be living in the moment. We dance to communicate our emotions, our capacity for intimacy, and our sexual passions. Caymanians dance to the music in the fullness and essence of its interpretation."

"Wow! Jeff, I feel so ignorant, yet so enchanted with your description of the way Caymanians interpret life. In this context, I better appreciate Larry and Nancy's intimacy as an expression of what you're describing. Margaret was about to take the biggest risk of her trip with her next statement when Allison, approached from behind the couple and said,

"Hello. Are you people talking business?"

Quickly Jeff responded. "No, we are not. The warm up dancing will be over with the next song, and then Margaret will see what we Caymanians are all about. We dance to celebrate life, we dance to celebrate the victory of today, and we dance to celebrate our success of the time with passion and determination."

Margaret was intimated by the directness of Allison and Jeff. In fact, she was scared to death. Then, in a flash of wisdom, she remembered that her job was not about the culture of the islands, nor about her hormonal disarray; it was about facilitating the prosecution of the people running the Louisville Midtown Bank. That thought caused Margaret to focus on her job not on her feelings and protecting the potential of lowering her guard.

Indeed, the group leader announced that the warm up was about over. "Enjoy our last slow dance for the evening," and the director said, "and let us party the way only Caymanians know how."

In a pleading voice, Jeff asked, "Margaret would you grant me this slow dance and then let's party?"

Margaret's legs were shaking a bit, but in her mind, she asked herself, 'How will I know what feels like to dance Caymanian style if I don't try?'

So she pulled Jeff to the middle of the dance floor and let him lead. The moment she felt his solid muscular body against her solid shape, there was a spark of sexual attraction! He held Margaret's middle back with a solid palm extended, and she experienced the unique feeling of his hand. She turned her head towards his chest and instantly noticed the light smell of a citrus cologne. The smell relaxed her, and her body felt his legs. As they swayed very slowly he began to whisper the words of the song "Without you…, without you, I can no longer live…, without you, life is not worth living... These words made Margaret feel the meaning of Caymanian dancing. As he whispered the tune, he tightened his grip on her lower body.

Margaret began to perspire. The feeling of attraction was making her hormones jump as she described earlier, like crickets in the summer night on the patio of Ultra Mar. A sense of sexual attraction was about to overwhelm her Southern heritage of candor, politeness, and properness. Immersed in her personal dilemma, she failed to notice Larry and Nancy dancing next to her. Then she heard Nancy remark "Are you enjoying this last slow dance?"

Surprised she pulled back from the close, very close tip to toe, knee to knee and leg to leg feeling of Jeff's hard body, and in a loud voice to overpower the music Margaret said, "Oh. My goodness, gracious, this a terrific dance and it's time to get ready to party!"

How little she knew of the underlining meaning of her spontaneity, and the message she was delivering to Jeff. In turn Jeff, conscious of her cultural naiveté, celebrating her simplicity and with a jovial and playful voice, loud enough for the ears of Nancy and Larry said, "I'll make sure that she doesn't go overboard here."

To cool down the emotions and feeling of Margaret's enthusiasm, Jeff led her to pick up their drinks and walked to the end of the terrace overlooking the city.

In the interim, the tropical group playing the Caymanian music was taking a break.

At the edge of the terrace, with a drink in one hand and holding Margaret with the other Jeff said, "Margaret, I want you to look at the city for a moment, then when I tell you to close your eyes, please close them. Then, turn around and let me lead you a few steps in the opposite direction. Don't open your eyes. When we stop, wait until I tell you to what to do next. Then only look above your head and describe to me what you see. Are we in agreement?"

While admiring the lights and the city view, Margaret was tapping her right foot as if keeping tempo with a Caribbean song playing in her head. Then, releasing Jeff's hand, she raised her left arm and exclaimed, "Yes! I'm!"

Jeff smiled and nodded, "Please look to the farthest you can see the city . . . Remember what you see. Okay, now close your eyes, turn around and hold my hand tight." He led her for several dozen paces. Then, he said, "Keep your eyes closed and tilt your head towards the sky. Stay in this position for a few minutes until I direct you to open your eyes. Margaret faithfully followed his instructions. Then, she heard, are you ready?"

In surprisingly loud voice said, Margaret. "Yes, I am!"

In a very soft voice whispered into her left ear, Jeff said, "Please open your eyes and describe what you see."

"Wow! God! Wow! The sky is pitch black, filled with stars. There are millions of them . . . All sizes and shapes . . . They are whirling like I feel when dancing . . . They're so bright I can't describe the luminosity . . . The intensity. Their power makes me feel insignificant before the magnificence of God's creation!"

Jeff then said, "Describe the city skyline."

"I can't, I can't remember. This is all I want to see and remember for the rest of my life. Let me be here in silence. Let's put these drinks away, I want to lay down flat on the floor looking to the sky, I want to experience what you are showing me unencumbered by anything other than to know that I will remember this moment, and you, Jeff forever!" Jeff remained standing in silence, looking at Margaret, who was staring at the night sky, oblivious to the hot music that had started again. He admired her simplicity and beauty.

The music stopped. A raincloud swept in, and it began to drizzle. Jeff took Margaret's hand and said, "Please let's go inside before we get wet."

Back inside, the server was waiting with towels on hand. "Thank, you," said Jeff. "Please bring us two cups of hot rum, no Coca-Cola, please.

"Yes, sir. It will be a few minutes because we are making hot drinks for most patrons," responded the waiter.

"Where are Nancy and Larry?" asked Margaret.

"I don't see them, however, there to your right by the flower vase are Allison and Thomas. Let's join them while waiting for our hot rum;"

"Hello, guys, where are Nancy and Mr. Jordan?" asked Margaret.

"They left shortly before the music ended," Allison said. "They had a meeting with someone at the hotel and requested that you relax and enjoy the evening. We'll take you back whenever you'd like to go."

"A meeting at two in the morning?" Exclaimed Margaret.

"Oh, yes dear," Allison replied. "In the Caymans we are about money and time is money. Whenever a client calls for a meeting, we have no problem, whether day or night. This is our culture. Money runs our country and our time is valued by how well we invest it. However, we Caymanians have a particular bucket to devote to fun and living as we are now. On the other hand, Larry and Nancy can't miss an opportunity to make some real money, no matter the time, or the place. Even tonight we had several side meetings with potential investors and all were most successful."

In a professorial voice, Thomas said, "Culture binds us, give us meaning and provides us with solid foundations; it surround us, entangles, and supports our daily lives."

"I'm perplexed about the big money game. What is the connection between money and greed?" Margaret asked.

In a near ceremonial tone, Jeff said, "Margaret, money is good. To have an abundance of is better. It allows us to fulfill our destiny and do what we enjoy doing. On the other hand, greed is evil. Greed is the endless appetite to possess luxuries of all kinds, whether for our own pleasure, just to display, or to own as a show of power."

Allison nodded vigorously. "For example, a good friend of ours has a top notch position in one of the largest banks in the world. He has been earning over six figures a year for at least ten years, that we know off. He lives in a beautiful but modest home, drives a new Mercedes-Benz, dresses well, and takes vacations at least twice a year. In the other hand, his best friend, and direct competitor earns about the same. He is also single, has a penthouse in the city, a luxurious home on the beach, a sixty foot Glastron boat, drives a Ferrari and collects famous paintings. He never goes on vacations, nor does he take the time to party as we are doing tonight. That is an example of the difference between having money and being greedy."

At that moment, the waiter arrived. "Here are the hot rum drinks with cinnamon and clove, please be careful, they are boiling."

Margaret's curiosity about her drink got the best of her. She took a sip and tasted apple cider with Coca-Cola, and exclaimed, "My goodness it is very, very, very hot." Please be careful you guys!

At four-thirty in the morning, while enjoying Calypso music and real Caymanian dancing, she remembered to call Mr. Ellis. To prepare and avoid being noticed, she asked Jeff to see if he could arrange a quiet place where she could make a private telephone call to her father who was leaving for London in less than thirty minutes.

Chapter 30
CALL TO ACTION

Immediately, upon hearing Margaret's request to call her dad, Jeff said, "Of course. Please follow me to the elevator. Here is my card key to the Executive Penthouse, where the officers of this club are located. You'll have total privacy there. After you're finished, all you need to do is insert this card key into the elevator, and it will open automatically here. I'll wait for you when the door opens."

"Thank you, Jeff, which is very kind of you. I'll be back in a few minutes."

At exactly five o'clock Margaret rang Mr. Ellis and when he answered she said, "Good morning Mr. Ellis."

"Hi, Margaret, thank you for calling. Are you having a good time at the Bankers Club?"

"How do you know where I'm?"

"Margaret, by now you should be aware, I know stuff," said Ellis.

"Now, I do Mr. Ellis."

Without any further comments, Ellis said, "Margaret, the following day after you return to Louisville, I need you to make up an excuse and come to Washington first thing in the morning so you can be back at the bank by before 4:00 p.m. the same day. Call me on this number, and I will give you the secret plans for the day. An agent named Marisol will be your only contact. She'll pick you up at your usual Starbucks. You will leave your car there and be prepared to give Marisol your car keys. She will make sure you will have your car parked where it should be when you return to the Louisville Midtown Bank."

"Understood, sir."

"Good I will see you when you get here, keep your eyes on the job and your ears and mind on the music playing. Do not leave early. When your host suggests it is time to go, then go and get a good rest—By the way, I expect you to win the tournament on Saturday. Have a good time," Ellis concluded.

"Thank, you Sir."

Margaret noticed a restroom just outside the elevator. She took a few minutes to look fresh and ready to party. When the elevator door opened, there was Jeff with two cups of hot rum in his hand. He offered one to Margaret.

"Hi, Jeff. Thank you for waiting for me, that was sweet of you."

"It was my pleasure. The outside temperature is getting cold, and the best remedy we have is dance and hot rum; it's good for our health and an excellent companion to the Caymanian spirit." He took Margaret's right hand and led her towards the living room where Allison and Thomas were engaged in deep conversation with another couple.

"Let's not interrupt Allison," said Margaret.

"Good idea," Jeff responded with a smile. "Why don't we sit by that water fountain, and while the band is taking a break, you and I can get to know each other. Okay?"

Margaret's mind was on the call with Ellis and focused on Jeff's presence. At the same time, she was feeling guilty about Johnathan and her loyalty to him. However, she could not deny that she was totally attracted to Jeff. Her mind was in a little turmoil as they walked towards the water fountain. The sound of the water was soft, and the smell of the sea inviting, and Margaret couldn't help but relax. Without realizing that the hot cup Jeff gave her was real rum, she took a sip and exclaimed, "Wow! This is hot." She was obviously a little distressed.

Jeff, alarmed by Margaret's reaction, took the cup and at nearly the same time, a vigilant waiter took the cup from Jeff and politely asked, "Are you, alright Madam? Don't be concerned. For many people, the hot rum with clove can be a little high." Margaret smiled at him and then turned to Jeff.

"Thank you, Jeff, I'm okay. This drink will be right. My mind was with my dad, and I carelessly took too big a sip."

They were sitting on a love seat. Margaret continued. "I'm excited about my Dad's trip to London. He receives the right news that a book he launched a year ago at the Book Expo America, in New York, made the bestseller list in the UK."

"Please give my congratulations to your father. What is the title of the book?"

"It's called, how do emotions drive money decisions? The subtitle is EURO."

"The title is intriguing, and the subject is my passion," said, Jeff. "I'll buy it tomorrow, and when you return next time, I'll give you my impressions."

While talking, Jeff held Margaret's left hand as lovers would, and said, "It sounds like you and your father have an excellent relationship and you care about his work, so the call was a good call for both of you?"

"We have a close relationship; he is a good guy and great friend. I can talk to him about anything and always he has either an answer or useful advice. I trust him. That's the real bond between us." Then, she quickly asked, "What about you?"

"Well, my father is the former Governor of the Caymans and, from his military career, tough as nails and demanding of my sister Lucia, and me. We're both investment bankers. She is with Wells Fargo International. She's smart, attractive, and a great mom. She has a ten-year-old daughter, Jean and a six-month boy, Ken. She has a special place in my heart and she's saved my good name more than once." Then, in a sadder tone, "Our mother died five years ago in a plane accident when landing in Havana. That night, there was dense fog, the pilot missed the runway and crashed into the reef. The thirty-eight people on board, including the crew, lost their lives, my mother among them."

Margaret's upper body turned towards Jeff with her right-hand she held his head and kissed his side of the face. "Oh, sweetheart, I feel sympathy for your plight." Then, realizing how familiar she must seem, she backed away and said, "Oops, sorry Jeff I got carried away with my feelings and the tragedy of your story."

"No, Margaret, there's nothing to apologize for. Your feelings betrayed you. Remember this, our words are born in our hearts, and when opinions are expressed spontaneously, they are true to our inner sense because they come from deep inside our subconscious mind."

Margaret was lost for words. Thankfully, at that moment the music started playing again. She said, "Let's go dance, I'm warm now and don't want to drink anymore."

Jeff and Margaret danced to hot music, Calypso, and slow, slow, very slow ballads, until five in the morning. All of a sudden, Allison approached and said, "You people, the party, is over. We need to take Margaret to the hotel and be at the bank by eleven-thirty when I'm to meet a new mega-investor coming from Colombia. He and his family own Bavaria, the oldest and largest beer brand in South America."

Jeff was still holding Margaret by the hand as they walked to the front of the club. While waiting for the cars to be brought by the parking attendant, Allison asked Jeff, "Do you have any appointments this morning?"

"No, my calendar is clear until 4:00 p.m. Why?"

"Jeff, would you do Thomas and me a favor? Please take Margaret to the hotel? It's on your way, and we live in the opposite direction. Do you mind Margaret?"

"Not at all! I feel safe with Jeff, and I'm pleased he doesn't have business to attend until four in the afternoon," Margaret said with a certain excitement in her voice.

Jeff and Margaret had to wait for some time for Jeff's car to show up. Meanwhile, the temperature was dropping, and Margaret started to shiver slightly. They continued to hold hands as was natural as a couple in a relationship. When Jeff noticed that Margaret was trembling, he took his coat and placed it on her shoulders. She looked at him with the eyes of a woman who just might be falling in love. At that moment a new silver Mercedes-Benz 500 SL showed up.

"Here we are honey, let's go home," said, Jeff.

Hum. 'Honey, let's go home,' was music to Margaret's ears. However, all of a sudden, in her mind the morning news alarm sounded. 'Sika Virus, a mosquito-bite infection.'

"Oh my goodness! I totally forgot I have a telephone conference call at eleven this morning," exclaimed Margaret.

As they drove off towards Seven Miles Beach, Jeff said, "No problem, I'll make sure you're awake in time for your call."

Jeff's mind was contemplating his desire for intimacy with Margaret. The passion grew with each mile driven. At the same time, he realized that any quick attempt to get Margaret to agree to let him sleep with her that night would ruin the possibilities of a meaningful and lasting relationship and would damage his professional reputation.

Margaret immediately thought,' what does he mean? Is he planning something? Please, Lord, help!'

Upon arrival at the hotel, Jeff said, "This is what we're going to do. You're going straight to bed. In five hours, I'll come back, and we'll have breakfast together and make sure you're alert before your conference call. Then after you're finished, I would like to invite you for an outing and continuing getting to know each other, what do you think?

"Honey, I love it," said Margaret.

Jeff opened the car door and walked with Margaret to the lobby. She totally forgot she was wearing his jacket and turned around and kissed him on the mouth. In turn, he held her tight, and, while kissing her, removed his coat. "Honey, I'll see you here in five hours. Sweet dreams."

As Margaret walked towards her room, her mind floated over the evening's events. She could think of nothing else, except how the sky full of stars moved her, how attracted she was to Jeff and the feeling of security he gave her.

At 10:00 a.m. the next morning Jeff arrived at the hotel and, not knowing Margaret's room number, he went to reception and asked the attendant to connect him with Ms. Gianelli's room.

On this day, Chayton was on duty and said "One moment please, Margaret's phone rang and rang, but there was no answer. He tried again, the same result. Then Chayton called Kathy, who had just arrived at her duties. "Kathy, please come to the front desk, I have a visitor for Ms. Gianelli."

"I will be right there."

"Sir, may I have your name please?" Asked Chayton.

"Jeff McNeil, with J.P. Morgan."

Kathy, this is Mr. McNeil. He is looking for Ms. Gianelli, I have called her room, several times. However, she's not responding. Would you please take care of Mr. McNeil?"

"Mr. McNeil, I'm Kathy, Ms. Gianelli's personal assistant, would you like a cup of coffee while I locate Ms. Gianelli for you? It may take a few minutes. I will find and be back as soon as locate her."

"Thank you, I'll wait here." Said Jeff.

Promptly Kathy went to Margaret's room and knocked, but there was no answer, then she opened the door and said, "Ms. Gianelli, I'm Kathy, are you here?"

In a barely audible voice and sounding very sleepy, "Come in Kathy."

Chapter 31
SURPRISE PACKAGE

"Surprise! Surprise, it's time to get up! There's a tall, most attractive Caymanian man in the lobby. He wants to see you, He says his name is Jeff."

"Oh, honey! Are you here?" shouted Margaret as she sprang to a seating position in bed.

"No, no, no I'm not your honey. It's Kathy."

"Oh, Kathy!" Margaret said to cover her momentary confusion. "He's my gift from last night, he's beautiful, I'm so attracted to him, that if he had asked me last night to stay with me here in this very bed, I would have said, yes, here I am!"

"Okay," said Kathy, smiling. "For now, let me help you to get ready. He's wearing white and yellow, so let's make you look your best so that honey will melt in your arms!"

In a tone of a hurry and quasi-desperation, Margaret said, "I'm supposed to have a telephone conference at eleven this morning, and he kept his promise to be here an hour before to have breakfast with me in preparation for my call, what am I to do?"

"Don't worry. At eleven sharp, I'll be your conference call. My name will be Ms. Winder. For now, I'll go and let him know you'll be in the lobby in a few minutes, Okay?"

"Thank you. I'll be ready in a flash," said Margaret.

Kathy hurried to the lobby and in a very business-like manner said to Jeff, "Mr. McNeil, I found Ms. Gianelli. She is finishing some papers for her conference call from the States, and will be here as soon as possible," Then she returned and found Margaret getting a yellow and white outfit ready to wear

"What did you say?" Margaret asked.

"I said, you were finishing some papers in preparation for your conference call from the United States."

With a sense of relief, and in a confident and fully awaken voice, Margaret said, "Thank you, Kathy, I mean Ms. Winder. It was awesome!"

Margaret, accompanied by Kathy, briskly walked to the lobby. Just before they enter Jeff's view, they noticed he is talking to another equally handsome man. They stop. While waiting, Kathy asked, "How was your time last night?"

"Oh dear! Oh. My goodness, we have to talk about it after my conference call. You know, being with him were some of the best moments of my life." Said Margaret.

At that moment, Jeff turned and saw Margaret. Kathy went ahead and said, "Mr. McNeil, here is Ms. Gianelli, have a good day."

Looking at Margaret with puppy lover's eyes, Jeff said to Kathy, "Thank you, very kind of you to find this beautiful woman." Jeff's friend was standing in silence capturing the whole episode, a pleasant smile on his face.

"Good morning honey, I'm happy to see that you kept your promise," said Margaret as she kissed him on the mouth.

"Honey, this is my best friend, rival, and notable workaholic, Peter De Santos, who is here to see one of my prospective clients. However, the best investment of my life and my time is you, Margaret!"

"Oh my goodness! What am I to say? You two are made for each other. Ambitious, determined, and equally handsome cats!"

"What a jewel you found, JJ," said Peter. At that moment, a short, robust looking man wearing a Panama hat, and an equally healthy female with a similar hat stopped a few feet away. Peter said, "It is a pleasure to meet you, I hope you, and JJ would consider this evening, a little Champaign sea tour of the islands. I'm free from seven to eight. JJ, please call and confirm. Now, I'm going to work on making some money!"

"Okay, Peter, we'll call if that is what my honey would like to do!"

Peter walked away and greeted the couple, waiting for him.

Let's go to my house and have breakfast there. You can take the call, and if convenient we can determine, how we would spend the day, so we can get to know each other a little more," said, Jeff.

They got into Jeff's car and when they were almost there when Margaret, suddenly exclaimed, "Honey! I know this area, I was here yesterday, taking possession of that pink house, over there with the little palm tree to the side. The bank bought that house from Prince Aamir from Saudi Arabia."

"Prince Aamir, did you say?"

"Yes. Prince Aamir of Saudi Arabia," Margaret repeated.

"Well, honey, the world is a small handkerchief. Prince Aamir is the Finance Minister of Saudi Arabia and my longtime client. Yesterday, we spent much of the day revising his investment portfolio and agreeing on a new investment strategy, until three-thirty in the afternoon, when he said, he had some other business to attend before departing for Miami."

"So, we have one business thing in common. The Prince sold that pink house to our bank, and we closed the deal yesterday at four in the afternoon," said Margaret.

"Honey here to the left on the corner, the big white and terracotta color house is my house, and I hope to say some day, "our house."

From a distance a beautiful German shepherd ran at full speed from the beach, and jumped on Margaret, as if she were a longtime friend, returning from a long absence. It licked her face, and then jumped on Jeff, then ran back at full speed to the beach and jumped on Esther, the housekeeper, who was sunbathing, while playing with the dog.

Jeff, at the top of his voice, called, "Esther, we're here for breakfast."

"Sir, I will be right there, please give me a minute to collect my papers, and calm Itania down. She's going crazy over your visitor."

Jeff took Margaret's arm and in a modulated tone said, "Come honey; this is where I am when I'm not working, or attending a business meeting, or charitable function. I love to stay at home, I love to study, and I like to dream, waiting for the Lord to show me YOU!"

They entered through the front door and immediately Margaret stopped, eyes open wide.

"Wow! Look at the view! It's as the sea is pounding onto your large windows. There is an extraordinary feeling of the ocean in your living room. No wonder you enjoy staying at home," Then she turned and looked at Jeff, as he was a view as equally magnificent. "Who calls you JJ?

"That was my mother's name when I wasn't taking care of my obligations. Whenever I hear JJ, it translates as 'pay attention!' It's not necessarily bad, it just makes me stop for a moment and pay attention to the caller.

At eleven o'clock Margaret's phone rang. She was so distracted by the view that she failed to answer, and Jeff said, "Honey, your phone is ringing, it may be your conference call. I'll be upstairs. Feel free to take your call in my office but close the door; Itania will run in at any moment, and she doesn't respect telephones or anybody for that matter when she wants to show affection."

Jeff shut the door to his office as Margaret said, "Hello…? Yes, this is Margaret Gianelli. Ms. Winder, I appreciate you calling, please know that I'm out of the country. May I call you back at the registered number on my phone?" Margaret hung up and then punched a button. "This is Margaret," let's renew our call please." She paused, listening. "Oh, I see…, the situation last night was one that can't be put into words… Yes, the package was divine in all respects. The bow, the wrapping tape, and the box were solid. When I tore open the wrapping, the feel of the box was smooth to the touch. It smelled delicious; there was a suggestion of citrus, so very enticing I didn't know whether to open the box, hold it tight, or simply eat the inside. Oh. Yes! I will be playing golf tomorrow. We should be finished by four in the afternoon, I will be in my room at that time, please call me then, better yet, I will call you, so we can conclude the report for the Senator."

"Thank you, so much "Ms. Winder." We'll talk tomorrow," Margaret concluded.

She opened Jeff's office door, and sure enough, Itania was sitting and waiting to jump. She nearly knocked Margaret to the floor. Jeff, hearing the commotion, rapidly showed up and in a commanding voice, "Itania, down!" Instantly, the dog laid down and looked at Jeff as if to say 'I wasn't doing anything wrong.'

"Thank you, honey," Margaret said, catching her breath, "she is lovely and would love my German shepherd, Rome,"

"Rome's a male? He'd be fantastic company for Itania. Her hormones are jumping since last week, and the only way to calm her is to take her for a boat ride on the ocean. She loves the water, and when a big fish shows up, she jumps in to chase the fish to no avail," said Jeff.

"Honey, who else calls you JJ besides your mother?

My best friend Peter, who grew up with me, has always called me JJ." Jeff pushed a button to lower the top to bottom translucent shades to block the brightness of the sun reflecting off the water, "Please turn around, and let me show you the rest of my place. This is the dining room. I only use it for formal occasions."

At that moment, Esther arrived from the beach.

"Margaret, this is Esther, my house administrator. To her credit is the immaculate condition of my home, my car, my golf equipment, and the health of Itania and me. She feeds us, and our health is her top priority.

With a slight German accent, Esther said, "Nice to meet you Madam Margaret."

"The pleasure is mine, Esther," said Margaret.

"This morning, before picking you up at the hotel, I called my office and changed some appointments so I can spend the day with you. We can talk, and get to each other know more." He raised his arms, palms to the sky. "I'm showing you who I am. I'm a romantic at heart, I love music, love the opera, and classical piano and strings. Also, I love Jazz, Caymanian tropical, and slow ballad music. I'm a voracious reader. I like to read subjects I don't know anything about, I love to study and learn every day. Unless I learn something new each day, I feel incomplete. That is why I read the Book of Life, in the morning, and evening, no matter the time I get home. As you know by now, we Caymanians are about money. However, I'm about blessed money, and plenty of that comes my way, in the form of new and repeat business."

Esther's in a loud voice from the kitchen, said, "Sir and Madam Margaret, breakfast is served under the canopy on the terrace. I wish you both a lovely day, I'm giving Itania a nice long ride on my boat and we'll be back at five this afternoon."

"Have a safe day," said Jeff.

Margaret stood during this exchange looking at Jeff's shelves. "I see what you mean. Your house sounds like my father's office; there are more books than free space,"

Then Jeff led Margret by the hand to a spiral stairway. "This is the day dining room: there to the left is a guest studio, to the right the guest bedroom. One more floor up and here is my room."

With an admiring tone, Margaret exclaimed, "Your bedroom takes the entire floor, and from the headboard of your bed, you are facing the Caribbean! What a view! It's so romantic."

"Let's go up one more floor, and that is where I love to spend time early in the morning and late afternoon," said Jeff.

The terrace overlooked the Caribbean. It was fenced with Italian water drop posts ten inches in diameter and decorated with seven, ten-foot tall palm trees, planted in large terracotta planters. These trees were strategically located to block outsiders from invading Jeff's privacy.

Margaret was spellbound by the site's beauty. Then, all of a sudden, Rachmaninoff's Piano Concerto Number Two was playing on the terrace loud enough to drown the surf.

Margaret couldn't help her emotions and briskly turned into Jeff's' arms and passionately kissed him. Then, she said, "This is my favorite classical piece, I love it, love the power it represents, I love you JJ!" He held her tightly."

I believe I'm falling in love with you, Margaret. I'm planning to know all about you between now and the time of your departure to Louisville."

Quick thinking Margaret, discerning the potential consequences of her hormonal disarray, the weight of her spontaneous reaction to the music, said, "Honey, let's have breakfast, and you tell me what you want me to know about you. Because I will be coming back within thirty days to complete two assignments Mr. Jordan entrusted to me. Then it will be my turn to open up and let you know who I am."

"That seems fair," Jeff responded.

While listening to Rachmaninoff, they ate a light breakfast of fresh fruit, yogurt, lavender tea and fresh oven baked bread. Then, as agreed Jeff related the background of his life from as far back as he could remember, laughing a little, and at times feeling near tears. All the while Margaret and Jeff held hands, touching each other's hair, passing kisses and caresses to and fro.

At two in the afternoon, Jeff said, "Honey, I'm a good cook, I gave the recipe of my mother's dish to Eric, my friend, and the Chef at the Blue restaurant in the Ritz Carlton Hotel. I'm going to prepare for you seared cobia in red wine sauce, beluga lentils, and bok choi with a citrus mustard emulsion. What do you think?"

"Honey, that sounds delicious, and I'm hungry," said Margaret. Then she added, "I'm not a cook. However, I'm a good team player and willing to learn to make our lunch a time to remember."

Let me go downstairs to start cooking. Meanwhile, feel free to roam around this house as in a discovery trip. I want you to feel free like I'm giving you full access to open the book of my life."

Margaret was lost for words. She could not imagine that the man she just met less than twenty-four hours ago was capable of being so real and transparent. After a moment of bewilderment, she regained control, and in a soft voice, said: "Do you mean, I'm free to walk around, be curious, and ask questions?"

"Yes, honey. That is what I want you to do, to become intimately familiar with every corner of this house, to experience what I feel when I'm here. I want you to be able to picture in your mind where I am when you are in Louisville, and we're speaking on the phone. This is my vision of spending time away from you while remaining close. Because unless we are able to see in our mind's eyes, and understand what we are about, the separation in time, and distance will hinder our growing relationship, rather than enhancing our understanding of each other to move closer, and respond to the Lord's will for our lives."

"Okay, JJ! I will do as you say and if I have a question, I will come downstairs and ask, or if need guidance, I'll pray," said Margaret.

"It's settled."

Then the music coming over the speakers turned to Caribbean tropical themes. Margaret, with the curiosity of a woman, began a real estate like walkthrough inspection, looking at every nook and corner, opening doors, closing other doors, touching shirts, watching the precision lining of his underwear, the color coordination of his shirts, suits, ties, socks, and shoes.

While Margaret was going through this exercise, her conscience was growing dark, thinking that she was betraying Johnathan. The conflict in her heart grew as she subconsciously compared Jeff's bright, orderly personality to the disarray of Jonathan's apartment and the money he spent on emergency clean ups when friends came to visit him. In a moment of inner conflict, she sat on the floor at the foot of Jeff's bed looking at the majestic power of the sea. For a brief moment, in silence, tears rolled down her rosy cheeks.

Margaret at this time did not know what to do, did not know if her jumping hormones were the culprit, or whether she really was falling in love with Jeff. Then, in anticipation of the possibility that Jeff might come up and surprise her, she went to the main bathroom to freshen up and straighten her already wrinkled dress. When she opened the door, the brightness forced her to look to her left. At the top of her voice, Margaret exclaimed, "Wow! I could never imagine the ocean in a Roman bathtub! What a lovely site! I'm feeling sexy! Boiling! If I didn't have principles, I'd undress and call, JJ! JJ! Come here." As she was checking her makeup, she saw Jeff in the mirror.

He was leaning against the open door, looking at her with wistful eyes. In a loving, soft voice, he said: "Honey, your wishes will come right after lunch, after dinner, after a sea ride, after the golf tournament tomorrow, and after you return from Louisville being sure, you are feeling then as sexy, and hot as you are feeling now!"

Margaret was embarrassed by being caught expressing her real feelings. With a red face, and in a sweet tone she said, "Honey. JJ. My sweetheart, I apologize for my exuberance, I'm feeling so passionate today that has done things and said things that in my normal behavior, I would never do."

In an equally friendly tone of voice, Jeff said, "Let us jot down this partial deposit of who you are, to your new investment account to be open upon your return from Louisville.

To divert the situation, Margaret said, "You are a fair man. Is lunch ready?"

At that moment, the music changed to slow dance tunes and immediately Jeff said, "Honey, before lunch, let's dance right here in my room, and we can slowly dance to the dining room and dance until we are so hungry we'll have to stop. He pulled her onto his muscular chest. There Margaret began to lean into his neck and feel the power of his ocean-swimmer legs. They danced for a couple of minutes, and then she said, "My JJ I'm hungry."

"Good. I am too, so let's go down and enjoy the view and the food."

Again, from the day dining, table one could see the ocean, Margaret asked, "Is this house designed so that one can see the ocean view from everywhere?"

"Yes, honey. Peter's father, Arnold is the most famous architect in the Caribbean islands, and he designed this home specifically for me and my lifestyle, and I love it. That is why I'm happy at home. This is me. This is what I worked hard to own and paid for in full. I'm former SASR, and we are aquatic people."

Margaret looked at him quizzically and almost embarrassed, she asked, "What is SASR?"

In an assured voice, Jeff said, "The SASR is the number one British Special Forces unit; the United States Navy SEALS are number two in the world."

"So, you are like a fish in the ocean, on the dancing floor, and in the kitchen, are you?

'Yes, honey I can communicate with dolphins and they know me. When you return, I will take you a few miles into the ocean and show you what I mean. Are you a good swimmer?"

"Oh. Yes!" Margaret responded. "I swim in my bathtub and instead of living dolphins my duck rubber swims around me and the bubbles!" The laughing got so loud and vivacious that Jeff did not notice the cobia beginning to smoke. "Honey, honey turn around and push that red button, please. It's the rapid smoke extractor. Let's say that cobia is feeling sexy, sweltering, and the heat is taking over the cook's attention!

Lunch was a unique experience while outside it rained in a sudden, tropical downpour. Now, light jazz piano music was slowing the mood and setting the tone for more of Jeff's life disclosures. Margaret cuddled on his chest on the sofa facing the ocean. Time was passing so fast that at 5:00 p.m., Itania made a grand entry and jumped on top of Margaret and Jeff. There was copious face licking right and left. Suddenly they heard Esther commanding voice. "Platz." The dog ended her show and laid down next to the sofa, facing towards the ocean and behaving as if waiting for the next attacking command.

Margaret was feeling intense sexual desires, and realizing the potentially irreversible consequence of letting her cricket hormones take over, in a matter of fact tone of voice, said, "My honey. My JJ, as much as I want to stay longer, I have to complete some work before seven this evening and must take some time to change gears from romance to deadly serious business.

Chapter 32
ODDS

At six in the evening, Jeff brought Margaret to the hotel, and after a long time hugging and kissing in his car, he said, "Honey, please rest well tonight. Tomorrow at the Golf Challenge we're in competition, I'm playing with the J.P. Morgan team, and we're committed to winning!"

Well, my sweet JJ. My honey, we from the Caribbean Louisville Midtown Bank will be the winners. The chance to excel is enough motivation for me to focus on relaxing, doing my work this evening, and being ready to win like I'm accustomed to! So good night, my JJ! My Dolphin friend!"

Upon arriving at her room, Margaret called Kathy. When she got voicemail, Margaret left a message. "Hello, this is Margaret, when available, please come to my room, I have some news to tell you; I want to call my parents and, depending on our conversation, call Johnathan,"

After two minutes Kathy called, "You, sound like something has, or is about to happen, right?"

Margaret said, "You could say that. Right now I'm up to my ears with live crickets on one side, alligators on the other, Johnathan waving at me while Jeff is throwing himself into the ocean to save my skin."

"That sounds a bit complicated. However, I have the "Winder' pill that can suck all the crickets, kill the eight-ton alligator, put Jonathan to sleep, and eat Jeff for dinner." said Kathy.

Margaret laughed out loud and said, "Kathy, I will see you when you get here."

In just a few minutes Kathy knocked at the door, but Margaret didn't answer. "Hello Ms. Gianelli, I'm here." Then Kathy used her master key to enter the room and found Margaret sound asleep on top of her bed, fully dressed and holding onto the flowers, Jeff had brought her in the morning. Kathy decided to let her sleep and quietly returned to her duties. On her way she saw Larry and Nancy arguing near the lobby. Kathy made sure they didn't see her.

At 10:15 a.m. Margaret woke up, and after seeing she was still dressed and on top of her bed, she called Kathy and said, "Are you still at the hotel?"

With a sympathetic tone, Kathy said, "No, Ms. Gianelli, I'm almost home, however, if you need me I'll be happy to return and see if I can bring you the "Winder' pill."

"Oh. That's okay Kathy. I guess the Lord wants to talk to me alone, I'm going to take a bath and keep the ears of my heart open because this "Winder' pill either kills the pain or puts me back to sleep. You understand, don't you?"

"Yes, Ms. Gianelli, not only do I know, I feel for you because I'm working at the hotel due to a similar situation," said Kathy.

"Oh. That's interesting. If you don't mind, please tell me your experience. Maybe that's the Lord using you to talk to me,"

"Let me park my car, go into my bedroom and will call you back in a few minutes. How would that be?

Margaret said, "Great, in that case, I'll take a shower and be beautiful and cozy in bed when you call."

"Okay, I'll call you," said Kathy.

Forty-five minutes later, the phone rang. There was no answer. A few minutes later, Kathy called again, and this time, Margaret picked up. "Hello Ms. Gianelli, are you alright?"

"Yes, I am. Perhaps while I was singing, 'Happy' at the top of my voice and didn't hear the phone, sorry," Margaret then proceeded to give Kathy a blow by blow detail of her breakfast, and lunch with Jeff.

After she had finished Kathy said, "Well . . . As I told you a little while ago, I had a similar situation, except no 'Winder' pill. I came to the Cayman on a Caribbean tour seven years ago, as a pre-wedding getaway gift to myself. I came with my sister and Mitzi, my best friend. We went out one evening, and our car had a flat tire. It was raining like crazy, it was darker than anything I ever remember when a handsome Caymanian and his friend stopped and helped us change the tire. He asked me my name and where we were staying, and I told him. The next morning the desk clerk called my room and said Ms. Bloomington, I'm sending a lady with a gift for you' 'A gift for me?' I said, and he said, 'Yes, the florist delivered a bouquet of roses for you.'

Kathy's eyes were shining with the memory. "I was so anxious, curious and at the same time excited to discover who could have sent me flowers, I didn't know anyone in the Caymans. Ms. Gianelli, when the lady knocked on my door, I was shaking, and my voice sounded like I was giggling…"

Interrupting in an excited voice, Margaret said, "Please, don't stop! Tell me who the mysterious sender was?"

"The Human Resources Director of this hotel, and since two weeks after my return to New Your, my present husband! We have a three years old girl, and we both work at the hotel, my mother lives with us and takes excellent care of our daughter Gina."

"Oh. Kathy, I'm so grateful, because now I can go back to sleep and be ready to win the tournament tomorrow. Thank you, thank you, Kathy for your beautiful story, thank you for your unconditional friendship. Then, Margaret asked, "Are you on duty tomorrow?"

"Yes, I am. I'll see you after the tournament, good night Ms. Gianelli."

"Good night, Kathy!"

Soon it was 6:00 a.m. on Saturday; a beautiful but windy day, the temperature was 65° and the prediction for midday was 85°.

Margaret was on her knees, talking to God and in a loud voice, asking, "Please speak to me. I need to hear from You, Lord. I need to know what's up with Johnathan, I'm feeling depressed. I need you to talk to me about what to do or say to JJ. I'm in trouble; my heart is not at peace. I'm supposed to be part of the winning team. However, my mind is being pulled in two directions. You brought me this assignment, now I'm asking to get me out, or direct my heart. Please, Lord, be merciful to me, please, please."

At 8:30, Margaret's phone rang. It was Nancy. Her voice was worried, almost hysterical. "We're here at the golf shop and our starting time is nine. Get moving and be here on the double!"

"Hello? Sorry Nancy, I'm tied up," Margaret responded.

"What do you mean you're tied up? Who is there with you, that you can't be here?

In a calming, soft and whispering tone, Margaret said, "Nancy, I'm talking to God right now about winning the tournament, and other heavy-duty stuff. Please, Nancy, relax. I'll be there as soon as I hear the answer but until then I can't move. You have no idea, how tough it is to get off your knees when they're glued to the floor. You have no idea who the competitors are. Yesterday afternoon, I heard that the British are coming, and sending people from the SASR team to play! You know those are the guys who eat our SEALS for lunch, and as far as I believe, the only one who can help us eat SASR, SEALS, and tigers in this tournament is God!"

There was a pause, then Nancy replied in a more smooth voice, "Look, you crazy nut, get over to the pro shop as quickly as you hear the answer, we have some big money on the plate, so add this request to your conversation menu."

Immediately Nancy told Allison and Larry the details of her conversation with Margaret. In a modulated voice, Larry said, "Based on my observations of Margaret, she has steadfast faith. Her belief system is so powerful, she may be the one eating SASR, SEALS, and

AIRS. Should that happen, I may be saving some heavy duty money, or making me some real money."

Just as Allison was about to make a comment, Margaret suddenly appeared.

"Good morning Mr. Jordan, Allison and you Nancy, good morning again."

We have ten minutes before the starting tee, said Nancy, "What's God's word?"

"He does not speak like you and me. He whispers into our hearts," said Margaret.

"What did He say?" Larry asked.

"To the best of my human recollection, in summary," said Margaret, "You people keep a good attitude. Don't use foul language even if you miss the shoot; don't belittle anyone, and love one another as He loves Mr. Jordan, Nancy, Allison, and me. As to the animals, He said, fear not because I am with you! That was all he whispered in the ears of my heart.

"Okay, we're up!" Nancy exclaimed.

JORGE RIVERA

Chapter 33
SUDDEN DEATH

The Chamber of Commerce Annual Golf Challenge was on; the morning temperature was rising steadily; the winds were fearsome, blowing forty-five miles an hour; the team member's nerves were tight as violin strings.

During the game, there was little or no conversation. The players were focused on the match and winning was on everyone's mind and heart. It meant a great deal to all, although in different ways. Larry and Nancy had open and side bets worth the heavy-duty money, Allison's efforts to give her bank international exposure was at stake, not to mention Margaret's reputation as a professional player. Also, Margaret knew that Jeff McNeil, her "JJ," was out there with the J.P. Morgan team, determined to show how the SASR could defeat anyone alive. For her, the competition was double jeopardy.

However, she also remembered her father's words: "When in danger, pray, and remember God is with you, and there is always someone better that you are." As her turn came, she walked up to the tee and in a loud and absolutely confidence voice, said, "Lord, this is your game, show us how to play it."

In unison, the team said "Amen!"

The front nine did not go as expected. Larry and Allison missed the green on two consecutive holes. Nancy was playing par with Margaret; the silent tension was felt a mile away. Coming to the last hole, the island green, Allison got a hole-in-one. She was speechless, and said, "I just copied Margaret, and played a four iron. What an experience! My very first, hole-in-one, after fifteen years of playing golf!

Regardless of the average team score, the hole-in-one was a shot of adrenalin. It was a sign. Nancy yelled, "We'll win, and I'm making some real money when we do. Also, Allison has a surprise, so does anyone who can bring up the team score to win the golf tournament. Larry and I said Nancy are playing against three other banks, and if we lose, my personal profits from the house deal will go down the drain."

In silence, Margaret listened to the outburst about the gambling, and she noted Larry's silent reaction.

Each team member played the last nine holes exceptionally well. In fact, on the last hole, Nancy scored a hole-in-one, and so did Margaret. With such fortune, it was hard for the Caribbean-Louisville Midtown Bank not to feel victorious, and already they were celebrating at the clubhouse. When the last team completed the final hole, everyone came out to hear the result.

The tension, suspense, and silence were healthy as the President of the Chamber of Commerce stepped to the microphone to announce the results. He tapped and cleared this throat and finally, he said, "Ladies and Gentlemen, we have a tie! J.P Morgan will play three holes sudden death against the Caribbean Louisville Midtown Bank." There were gasps from the crowd as the president continued, "To make this fair the Chamber of Commerce Board of Directors will randomly select the name of the player that will represent each team. "Please, everyone should move to the Seventh Tee to cheer the players on. Listen, please, all participants gather and wait at the Seventh Tee for my announcement, thank you!"

Larry, Nancy, Allison, and Margaret were dumbfounded at the decision, because after ending with the spectacular double holes-in-one, they had been sure of victory and had been planning a big victory party.

Margaret was especially dumbfounded. She thought, 'if I'm selected to play, I might be playing against Jeff, and that will be too much for me. Out loud she said, "Lord, please hear my prayer! Let some else to play, not me!"

A member of the board of directors came up and handed the president a slip of paper. The Chamber President read it and then said, "Listen up! Listen up! All teams! From the Caribbean Louisville Midtown Bank, shooting first will be Ms. Nancy McArthur! From the J.P Morgan Team, Ms. Kristy Rogers. Good luck and cheers to the champions."

Margaret, in a friendly tone of voice, approached Nancy and said, "Let me be your caddy, Nancy. We'll team up to read the topography, and I can guide you. I know we'll eat the SASR, the SEALS, and the AIRS, and any other animal they send our way."

"Oh. Margaret, that's wonderful! Please, be my caddy and reader."

With exuberance in his voice, Larry said, "Margaret, that's a brilliant idea."

Allison nodded. "I agree. Who can be a better caddy and terrain reader than Margaret? After all, she's the only professional player on our team. Go for it and let's take the trophy to the lobby of my bank."

At the Seventh Tee, all eyes were on Nancy. While standing in the line of fire, in a delicate tone of voice, Margaret said, "Focus on the far left side of the green. Slowly bring the driver back, paralleled to the ground, relax while coiling your upper torso, when you feel that's all you can go back, in your mind, attempt to kick the ball with your right knee and let it go!"

As Nancy uncoiled her upper body and shot, there was a "click!" sound. It indicated that she had hit the ball on the club's sweet spot. As planned, the ball glided left but the wind pushed it right, and it fell and bounced in the center of the fairway.

As Nancy saw her ball stopping, she turned to Margaret, "You are one hell of a caddy!"

She smiled, "we'll win this babe and make some real money!"

The second shot landed Nancy's ball within a few inches of the flag. This made her more excited and expressive. Then Margaret turned towards her and in a soothing voice said, "Nancy, please blank your mind of everything and focus on my voice. Relax, and become one with the target. I'm giving you the same advice my university coach has always given me. Do you understand? Are we in agreement?"

Nancy nodded vigorously. "We're in agreement, I want to win this more than anything."

Each and every shot was pre-planned and executed to perfection. At the last tee, facing the island green, in a quasi-commanding voice Margaret, said, "Nancy, do you see the far left top branch of that last palm tree?" Margaret pointed, "That one, behind the green? That is your target! I want you to stand behind your ball, without taking your eyes from the target. I'll put a four iron in your hand. Hold the club lightly but, correctly, the Ben Hogan way. Do not look at anything else. Don't hear anything. Breathe slowly in and exhale slowly out. When you are on the target's vertical and horizontal cross hairs, slowly pull your club back and let it all go!"

In a passive voice, Nancy said, "Understood!

Kristy's shot landed in the water. Then it was Nancy's last chance to win or tie the score and force an additional hole to play. Margaret was to her right, tossing blades of grass in the air. Then she approached Nancy and said, "Describe what you see, and tell me what you are feeling."

In a voice, sounding as if she was speaking into a hollow pipe, Nancy said, "I see the thick palm branch hanging over the green, I'm feeling as if I'm touching it with my hand."

Margaret whispered, "The flag and your hand are one, go ahead and place the ball into the target cup."

Without a word, Nancy brought her club slowly back parallel to the ground, simultaneously cooling her body. Then with a right knee kick towards the ball, she uncoiled her upper torso to make a powerful shot.

The ball whistled against the fierce wind. It was almost suspended in the air; then slowly it descended onto to the surface of the green, rolled slowly, very slowly to the right and stopped at the lip of the cup. A few seconds later the ball disappeared. Nancy remained as if in a trance. She didn't realize she just scored another hole in one and won the tournament for the Caribbean Louisville Midtown Bank.

The cheers and screams brought Nancy back to her senses, and she said, "Margaret, what a coach you are! You won this tournament. I'll never forget this extraordinary experience as long as I live."

At the celebration dinner, Jeff and Margaret were so wrapped into each other that Margaret missed her name being called by the President of the Chamber of Commerce to receive the award as the tournament's best player. Time was moving at the speed of light for Margaret and Jeff, nothing was as important as to establishing a clear method of communication and personal priorities for their next face-to-face meeting, anticipated within three weeks.

Sunday, at ten in the morning, Jeff appeared in the hotel's lobby to say goodbye to Margaret. Instead, he found out from the receptionist, that she just left for the airport. As if racing in the Indianapolis 500, his Mercedes Benz drove with such speed it produced a whistling sound when passing the trees lining the road to the airport. He arrived in time to give her a hug and see her off to Louisville.

Once on the plane, Nancy said to Margaret, "Margaret, there is no question that you are in love with Jeff, and he with you. Last night Larry and I decided that observing you two was simply precious and decided to wait until now to give you in private, the last surprise of the tournament."

"What is it?" asked Margaret.

With a smile and in a kind voice, Larry opened his briefcase and handed Margaret a large manila envelope, marked "Hole in One Winner."

"Do I open it now, or in private?"

"Go ahead open it now," Nancy said.

Slowly, and carefully, Margaret opened the envelope. Inside there were six bundles of ten brand new $100 bills each.

"Wow! What's the meaning of this money?" asked Margaret.

In a matter-of-fact tone of voice, Larry said, "The first $1,000 represents a side bet between Nancy and me, for your hole in one. The remaining $5,000 is your cut of the bets between three other banks and us."

"Mr. Jordan, what do you mean my cut? I didn't bet, nor did I contribute any money to the betting pool."

Nancy smiled. "Don't worry. This is just ten percent of the $50,000 wager on the outcome of the tournament."

"Wow, Wow! This is real money, I can't wait to see Prince Aamir's face when I tell him the story of my making real money in sudden death," Margaret exclaimed.

Hearing Captain Rogers, announce that they would be landing shortly in Miami Margaret asked, "Are we already in Miami? The time is passing so fast, I'm in complete shock!"

Looking out the window and returning her attention to Larry, Margaret said, "Thank you so much, I'm going to enjoy every bit of this money, I will use it to return to the Caymans during my two weeks vacations."

At the airport, while the aircraft was undergoing TSA inspection and refueling before continuing on to Louisville, Margate called Jeff. His phone rang four times and when to voice mail "This is Jeff McNeil, I'm not available to take your call, please leave me a detailed message, including country and area codes and telephone number. I will return this call within 24 hours. Thank you. Beep…!"

"Honey, it's Margaret. Thank you for rushing to see me off the airport. That means a lot to me. My JJ, we're in Miami, and while the aircraft is undergoing inspection, I want to tell you, I'm planning to return to the Cayman and spend my two weeks vacations with you. I just made $6,000 unexpected money, and strongly feel that the best investment of this real money is to do whatever you'd like us to do, as long as we are together. More details when we speak from Louisville, I love you my SASR man!"

At two o'clock in the afternoon on Sunday, upon arriving at Bowman Field Airport, in Louisville, Carlos was waiting by the arrivals exit. In a matter of fact tone of voice, Larry said, Carlos, please take Margaret to her house, while Nancy and I caring for some business here at the airport. We will be waiting for you at "Bistro Le Relais."

"Very well, Sir," said Carlos.

In a friendly voice, Nancy said, "Margaret, last night Larry and I decided that all of us will be taking Monday off, and we'll continue with the agreed upon plans on Tuesday. Please enjoy a free Monday. I'll see you on Tuesday to turn over to you my office because I'll be on vacation as of Wednesday."

"Thank you for the time off, I'm planning to sleep and rest. This week has been a real experience, and I feel exhausted," said Margaret.

On the way to Margaret's house, Carlos asked, "How was your trip, Ms. Margaret?

"We had a productive time, and won the Chamber of Commerce Golf Tournament, besides I met a real Saudi Prince and the man of my dreams!

"That's wonderful. Ms. Margaret. Congratulations," said Carlos.

"Thank you, we are already here. Look Carlos! Rome is going crazy, I better be ready for a welcome licking and keep my eyes covered,"

"Shall I put the golf equipment and your carry-on bag in the garage?"

"Yes, please." Margaret noticed her little brother Bobby, his friend, Jonny, and Rome playing and chasing after a tennis ball.

"Hey guys," she shouted when she got out of the car. "Where are mom and dad?"

Sure enough, Rome came running up and licked Margaret's face, Bobby's and Johnny, moved to the end of the front lawn and back. Over his shoulder, Bobby said, "They're upstairs watching the football game, and we're playing until mom calls us."

"Ms. Margaret, is there anything else you need?" asked Carlos.

"No, thank you, Carlos. Have a nice rest of the weekend."

She turned and watched her brother for a moment. Then she shouted, "Okay, guys, I'm tired from my trip and want to sleep for a little while till mom and dad are free. Please, don't disturb me, nor mom and dad, okay?"

Bobby and Jonny, shouted back, "Okay, okay! Bye, bye, baby!

Chapter 34
MISSION

At six o'clock in the morning on the first Monday of December 2014, it was cloudy almost dark; the weather was 29 degrees Fahrenheit in Woodland Hills. The fresh aroma of Hazelnut coffee woke Margaret Gianelli. She checked her iPhone's calendar and in a loud voice, exclaimed, "Mom, Mom…, I'm here, I arrived yesterday and fell asleep. Are you in the kitchen?"

From downstairs came her mother's reply. "Yes, honey, I'm in the kitchen. Come on down, and have some coffee before the troops are awake and we can't even talk."

Margaret rushed downstairs in her pajamas, and exuberantly whispered, "Oh, my goodness Mom, I'm feeling great, and I mean great! I feel like I've never felt before."

"Here, be careful this coffee is piping hot. Before anyone gets here, tell me all about your trip, I'm dying to hear all, and I mean all, in detail. You look radiant and beautiful. There is something exciting about you. There is no greater reward to a mother than to see her child blossom and sparkle."

"Well mom, this is going to be just an appetizer because I must be at the bank at eight o'clock sharp. Therefore, here are the facts and the facts only. Details, this evening when Bobby and Rome are asleep. I'm in trouble mom, and deeply in love with Jeff."

Before Margaret could finish Janet jumped in, "Jeff! Who is Jeff?"

"Well mom, Jeff is the son of the former Governor of the Cayman Islands, his mom, a former investment banker died in a plane accident while landing in Havana, Cuba. He is half an arm taller than me—this much." She shows Jeff's height with her arms half extended over her head. "He is Creole, with beautifully light olive skin, expressive brown eyes, shiny black hair, nice size ears, thigh neck, broad shoulders, muscular body, like the iron man of last year's state competition. Oh, mom! His lower back and legs are like steel. He is an SASR man, a swimmer." She took a breath, "Jeff lives in the Seven Mile Beach, in a beautiful three-story home, immaculately clean, and organized as an inspection-ready military palace. The house has a magnificent ocean view. It is right outside every window, no matter whether you are in the living room, dining, kitchen, bathroom or bathtub."

Alarmed by the word tub, Janet jumped and said, "Bathtub? Did you mean bath? I will be very upset if all of a sudden I need to explain to my friends and neighbors, where this little crawling caiman or crocodilian came from."

"Oh mom, please …,"

But Janet would not let Margaret talk. "Look, sweetheart if you are already carrying one of those green reptiles, make sure you go today and see Dr. Ross. She'll give you a test, and depend on her diagnosis; we can go to Louisville and spend your dad's money shopping to build a cage to keep this little animal.

"Mom, mom. Mom listen! I did not give Jeff my virginity," said Margaret, taken aback by her mother's language, to say nothing of her insinuation. "No, Madam, if you think my hormones were jumping as crazy as crickets in a hot summer night you are sadly mistaken and please save your shopping energy for maybe next April," With that she ran upstairs to get ready to go to "Starbucks" where she would be meeting Agent Marisol.

When she came downstairs, she felt calmer. "Mom, have a good day, please tell dad that I need to talk with him this evening when I get back from work. Give Bobby and Rome kisses for me,"

"Hone, honey, breakfast is ready, and I'm about to serve it."

"Thank you, Mom bit today I'm out of time, I will eat a good breakfast at the bank, Bye Bye mom. I love you!"

In the car she called, Mr. Ellis as instructed. "Good morning, Sir. We're in luck, today. I have the day off, so I'm at your service. However, not to raise any suspicion, I must be back home by six-thirty this evening."

"You will have plenty of time," Mr. Ellis replied. "This is your mission: Special Agent, Marisol Macmillan is waiting for you at Starbucks. Have some coffee and eat a bagel with cream cheese. Please hand your car keys to Agent Macmillan. She will take you to the airport and accompany you on board a military plane to your destination. Upon landing, you will be met by specialized personnel. The operation's code is 'COBRA.' You will be transported to where I am waiting with the Inspector General, Ms. Crystal Reyes. Do you understand?"

"Understood, Sir!"

Upon arrival at "Starbucks, Margaret got a surprise! There sitting at the far end table away from view sitting and holding hands was Johnathan and his ex-girlfriend, Krystal!

Agent Marisol approached Margaret and said, "Ms. Gianelli, shall we have some coffee and bagels before going to play?"

A bit shook at seeing Johnathan, Margaret said, "Please, let's order, and I need your assistance on a personal matter."

"Of course," said Marisol.

While waiting for the coffee, Margaret related to Marisol her love issues and asked the agent to accompany her as she delivered the bad news to Johnathan before departing on their journey.

She nodded. "Let's go do it before ruining our breakfast . . . the last meal you are having before a particular flight to meet the head COBRA."

They walked to Jonathan's table and stood a few feet away for a few seconds. Jonathan turned and saw Margaret. His face turned red as a tomato, and with a quiver in his voice said, "Hello Margaret, I'm here with Krystal because her mom died yesterday!"

In a matter-of-fact, voice that was colder than an iceberg Margaret said, "Hello, Johnathan, Hi Krystal, this is FBI Special Agent McMillian. She's my friend. I have asked her to be a material witness to the return of your expensive diamond ring. Also, to listen to the irreversible consequences of your actions." Margaret took a breath. "Last time I caught you right here, not holding hands, but knees. That was an accident as you put it, Johnathan. The second time it was my fault because I did not announce that I was coming to lunch here. At the time, I considered the situation and felt "nobody's fault." This time, it's clear that if I forgave you again, I'd be stupid. Therefore, here is the ring, relax and enjoy the rest of your life!"

Marisol and Margaret turned around, picked up their order and ate and talked while enjoying coffee and beagles. All of the sudden, Jonathan was kneeling next to Margaret. "Sweet Margaret, my traveling golfing queen, please forgive me one last time. This will never happen again, I swear."

In a cold but polite voice, Margaret said, "Johnathan, get up. I respect you as a person. However, kneeling in public is like Judas denying knowing the Lord. Go in peace, apologizes to Krystal for humiliating her in front of Marisol and for lying to me. Further, I don't have the time for you. We must finish our coffee and go. We have important things to do."

"Well Margaret, if that's the way you want it, this is it, and in a loud voice, so Kristal could hear him, Jonathan said, "Our wedding engagement is finished! Go and have a lovely time playing golf and eating turtles!"

With a soft and joyous lilt in her voice, Margaret responded, "Thank you for your blessings!"

In an admiring tone of voice, Marisol said, "No wonder you were selected for this assignment, you have class, and you are as cool as a cucumber out of the refrigerator. I'm impressed."

"Thank you, Marisol, the more I work and experience real life in the real world, the more I'm learning that emotions are both profitable and disastrously costly."

"Hum . . . I never thought about that. We've got to go now. COBRA is waiting. You drive." At the Bowman Field Airport, as they were walking towards the security checkpoint Marisol handed Margaret her official FBI Special Agent badge. "Just follow me and do exactly as I do."

Leading the way and walking briskly, Marisol and Margaret whisked through the security checkpoints and arrived at Gate Four. There, Marisol showed her badge and told the attendant. "My colleague, Special Agent, Margaret Gianelli is the only passenger on board the United States government flight 745, destination confidential. The flight manifesto is also secret. Does she need a boarding pass?"

"Yes, Madam, I'm printing it. May I have a positive identification?"

Margaret handed the charter flight gate attendant her driver license. "Thank You, Special Agent Gianelli." Marisol and Margaret walked down the ramp and continued about 700 feet to a small, gray unmarked jet, similar to the one Margaret returned from the Cayman Islands the day before.

Once inside the aircraft Marisol turned and told Margaret, to select a seat and fasten her seat belt. Then she knocked at the pilot's cabin door, and announced, "COBRA, your passenger Special Agent Margaret Gianelli is on board and ready to depart as soon as I close the cabin door behind me." Then Marisol asked Margaret for her car keys, and said, "Have a safe trip, I'll see you right here upon your return."

"Thank you, Marisol."

Margaret was rehearsing in her mind the recent experience in the Cayman Islands. Sure enough, a male baritone voice came over the speaker system" This is your pilot, COBRA, please fasten your seat belt and follow the exact instructions on the laminate card inside the pocket of the seat in front of you. We are ready to depart. Relax and enjoy the flight Special Agent, Margaret Gianelli." Beep.

Margaret pushed back into her seat as the aircraft accelerated into the sky. Soon she could only see the clouds and was reviewing in her mind her feelings about the separation with Johnathan. A sense of peace overwhelmed her to the extent that she fell asleep until the voice came over the speaker, "COBRA. We will be landing in twenty minutes, please be sure your seatbelt is securely fastened. Thank you."

Within minutes, Margaret saw the color green and the ocean. Her heart started to jump like a scared rabbit, thinking and reminiscing about her time with Jeff. Soon, the aircraft landed at Robert Owens, the same airport she departed from the day before. She was totally intrigued as to why the plane had stopped at the far end of the runway. However, she asked no questions. The aircraft taxied for a few feet and stopped, and the speaker system announced, "Special Agent Gianelli, we have arrived at your destination, please remain seated until an outside crew in U.S. military uniform enters the aircraft and calls your name. Have a pleasant time." Beep.

The Cabin door opens, and a uniformed U.S. officer entered the aircraft and said, "Special Agent Gianelli?"

"Yes, I am!"

"Welcome, please follow me," he said.

At the top of the exit ramp, Margaret saw only the long runway, grass, and palm trees. At the bottom standing at attention were three uniformed men, one next to a military van with the side door open, the other standing in front of the van and a third near the right driver door. The welcoming officer said, "Special Agent Gianelli, while you are here these men will be your transportation and security escort. They are U.S. Navy SEALS and trained to protect you and ensure your safe return. Have a good day."

"Thank you, sir," said Margaret.

Once in the van Margaret was slightly bewildered. No one said a word as the driver sped away down a long road. There was nothing to see, and no one was anywhere. Then they arrived at a gate. Two guards snapped to attention, saluted and then opened the gate. Outside the airport perimeter all of a sudden, Margaret began to recognize her surroundings, the place looked like the way to Seven Mile Beach. Wow! Her heart started thumping in her chest. Anticipation was mounting. Indeed, it was the way to the property bought from Prince Aamir.

Then, the van turned right and there in full view was Jeff's home. Margaret exclaimed in a loud voice, "Oh. My God! Oh. My God! I'm here, I'm here."

The SEAL seating to her right asked, "Is everything alright, Madam?"

"Yes, right, right." All is wonderful and can't believe that I'm back here this soon.

The SEAL, looked at Margaret and in a concerned voice, asked, "Is it there anything we need to know before you disembark from this vehicle?

In an inquisitive tone of voice, Margaret ask, "Where are we going?

The SEAL said, "That white house on the corner is the private home of our joint effort SASR-SEAL commander. He is the one you are meeting along with two other people. They should be already in the house. The speaker, a chief petty officer, commanded the SEAL sitting on the front left of the vehicle to verify and report.

Within a minute, "All clear, sir."

When the SEAL turned his body towards Margaret to let her know it was time to disembark, she saw his name tag, read, "McIntyre."

"Let's go Madam Gianelli."

"Officer McIntyre, please give me a minute to relax. There is more emotional stuff going on than I can handle."

McIntyre, sensing Margaret's state of mind replied, in a gentle voice, "Look right at my eyes and do exactly as I do." The two of then began a relaxation exercise of breathing and slowly moving each essential part of their bodies. This lasted less than three minutes.

Then, in a confident voice, Margaret said, "Thank you, I'm ready for action!

"You sound like a SEAL woman," said McIntyre.

"Sorry I'm an SASR lady," said Margaret.

"Oh! Our Commander will be proud on hearing this," said McIntyre as they departed from the van. Shortly after he rang the bell on the front door.

Esther opened the door, and called out Sir Jeff! Sir Jeff, Lady Margaret is here with three SEALS.

From the terrace, he yelled, "She must be a gem to be escorted by three SEALS, I will be down in five minutes. Let the men go, and call Itania, she is running on the beach to say hello to Lady Margaret. As soon as we are ready, I will call for the gem Lady to come up and join us on the terrace!"

Margaret hugged Esther and feeling exuberantly happy asked, "Who's upstairs with Jeff?"

"I don't know their names. All I noticed was a man and a woman, and they've been there for some time," Esther replied. "May I recommend that you put on that full body dust cover? The moment Itania sees you, there is no way I can stop her, and Sir Jeff cannot be disturbed.

With and obvious delight in her voice, Margaret said, "Call the dog in, I'm ready to demonstrate in action I'm a real dog trainer.

"Itania, Itania, come here now!" commanded Esther.

Within a minute or two there was a bang! Margaret knocked on her back, and Itania's front paws were on her chest, the dog licking her face and intermittently barking. Finally, in desperation, Margaret yelled "Platz!"

The obedient dog laid down next to her firm body, looking as innocent as a babe watching TV.

Esther was laughing, and with a clean, moist towel in her hand, said," Lady Margaret, I think you need to freshen up and redo you face, it looks like you just came from a combat zone, you have about three minutes before Sir, Jeff calls you upstairs.

After a bit of refreshing, Margaret asked Esther, "How do I look?"

"Lady Margaret," said Esther, "You look fresh, beautiful and deeply in love. I have been with Sir Jeff for twelve years, and you are the first woman who I know to return to this house. However, more important is that Itania lets you in the house. Whenever she senses anyone that could harm Sir Jeff or me, she does not yield even to the ….you know the command word. She is a trained guard dog. She comes directly from the U.K formed by the SASR canine unit. Some of our neighbors have small children, and when they're playing on the beach, even if their parents are around, whenever a stranger approaches one of them she stands in front of the child and forces the person to return where they came from. In exchange for her police duties, all she wants is to play with a ball or Frisbee."

"That's wonderful," said Margaret.

A loud command voice came from the terrace, "Esther, please escort Lady Margaret to the garden and prepare the kitchen, I'll be fixing lunch for our guest." said Jeff.

"Yes, sir we're on the way!" Upon arriving on the terrace, Margaret exclaimed, "Mr. Ellis! Mr. Ellis and Ms . . . I'm sorry. Good morning! What a surprise!" With a dazzling smile, she said, "How are you Sir Jeff!"

Immediately Ellis, said, "This is Ms. Reyes, the Inspector General, and our Big Boss!

Without ceremony, Jeff said, "While you talk with Ms. Gianelli, I will go downstairs to prepare lunch so we can send Ms. Gianelli back in time to show up at her home before seven this evening. Thus, our time is at a premium.

Ellis nodded and said, "Margaret, The Inspector General has asked us to meet here because Jeff is the Joint Commander of High Water Group, based in Brussels. He is retained by the U.S. Treasury and The Crown of England to oversee the Financial Intelligence Units. The primary function of this outfit is to detect, identify, analyze, and frame the prosecution of financial crimes, regardless of place and time. He is also Chair of the Assets Recovery Group, working in coordination with the Departments of State, regulatory institutions, Interpol, and their collaborative law enforcement units."

Margaret was listening as she always did when Ellis spoke. Then, Reyes said, "Margaret, Ellis, and the FIUs have read your daily reports. They are concise, objective, and actionable. We have asked you here because your effort has an international reach and impact. The Commander learned of your name as the principal prosecuting liaison in the Louisville Midtown Bank case less than an hour ago. She said, 'I knew it, the Lord is responding!' Something like that." Reyes paused and gave Margaret a tight smile. "Ellis is assigning you to a new case once the arrest and processing of the people of the Louisville Midtown Bank are completed. The issue we want you to know is that to be credible, I will also order your arrest and incarceration.

Margaret with both of her hands on the sides of her head exclaimed, "Oh. My goodness! I need to take a moment out, please! I need to look at my face in the mirror and quickly ask a secret friend for advice. I'll be back in a moment, may I leave you, please?"

"Yes, take your time," responded Reyes.

Margaret ran downstairs expecting to see Jeff. He was not around, nor was Esther or the dog. She was near panic. Shaking entered Jeff's bathroom. There she stood spellbound seeing the power of the pounding waves against the beach. An ocean storm was approaching. Margaret was so taken by the sight that she forgot for a moment about the arrest and incarceration issues.

Upon returning to the terrace, she found Ellis, Reyes, and Jeff, standing ready to go downstairs for lunch. At the table, Ellis asked Jeff, "Please lay out the mission, so we all can hear your plan and discuss the potential risks and how these will be mitigated."

In a modulated tone of voice, Jeff said, "Let us eat lunch first, then we all can see the drawing plan and discuss details. Is that agreeable with all of you?"

Margaret, her face reflecting relief, said, "If Jeff is the architect of the plan, I have no problem with being arrested or incarcerated, as long as my family does not get involved in any part of the process. A mistake on that aspect could have unavoidable consequences, especially for my father.

After lunch, the party moved to Jeff's office in the basement. He opened a full-size bank safe door behind a movable bookshelf. There was a semi-circular room, staffed with fourteen men, seven from the British Special Air Service Regiment (SASR), and seven U.S. Naval SEALS supported by logistics specialists of three U.S. and three British military women. They were sitting and some standing in front of monitors showing graphs, maps and pulsating red dots on their screens.

This room was one of the strategic command centers of the High Water Group, the World Financial Intelligence Unit. Large computer monitors covered the main wall. There was an observation deck with swivel chairs for seven people. Jeff showed Reyes, Ellis, and Margaret to their seats. Then Jeff picked up a microphone, "Delta Team! To my right is Madam Crystal Reyes, The United States Special Inspector General for the Trouble Asset Relief Program. To my left are Mr. George Ellis, Special Counsel to The Inspector General and Special Advisor to the High Water Group. Next to him is Madam Margaret Gianelli, FBI Special Agent, and U.S. Treasury Prosecutor Liaison. We are going to review the operation KALI for all American assets. And for all international assets, we will consider the operation AIR surgical strike." Jeff paused for a moment, then continued speaking to the people seated around him. "With due consideration for the ancillary impacts, this is the proposed plan for your approval. The staff is showing the routes of access from the most recent architectural drawings obtained from the relevant jurisdictions of the following properties. There, on the central monitor, is the bank.

"The next sequence of drawings on the other screens shows the title documents that correspond to the real estate properties and unimproved land holdings. Also, you will see details on bank accounts, safety deposit boxes, insurance policies, vehicles, and artworks. These are the actionable facts we have at this time in the names of Larry Jordan, Nancy McArthur, Roy Lubec, and Keith Jones. Also, actionable facts on the multiple homes located in various states within the United States. We include other assets as recovery candidates. These properties are located in Honk Kong, St. Thomas, and three others locations in the Virgin Islands, and Singapore. We are in direct contact with the corresponding government representatives in each country. All that is needed is your final approval so we can set the precision strike, at a simultaneous time on all targets."

Jeff, in a commanding tone, said, "Delta Team, take ten!" This indicated ten minutes of deliberations among the team and the decision makers. The team could hear the decision makers, but they could not understand the team.

Jeff turned to Reyes, and asked, "May I have your observations and identification of potential risks?" Then he turned to Ellis and Margaret and asked, "Please give me your best estimate of the potential success of conducting both operations simultaneously given the facts you have now."

Reyes: "The only potential risk I see is what if the subjects are not where you expect them to be?"

Ellis: "Given the time zone differences, a simultaneous strike could present a potential risk."

Margaret, "The issue to consider is the cultural differences and calendar time of the AIR attack.

Jeff, announced, "Deliberations are over! Let us hear from the team leaders. You have six minutes to define the risk, and provide an actionable solution."

Delta, male team leader: "We determined the KALI operation, a low level of risk. The solution is to ask the local law enforcement to shadow the subjects for ten days to confirm patterns of behavior before setting the strike time.

Alpha, team leader, "We recommend that the AIR surgical strike be evaluated for implementation on a separate country-by-country basis to ensure one hundred percent success."

Jeff nodded. "Thank you team leaders. Madam Reyes, we have concluded deliberations and now need your decision."

Standing and reflecting the body language of the leader in charge, Reyes said, "On behalf of the United States Government and my Agency, I thank the members of the Alpha and Delta Teams for a job well done, and you Jeff for your leadership. My decision is to move forward to execute your plan. It has my approval as of this moment. Please keep Mr. Ellis, and Ms. Gianelli informed.

Then, she turned toward Ellis and said, "We have another meeting with the Governor in thirty minutes."

Waiting at the front of the house was the transportation for Reyes and Ellis, and Margaret's military van.

After the Reyes party had departed, and on her way to the van, Margaret turned towards Jeff, who was standing at the door and said, "Thank you JJ. Please give my thanks to Esther, and give Itania a hug and kiss." She gave him a dazzling smile.

Upon arrival at Bowman Airfield in Louisville, Marisol was waiting to take Margaret back to Starbucks. As she was sitting to brief Marisol on matters relevant to her duties, she noticed Johnathan with a girl, not Kristal. With a deep sigh, she said, "Look Marisol, Don Juan in action! I'm blessed to have seeing him with my own eyes, and his shenanigans before committing marital suicide."

Time was moving at the speed of light, but life at the bank continued like an old machine, beautiful and comfortable. Larry met Tamara and assigned her the duties of preparing the weekly trades as Roy had trained her to do.

Nancy went on vacation to the European Alps to meet a large scale investor and to establish some banking relationships in Liechtenstein.

Roy remained in rehabilitation with Bertha by his side, mean as ever.

Keith agreed to take over Roy's job as Chief Financial Officer until Roy's health issues were resolved. He celebrated his wedding anniversary without irreversible consequences.

Jennifer was becoming a pal with Margaret as they often met at the hospital to cheer up Roy.

Rumors were circulating that Barbara had a lover.

Megan and Ralph continued spending dad's money and doing what they liked.

Margaret completed her bank assignments sooner than planned and invited Jeff to meet her parents. They liked him a lot. She also told her father about the imminent arrest and incarceration. In agreement with the strategy, Harry arranged that on the "D," as coined it, to take Janet, Bobby, and the dog to see a cabin located by the lake with the possibility of purchasing it after the New Year. All was going as the Lord has planned.

On December 23, 2014, at 4:30 a.m., local time in all locations in the Unites States, where the Louisville Midtown Bank, Larry Jordan, Nancy McArthur, Roy Lubec, and Keith Jones had recoverable assets. The arresting teams in all jurisdictions consisting of Special Agents from The Treasury Department, The Special Inspector General for the Trouble Asset Relief Program, the FBI, and its law enforcement partners, swarmed upon the parties and served the similar court orders. These were to search, identify and seize all documents, property, and related valuables located in and away from the places of business and residences of the bank and the people responsible for managing the bailout money provided by the U.S. Government to the Louisville Midtown Bank to keep operating during the financial crisis of 2007-2008.

At 4:00 am that same day, as instructed by Mr. Ellis and Jeff, Margaret took a vomit inducing pill. Escorted by Marisol, Margaret checked herself in the County Jail. Without delay, the Warden as a party to the plan ordered his assistant to outfit Margaret with a new orange jumpsuit and then placed her in a solitary holding cell awaiting the arrival of Nancy McArthur.

Sure enough, at 4:40 am Nancy was brought in by two deputies, wearing her new prison uniform.

As the cell door was opened, Nancy saw Margaret. She was curled in the fetus position against the wall on a steel bench, Nancy screamed, "Oh no. You don't belong here, Oh God! Oh God, poor Margaret, Why did they arrest you?"

Sobbing without stop, and in a desperate tone of voice, Margaret said, "I didn't do anything wrong, I'm in the bank for a little over a year. Did they arrest me for helping you to win the golf tournament? Or stealing money from the three banks you guys bet against? Are they gangsters? What am I to do? I can't call my dad or anyone, I haven't committed any crime. Nancy, please tell me what are we going to do?"

Equally shaken, but more in tune with the realities of her actions, Nancy sat by Margaret and held her, saying, "Margaret, it'll all be okay. We have enough money to buy the best legal counsel in the world to defend you and me. I will pay the legal fees and will compensate you handsomely for the pain and suffering. Please understand, there is nothing we can do until at least ten in the morning when I will call Larry and find out what is he going to do to get us both out of here."

"This place is horrible. It smells like death, I'm scared. If this is publicized, I'll go to China and hide for the rest of my life. My dad, oh my dad, oh my dad, he is my best friend, and I'm about to ruin his life and his diplomatic career. Nancy, this is too much for me . . . I'm getting sick. Margaret started to vomit while holding her stomach with both hands.

"Guard, guard, guard, please call a doctor Margaret is sick, very sick," screamed Nancy.

No one responded. The time seemed an eternity. "What time is it?" Nancy continued to cry.

There was no answer.

Margaret was shivering after the vomit subsided. There was silence, no one was coming.

About nine in the morning, a deputy comes to the holding cell, "McArthur?"

Nancy stood. "That's me."

"You have the right to make one telephone call. It's limited to three minutes. Do you want to make this call, or wait for the public defender to come and talk with you?

"I need to make the call, please." She and the deputy walked to a telephone fixed on the wall.

The deputy handed Nancy a card and said, "Insert this card and dial your number. After the other party answers, the call will be terminated in three minutes, and you will have exercised your legal right to a telephone call to notify the party that will arrange to bail you out of here. Do you understand McArthur?"

"Yes officer I do," responded Nancy. She proceeded to dial Larry. His phone rang and rang. Then the voice mail came on. She called again, and when Larry didn't pick up, she left a message in a desperate tone of voice. "You S#73it! Where in the hell are you, So&U4$#@! Margaret and I are in the county jail. Get your "Blankets" over here, and get us out of this stinking joint." Beep.

Nancy returned and said, "Margaret, I called Larry and left him a message that he is to get here as soon as possible to bail us out. Please relax and let's wait. How are you feeling?"

"Still nauseated…," said Margaret.

A few minutes passed, the same deputy returned, "Gianelli?"

"Here I'm in jail for something I don't know anything about."

"I'm not asking for your life story, are you Gianelli? Yes or No!"

"YES."

"You have a legal right to a telephone call, do you want to make it, or wait for the public defendant to talk with you, sometime this morning or this afternoon?"

"I will not call anyone, for I didn't commit any crime so will wait for the public defender, and I will expect an explanation for the grounds of my arrest," said Margaret.

About eleven-thirty, a fat, five foot one, unshaven, curly haired man, showed up in front of the holding cell and said, "Who is Gianelli?"

"I am. Are you the public defender?"

"Well," The man asked, "it all depends on whether you have any money to pay for your legal defense, or are you broke?

"Let's assume I'm totally broke, are you the public defender?"

"In that case, I'm your only chance to get out of this place within a reasonable period of time. Hopefully, before you are transferred to your new residence, and that depends on the nature and severity of your crime, if it's serious violation of law, you may end up in Fort Knox, where all hardcore criminals, or those that have attempted to screw the government, will end their miserable lives. You must tell me the truth. Otherwise, you will stay here for a long time.

In a shaking voice, Margaret said, "I will only tell you the truth if you say your name, so I can call God and ask Him to help me because He is the only one who can get Nancy and me out of this place.

"Okay, my name is Fausto De Victor, your pro bono attorney, a graduate from the University of Hard Knocks. Now, let's go to the interrogation room, and we will see how long you will remain in this jail."

Waiting in the interrogation room was Marisol, and she introduced De Victor as the FBI Special Agent, Organized Crime Unit. Together, they laughed with gusto. Marisol and Margaret departed following De Victor, who released Margaret after her only visit to a correctional institution without leaving a trace of ever being there.

JORGE RIVERA

Chapter 35
REWARDS

On Tuesday, Margaret went to the bank and found that the elevator to the floor to her office was out of service. She called security.

"Hello, this is Margaret, is the chief available?

"Hi, Ms. Margaret. Can you please come to my office, there's a major issue I need to report."

"Charles, I'll be there in a flash!" said Margaret. When she arrived, she greeted the chief.

Without preamble, Charles said, "The security detail on duty, led by Tom, reported that at four o'clock in the morning a team of Kentucky State Police, the FBI and Treasury Department agents, about twenty of them, entered the building. They handed Tom a court order and swept clean the executive offices, and Mr. Lubec' and Mr. Jones' entire floor. After twenty minutes they left with everything in brown file boxes. As they were leaving, they instructed Tom to 'block the 19th, and 20th floors. Also, that no one was to go on these floors until a judge says so.' I've been calling Mr. Jordan, Ms. Nancy, and Mr. Jones, but no one answers. Also, I called the hospital, and Mr. Lubec is no longer there. So, what do you suggest we do?"

"Charles, I'm going home and be available on my phone. Please go to the police and find out what's happening and report back to me as soon as you have the facts. I will only need to know the facts so I can call Nancy, who is in Europe, for further instructions."

At home, Margaret picked up the newspaper and on front page she read. The Cabot Estate filed in Federal Court a multimillion dollar lawsuit against the Louisville Middle Town Bank, and its officers."

"Dad, dad, dad, are you here?" she shouted.

Bobby responded, "Mom and Dad are across the street, Johnny's father is sick."

"Okay, please go and tell dad I must speak with him right away," asked Margaret.

When her father came through the door, Margaret showed him the newspaper. "Look, Dad, you predicted this outcome right on the money. Now that I have my two weeks paid vacations, and no one is running the bank. This afternoon I'll go and see Karen to authorize my time off, and spend it with Jeff."

"Sweetheart, after being in prison, you deserve some time off to readjust to civilian life. Go for it. We like the guy and feel comfortable that he is honorable," said Harry.

With great anticipation and a feeling of accomplishment, Margaret said "Thanks, Dad. I'll see you tonight. I'm going back to the bank, and then meet with Marisol so I can arrange a military ride to the Caymans for an immediate live report."

Margaret called Jeff and said, "JJ, How are you, honey? I have a success report on KALI, I'm in the process of making the arrangements, to depart from Bowman Airfield, tomorrow at seven in the morning.

"Honey, that's wonderful, I just received the tactical report, and your presence will verify the value of the KALI operation. Did you like the guys that picked you up last time?"

"Oh, yes those SEAL guys are okay. However, I would like to meet the British support female leader. She impressed me. Can she do transport escort?"

"Honey, the Delta Team is multi-tasking multi-use, Elizabeth will be your seating guard and the other two the same fellows will support her. I'll see you tomorrow my warm honey," said Jeff as they ended the conversation.

On arrival in the Caymans, Elizabeth, the British support female leader, said "Madam Gianelli welcome back. The Delta team wants to meet you and learn from the inspiration of your accomplishments. We have Commander McNeil's approval, so since he is in Havana until late this afternoon, I'm your host and personal guard."

"Wonderful, I'm equally excited to learn and cooperate as necessary," said, Margaret.

After meeting one-on-one with the Delta team, she decided to go to the house purchased from the Prince, and invited two male SEALS and two female British members of the Delta support team for a social get-to-know one another and learn as much as possible about Jeff's military personality.

The social gathering at the house was a success, everyone liked Margaret's sense of humor, and they arranged for a friendly game of golf after plans were discussed with Jeff.

Margaret decided to stay at the property owned by the bank. In the morning, Itania was barking outside as Jeff threw pebbles at the window. When there was no reaction after some minutes, he knocked on the door. There was no answer. He knocked again and again.

Then Itania took off towards the beach like a bullet. In a minute, both Margaret and Itania were on the ground, playing. Jeff stood by the house observing in silence and delighting in the relationship building between the real loves of his life, his dog, and Margaret.

"Hello, honey, how were your fight here and time with my guys and girls?" Jeff finally asked.

"My JJ, my honey, my sweetheart, after playing with this beautiful dog, and my time with the SEALS and SASR, I belong here. I'm planning to request my two-week vacation and stay here, I have a beautiful house, a housekeeper and a driver at my command, what are your thoughts?"

"Let's walk on the beach, and I'll give you my thoughts," said Jeff.

They walked, talked, and played with the dog and with each other. A mile and a half later, and around a corner with a magnificent view of the Caribbean Sea, Jeff said to Margaret, "Please turn towards the ocean and look as far as you can see. Then close your eyes, and when instructed, remain with closed eyes and pretend to look down twelve inches from the tip of your toes. With your left hand, feel Itania, she'll be sitting with your left leg. Touch her head, and then when I tell you, open your eyes. This time, looking down two feet away from your body. Is that agreeable?" asked Jeff.

"Yes, Yes, I agree," Margaret knew that something important was happening. And she stood frozen, with her hand on Itania's head looking slightly forward.

In a warm tone of voice and almost whispering, Jeff asked, "Can you sense my voice, can you feel where I am? Don't open your eyes, just respond to my questions as simply as you can with the first though in your mind. What am I wearing today? Where am I? And the last question, what are you feeling right now?"

With a cautious tone and a funny sound of her voice Margaret said, "You are wearing a pale green tee shirt, dark, almost brown shorts, and brown sandals. You are low on the ground, almost in front of me. I feel that you are the man the Lord has selected for me, and I can be safe with for the rest of my life."

Upon hearing these words, in a soft voice, Jeff said, "Slowly open your eyes, and look at the sand. Equally, slowly raise your sight until you see my legs, torso, and hands."

Okay, JJ, stop the delightful torture," said Margaret. Do I proceed now?

"Yes, my love, now," said Jeff. Immediately, he added "Express in words what you see!"

"Oh my God! Sparkles like the stars of our first night on the terrace, what is it? Oh my goodness, what a beautiful jewel!"

On his knees, with a two-karat diamond ring set in a black velvet box, Jeff asked, "Will you marry me on the last day of this year?" Margaret drops back to the sand falling like a brick, Itania bark in warning. Jeff extended his upper body and checked her pulse. He was about to place his index finger on her neck to verify her breathing when Margaret sprang to a sitting position and yelled, "I will love you JJ, for the rest of my life. I will honor you as an SASR woman shall, and I will make you proud to be the wife of the most distinguish FBI special Agent. Yes, Yes, Yes! I will marry you this December 31, 2014, where ever the Lord lets us be."

Filled with love and emotions impossible to put into words, nearly in silence, they returned to the house where Margaret had placed in a drawer a file titled KALI. With an enormous difficulty in separating the government assignment and her personal feelings of joy and excitement, upon arrival Margaret said, "honey since I am to return to Louisville later this afternoon, I would like to know the process to render my report. "Good, that will work well, because I must also return to Havana tonight, so let's have lunch at home, then we will meet with Alpha and Delta teams, and you proceed to present the results of the KALI operation.

Then, after you return from official vacations, we can devote our time to us, and, focus on the details of our wedding. Is that agreeable?

"Yes, yes, that is beautiful."

Lunch was so romantic and filled with expressions of dreams and fantasies, which hardly left time to eat. In a warm, soft tone of voice, Jeff said, "honey our private time is about to be interrupted…at that moment a male voice loudly called 'the situation room will be ready in ten.'

Margaret giggles a little as she was planning to engage in more kissing and hugging. However, Jeff stood up and said, "Honey we will go down the situation room, and you should render the report. Upon conclusion, I will take you to the airport and be your personal security detail to your transport, from there I will also depart for Havana.

"Attention!" Called a male voice on Jeff and Margaret arrival to the situation room. "At ease," responded Jeff as he and Margaret took a seat at the observation deck. On the microphone, Jeff said, "Special FBI agent and U.S. Treasure liaison is ready to report the outcome of KALI operation."

The room came to silence.

Please relax and listen, Margaret began "The KALI operation was executed as planned in this place. One hundred percent of known assets and information was seized without incident. The cooperating agencies and law enforcement partners from each jurisdiction performed an outstanding job.

The outcome of this operation was a just reward for each person.

The death of a Marjorie Cabot triggered the next prosecution phase of the Louisville Midtown Bank. In fact, Dr. Rasmussen, the spine surgeon who operated on Ms. Cabot was charged with professional negligence. The insurance carrier holding the professional liability insurance policy for Dr. Rasmusses, settle out court with the Cabot Estate for an undisclosed amount of money.

Mr. Larry Jordan, Chief Executive Officer, Ms. Nancy McArthur, Corporate Secretary and Investment Banker, and Mr. Roy Lubec, Chief Financial Officer of the Louisville Midtown Bank, pleaded guilty to the charges by the U.S. Government. They were respectively sentenced by the United States District Court for the Southern District of New York to ten years in prison where they remain today. The Louisville Midtown Bank was ordered to make full restitution to the victims, and pay punitive damages equal to twenty percent of the deposited amounts. The case against Mr. Keith Jones was continued.

Barbara Jordan in humiliation resigned as Chair of the Children's Hospital, and with her daughter, Megan and Son Ralph moved to London. Neither suspected that Larry's troubled past included gambling addiction, or that Larry had been having a love affair for the last thirteen years with Nancy McArthur.

Bertha Lubec was admitted to a mental hospital, where she remains today.

Elizabeth Jones and her daughter Jennifer continue their lives in Louisville awaiting the continuation of Mr. Jones case. This concludes my report."

"Thank you, Special Agent Gianelli for your brief, and to the point report."

An applause from the Alpha and Delta teams was the reward for Margaret.

"Carry on!" was Jeff's command as both stood up and departed for the airport. They arrived at the takeoff line of the runway as COBRA was ready to leave, a few tender moments at the foot of the stairway leading Margaret to embark the aircraft. Just before reaching the door, she turned around waved kisses to Jeff and disappear from view, within minutes COBRA was out of sight.

Three days later, Margaret returned to the Cayman Islands on her permanent vacation and devoted her time to Jeff, and their wedding plans.

And so, at midnight, on December 31, 2014, in an intimate ceremony at the Crown Estate, St. James Palace in London. Attended by Margaret's and Jeff 's families, and sixty banking and military friends, Margaret Gianelli became, Lady McNeil, wife of Sir Jeffrey McNeil, Knight of Her Majesty, Queen Elizabeth of the United Kingdom of Great Britain and Northern Ireland.

JORGE RIVERA

About the Author

Jorge Rivera, PhD, is a Behavioral Science Specialist, and Economist. Dr. Rivera is a member of the U.S. Council of Economics and Financial Literacy. He holds a senior consultancy status with the United Nations, The World Bank, International Monetary Fund, and the International Finance Corporation. Rivera is a Chief Executive Officer of American Hope Charities, and is a Commissioned Colonel, Commonwealth of Kentucky.